"So, I mean, is it a problem?"

"That you're a wulf?"

"Half," I say, holding a finger up and trying to laugh, though it probably sounds more like I'm choking.

"Not a problem for *me*." And now she grabs my arm to pull me along. She's touching me. She's holding my arm. We stop at her locker.

"Seriously? It doesn't bother you?"

She raises an eyebrow. "Did you think it would?"

"No. I'm not saying that at all, but it's the kind of thing you're supposed to tell someone who you're . . . getting to know. Full disclosure." Okay, maybe not full, but enough. For now, at least.

RED MOON RISING

PETER MOORE

HYPERION

NEW YORK

Copyright © 2011 by Peter Moore
All rights reserved. Published by Disney • Hyperion Books, an imprint of Disney Book Group. No part of this book may be reproduced or transmitted in any form or by any means, electronic or mechanical, including photocopying, recording, or by any information storage and retrieval system, without written permission from the publisher. For information address Disney • Hyperion Books, 125 West End Avenue, New York, NY 10023-6387.
Printed in the United States of America

First Disney • Hyperion paperback edition, 2012
3 5 7 9 10 8 6 4 2
V475-2873-0-14147
This book is set in Sabon.
Designed by Marci Senders
Library of Congress Control Number for Hardcover Edition: 2009040375
ISBN 978-1-4231-1939-5
Visit www.un-requiredreading.com

SUSTAINABLE
FORESTRY
INITIATIVE

Certified Chain of Custody
Promoting Sustainable Forestry

www.sfiprogram.org
SFI-01054

The SFI label applies to the text stock

For
  Ellen
    & Hedy
      & Jake
  with all my love

RED MOON RISING

PART I

Just before humans completely split off from their hominid primate ancestors, two separate mutations occurred, resulting in three different species: H. sapiens, H. vampyros, *and* H. lupus. *From a genetic viewpoint, humans, vampyres, and wulves are 99.6% identical. That four-sixths of one percent makes all the difference in the world.*

—Dr. Kavita Singh, *Critical Divergence: the Human, Vampyre, and Wulf Genomes,* 2007

By 1920, vampyres no longer needed to hunt humans. It was then that humans came to understand that vampyres were remarkably intelligent and could contribute a great deal to society. This was the turning point for the vampyre species.

—Bianca Fournier, age 17, youngest recipient of Pulitzer Prize for Commentary: "Late Invitation: The Vampyre Journey from Reviled to Respected," adapted from her doctoral dissertation

All around the mulberry bush
The poacher chased the werewulf
The werewulf stopped when he heard the first shot
Pop *goes the werewulf!*

—Nursery Rhyme

1
DANNY-SOMETHING

Feeling like you fit in as a freshman in high school is tough enough, but it really sucks when you're only half-vampyre.

It's obvious that I'm not full-blooded. I have a shorter, wider build than a typical vamp my age. I have vamp-blue eyes, but I got my father's coloring: olive skin and hair the color of burnt chestnuts. And even though my vamp immune system rejected most of the ink from the wulftag tattoo, it's still there if you look for it, like a hologram under my skin.

It's not that the other vamps openly avoid me. The ones who've known me since we were little know that I'm technically half-wulf, and the ones who don't assume I'm either half-human, or that I had the genetic treatments.

I look at the vamps sitting at the table with Claire and me: Bertrand, Martina, Oliver, Constance, Hugh. They're arguing about song lyrics, which they do all the time. Martina's my lab partner. I've studied for tests with Constance and Oliver. Hugh has had me over to watch movies in his home theater.

They're good friends, but I kind of imagined I would branch out a little once I got to high school.

"Are you *ever* going to shut up?" Claire asks me.

"What?" I say.

She pushes the purple headband farther back on her head. "You haven't said a word in ten minutes. What's wrong with you?"

"Nothing. Just thinking." I twist my neck until it makes a cracking sound, which I know grosses Claire out.

Thanks to successful genetic treatments, Claire looks full-vamp. She has ivory skin and pale yellow hair the exact color of plasma, cut in a bob. Her human mother died in childbirth, and her father married another vamp a year later. Everyone assumed she was full-vamp when she moved here, and she has no intention of telling them otherwise.

"You drinking the rest of that, or what?" she asks.

I pass over the bottle of SynHeme. Claire drinks, then makes a sour face. "Is this diet?"

"No. Why?"

She smacks her lips, way too many times, because she knows it bugs me. "Tastes thin."

"I watered it down a little."

She holds up the bottle so it's backlit by the moonlight coming in through the big glass cafeteria windows. "Gross," she says. But she still drinks it.

Though she rags on us all the time, Claire has no interest

in making new friends. She took a lot of crap last year after the locker room incident that started all the rumors about her being gay. Her entire safety net, every person who stood by her, is at this table right now.

Claire pushes the SynHeme bottle back across the table. "This is horrible," she says. "Why would you water down SynHeme?"

"My stomach's been bothering me." Even though I have the Thirst, SynHeme's been making me feel queasy lately. To distract myself, I look around the caf.

There are rich vamp kids at almost every other table. Guys wearing shirts that cost a few hundred bucks, girls whose spike heels or skinny jeans cost as much as some wulf families' rent. These kids are smart, confident, and good-looking. I would never sit with them.

Down by the serving lines at the other end of the caf is a single table of wulves. Eleven wulf kids in the whole place.

The vamp parents protested wulves' being admitted into Carpathia's Night High Gifted Program. But in the end, it all came down to money. The wulves who come here have families who can afford to live in town, so their kids are entitled to attend. Not that the wulf kids can hack the same advanced academics that vamps take. Wulves come to this building— which doubles as Millbrook High during the day—and take Carpathia electives at night. Even if they can't pass the heavy academic subjects, they still get "Carpathia Gifted Program" on their transcripts just by taking stuff like art and gym and health.

The wulf kids really stand out. They're built like wrestlers:

short, wide, and muscular. A lot of them have longish hair to cover their post-Change ears and their skull lumps. Some have facial ridges they never got fixed, even though their parents have the money for the surgery. I guess it's their way of saying, like, *suck it!* to the vamp kids. Same thing with the facial hair—some of them have goatees and sideburns. Or pierced ears and eyebrows. They do it because they can, and vampyre regen means we can't. But rebels or not, all of them have wulftags—the werewulf-head tattoo near the bottom of their right thumbs, each with a red circle around it, meaning they're registered and go to compounds every month.

"Hey! Check it out!" says a vamp kid a few yards from the wulf table. "Feeding time at the zoo! Here you go, moon-doggies!" he yells, throwing a handful of cold cuts at them.

Three wulf kids jump to their feet, but the two massive lunchroom safety officers get there first, hands resting conspicuously on the riot clubs hanging from their belts. They're humans, and it's hard to tell who they dislike more: the vamps or the wulves. To them, we must seem like spoiled rich kids or rowdy brutes. Most likely, they despise us equally.

"Don't even think about it, mutts!" a guard bellows at the wulf boys. One of the wulves, looks like John Fusco, is about to protest, then sees there's no point and sits back down. His friends follow.

Wulves are not wanted, and it's made clearer every day.

"Hello! Danny! Anyone home?" Claire raps her knuckles on the table three times. The chunky silver bangles on her wrist rattle.

"Yes, Claire, I'm here. I know you need my undivided attention."

"Believe me, I don't need *your* attention. Wherever *you* are is a place of weirdness," she says. She tilts the plastic bottle and drinks the last drops of the SynHeme. I look out the big windows at the white, waxing gibbous moon.

I hate all my classes, especially ninth grade Organic Chem. It's accelerated, so we'll be up to gross anatomy with cadavers during senior year and get med school credit. But I don't want to be a doctor, so what's the point?

Science is actually my worst subject, but I still finish my test in half the time Dr. Burke allotted. Dr. Burke is a new teacher, a human, and usually teaches this class to humans at the state university, so she always seems surprised at how quickly vamps learn. And this class is all vamps, with two exceptions. One being me.

The other is a human named Juliet Walker, who just now is leaning over her test. From this angle, with the moonlight coming in through the shades, I can see her eyebrows furrow as she works out a problem. I love the way she does that when she's concentrating.

I guess I stare at her a lot. I try to hide it, but sooner or later I'm going to get caught, and then I'll feel like the biggest idiot on the planet.

She started Carpathia at the beginning of the term. Bertrand (who seems to get inside information about anyone who's interesting) said a human girl was taking some of our ninth grade classes. He found out that she's actually sixteen and a junior at Millbrook during the day. Even as a junior in the human school, she must be *really* smart if she can handle Carpathia's core academics.

Juliet might be considered plain by vamp standards, but I think she's way cuter than the vamp girls. Her hair is dark-red and wavy, and she usually wears it in a low ponytail. She's not pale, tall, and skinny like all the other girls in school. Which is fine by me. I'm not pale, tall, and skinny, either. And she has a really nice smile.

I've said hi to her a bunch of times, but aside from that or "how's it going?" I've never talked to her; the fact that I have a crush on her almost guarantees I'll make an ass of myself.

The only girl I'd go to for advice is Claire, but then she'd mock me until the end of time. Claire isn't like other vamp girls, either, being that she's secretly half-human and not so secretly a lesbian, which I don't really get. I mean, she's never had an actual girlfriend, so even though she says she likes girls, how can she know for sure? What I'm saying is, she isn't judgmental the way most vamp girls are, but she might still find it weird that I have a thing for a human.

Most people say that interspecies relationships never work. "There are dietary issues," Mom has said a million times. "Conflicting schedules of sunlight restrictions. And that's not even taking into account the fundamental differences in morals, values, philosophy." Every kid—vamp, wulf, human—hears the same lecture all the time.

So I can watch Juliet Walker as much as I want. There's no way we'll ever get together.

After class I get a headache, then start to feel dizzy and sweaty as I head to my locker. My vision blurs and my stomach churns. I duck into a stall in the boys' room just in time to puke. It's blue, from the SynHeme I had at lunch. After I'm done, I rinse out my mouth. A vamp guy who I don't know, his white-blond hair gelled up into a pompadour, comes in. He takes a look at me, then walks across the boys' room. "What's wrong with you?" he asks on his way to one of the urinals.

I try to blink away the white spots in my vision. "I'm okay," I say. It comes out weak and trembly.

He looks me up and down. "You should go to the nurse."

"I don't need to." Still dizzy, I lean against the sink.

"You *look* like you need to."

"No, really. I'm fine."

I wake up lying on a fake-leather bed in some kind of cubicle. There's a small poster that shows a cartoon of a woman wearing white clothes and holding a syringe, with the words: *I'm a School Nurse: Armed with Needles and Not Afraid to Use Them.* The curtain is pulled open.

"Look who's awake," says a heavyset human nurse who's hovering over me. The bags under her eyes are probably from working the night shift at Carpathia on top of a day shift at Millbrook.

"Did I pass out?"

"You sure did," she says. "Did you happen to take a hematocrit reading this morning before you fainted?"

"Oh. No. I can't find my hemometer."

She shakes her head. She probably hears about vamps losing their portables all the time. "Before I check your blood, you might as well tell me. Did you do any drugs?"

"No." I try to sit up, but my head starts swimming.

"No blood thinners? Coumidex? Nothing?"

"Nothing. I've never taken anything like that."

"Okay, we'll see. You're Danny-something, right?"

"Gray."

She pulls my file. I see her take note of the big yellow-and-black sticker on the outside of the folder, which means I'm genetically part-wulf.

She takes half a vial, runs it through the meter, then attaches the tube to the needle and puts the blood back in me.

"You're anemic. Your crit is low and you're having a globin crash. Didn't you have lunch?"

"I had half a bottle of SynHeme and a sandwich."

"Half a bottle? Well, there you have it. You need more heme."

"I just puked. I won't be able to keep it down."

"We'll go IV, then. You need it."

She brings out a bag of clear VeniHeme and connects it to the needle she left in my arm, then hangs the bag from a hook on the wall. My heart skips a beat when the concentrated heme hits, then goes back into rhythm.

I notice that there's something stuck to my forehead. I touch it and feel gauze.

"You hit your head when you passed out," she says. "It was a deep gash, almost to the bone. Even if you have

14

strong regen, it could still take four or five hours to heal. That is"—she wags her finger at me—"if you have a nice big dinner and get plenty of hemoglobin."

I get home three hours before sunrise, and my little sister, Paige, is watching one of her celebrity-news shows on the wall TV. She doesn't look up when I come in.

"Hey," I say. "What's up?"

"Virginia Lanchester and Shane-Luke may get married," she tells me, eyes on the screen.

"Oh, no."

"Yup. And I predicted it the second she left Tad Snyder," Paige adds. Paige is the perfect little vampyre, her main interests being fashion and the publicly private lives of celebrities.

"Anyone else home?" I ask.

"Mom's shopping. Jess is out somewhere with her boyfriend." Paige tosses her platinum hair.

"So you're home alone?" I ask.

"No, Loretta is downstairs doing laundry."

"You do your homework?"

"Yes, yes, I did it," she says in the snotty tone she picked up from Jessica. "Do you mind? I want to find out who's getting custody of the babies!"

I just don't see the appeal of shows like this—celebrity gossip masquerading as news. But Paige is crazy for anything having to do with TV. She even loves the songs from commercials.

On the wall above the TV is the picture I always try not to look at (and I always fail). Mom insisted we have a "proper" family portrait done, in a photo studio. The photographer set us in front of a dark background to contrast with all the white skin and blond hair. Paige is in front; she's all-vamp. Her father, Troy, Mom's second husband, is behind her with a hand on her shoulder. He's got his other arm around Mom, whose blond bob and white teeth are almost blinding. In front of her is Jessica, whose genetic treatments worked completely, erasing any chromosomal hint of her father—our father. You'd never know she had a drop of wulf blood in her. She looks like a young carbon copy of Mom, but with long hair. Then, last and certainly least: me. Standing next to Mom makes my skin and brown hair look even darker. And with the black screen behind us, I'm halfway fading into the background. It's the four of them, bright and shiny, and then me. Like a wulf in sheep's clothing.

Sick of looking at the picture, I go into the kitchen and open the refrigerator. I'm looking and enjoying the cool air on my face, when I hear the front door open.

"Excuse me?" It's Jessica, right behind me. "Are you planning to stand there blocking the refrigerator until the sun comes up, or what?"

"That was the plan."

"Seriously. I'm practically hypovolemic. Get out of the way."

Since she's being snotty, I'm going to have to be obnoxious. I *slowly* pick up a bottle of SynHeme Gold, extra rich, triple hemoglobin, even though the thought of it makes my stomach knot.

"You are such a brat," she says. "Move it. If I have a

16

globin crash and need an infusion, I'm telling Mom it was your fault."

"Don't throw a clot," I say. I hand her the SynHeme Gold. "Here. I didn't want it anyway."

"About time," she says, twisting the cap off and drinking as she walks out of the kitchen.

"Yeah, you're welcome," I call after her, closing the door.

I go to my room and take out my textbooks. Before I get to my homework, I check my computer, but Claire isn't online, so I put on my iPoddMax, pick "Funny You Should Ask. . . ." by the Emetics.

I get in bed and pull the curved Sol-Blok canopy over me and snap it shut. My cocoon. I'm going to close my eyes for just a few minutes.

I wake up and get out of bed. The Sol-Blok blinds have already automatically rolled down over my windows, and the room is black. Since the light sensors on the roof activate the blinds an hour before sunrise, it means I've slept for at least three hours. Fantastic. Now I'll probably be up all day.

The only thing I have an appetite for at dinner is meat. Mom took one slice and ate half. She's filling up on vegetables and glasses of the Sangre-Vin that Troy brought back from his last business trip to Europe. Supposedly they ferment the wine with a few drops of actual blood, not like the completely synthetic heme that's added to California Sangre-Vins. Real Sangre-Vins are illegal in most countries, since it can be addictive if you drink too much. My guess is that Troy could get in some real trouble for bringing it back to the States.

I guess Troy's nice enough, but when you get down to it, the guy is boring. I have a feeling he knows it, too, which is why he tries to use slang and stuff to convince us that he's cool. Still, dull or not, when Mom met Troy, that was it. They got married, had Paige, and here we are. One big happy family.

Loretta comes in with her coat over her arm. She's short and built like a little football player. She has a lot of facial and cranial bone damage and scars from too many rough times at the compound. Even so, she still sings while she works, and she always has a smile for me.

"Excellent dinner tonight, Loretta," Troy says. "We should get you your own celebrity cooking show on TV. Like that Wulfghang Packe."

"Oh, I don't deserve a television show. I just know what you like."

Paige looks up at her, grinning through a mouthful of Fettuccini Caprese. Loretta smiles back at her, probably not getting that Paige is being obnoxious.

"Actually," Jessica says, "I was going to tell you that I don't like basil anymore, so could you not put any in my food from now on?" She gives Loretta her fake smile, the same one she gives the wulf custodians at school.

"If there's nothing else, I'll be leaving now, ma'am," Loretta says to Mom. She keeps her eyes lowered and holds her swollen-knuckled hands behind her back.

"That's fine, Loretta. Oh, I have a blouse at the tailor's. Could you pick it up next Wednesday morning before you leave?"

Loretta's already crumpled brows move even closer together. Like a body echo, her shoulders hunch forward, too. "Oh, ma'am. I meant to tell you. I got new papers served. The A3-221-F compound is full. They want me to go to the new one, A6-004-F. I have to appear on Tuesday for processing." She swallows hard.

Mom frowns. "Tuesday. Well, that's not very convenient. I don't know if Maggie will be able to cover for you."

"I left a message for her already. I should speak to her later today."

"Good thinking, Loretta. Please make sure it's all arranged."

"I will, ma'am." She gives a little bow. "Have a good morning, everyone." She smiles at us with her mouth closed. Even though Mom paid to have Loretta's teeth fixed (which I always thought was more for Mom's benefit than for Loretta's) she still stays tight-lipped when she smiles. Habit, I guess.

Loretta goes through the Sol-Blok photoshield double doors. I picture her outside in the sunlight, waiting at the end of the driveway for her husband to pick her up in his old car. It must be tough for them to split up and go to different containment compounds. I don't know if they keep males and females separated to stop aggressive males from killing the females, or to prevent unwanted mating.

Mom takes a sip of her Sangre-Vin, then spears a few string beans. "Did you want some heme, Dante?" She's the only one in the world who insists on calling me by my given name, which I hate. Almost as much as I hate her telling me when to eat and drink.

My stomach tightens. "No, thanks."

"You haven't had anything to drink," she says.

"Not thirsty."

"Maybe you ought to check your crit," Troy says.

"It's fine. Anyway, I left my hemometer in my locker," I lie.

"So use the one in the kitchen," Mom says.

"Mom, no," Jess says. "He always leaves it sticky."

"I do not. *You* do. And when's the last time you washed your hands? Who knows where they've—"

"Okay, that's enough," Mom says. "Just please go in and check your crit."

I get up and resist the urge to throw my napkin at Jessica. Instead, I put it next to my plate and go into the kitchen. If I don't use the hemometer and Mom checks the log, then she'll ask why I lied about it, and I'll get the "trust" lecture.

I take the monitor off the cradle, open the clip, and put my fingertip inside. The display blinks red; then numbers show up on the display, along with my heart rate.

Just like I thought.

"Hemoglobin is seven, crit is twenty-eight," I say, sitting back down at the table. "I told you."

Mom tilts her head a little and leans back in her chair. "Is something else bothering you?"

"No. I just didn't feel that well today."

She looks at Troy, then back at me. "That must be the third time this week. Do you need to go to the doctor?"

The more irritation I show, the more she'll question me. I have to keep cool. "No, I'm good. Really."

We eat in silence for a minute or two.

"That Loretta," Mom says. "I'm seriously thinking about letting her go and getting a human maid. It would be much easier to have one person."

"You realize you'll have to pay a human about twice as much," Troy says to her.

"I don't care about the cost. We wouldn't have to deal with the switchover every month."

"Wait a minute," I say. "Are you serious? You're thinking about firing Loretta because she has to take off early *one* day this month to register at another compound?"

Mom turns to me, her eyes steady, her face calm. "It isn't just about this incident, Dante. We have to go through this every month, and frankly, it's inconvenient."

"My guess is that she finds it pretty inconvenient, too," I say.

"I say ditch her," Jess chimes in. "No offense, but *seriously*. I can't stand looking at all those facial ridges. And she has BO." She doesn't even look up from her food as she says this.

"Nice way to talk about Loretta," I say.

"I'm just being honest," Jess says. "What do you think, Paige?"

"I think she looks gross." Paige twists her mouth and crosses her eyes.

I'm going to puke. "You have got to be kidding. Paige, Loretta's been with us since you were a baby."

"But her face is a nightmare," Paige says. Obviously something she heard from Jessica.

"Mom, are you hearing this? Jessica is completely ruining her."

Paige throws back her head and sings, " 'If your teeth have that hue, and they're just a bit too blue, new improved Blue-Shoo's the toothpaste for you!' " Just to annoy me.

"Paige, honey," Troy says. "No commercials at the table, please."

Mom is frowning at me. "Let's not get overdramatic."

How dumb am I, looking to Mom for help against Jessica? They're practically best friends. Mom is even wearing Jessica's Delicious Couture sweats. And Mom is the one who brought up the idea of firing Loretta in the first place.

Jessica shrugs. "Looks like I'm right."

"You're disgusting," I say.

Jessica turns a slow gaze on me. "*I'm* disgusting? It's *my* fault she smells like a wet dog half the time? She needs a stick of extra-strong Lupine Fresh. And her face *is* hideous. It's not *my* fault she's a wulf."

"You're half-wulf yourself! What makes you—"

"I'm not half-wulf. Not anymore." She points her fork at me and waves it up and down. "*My* treatments worked. *You're* the only one here who's half—"

Troy clears his throat. "Okay, easy now."

I take a few breaths. I'm getting mad, but they're all against me, at least about Loretta, so I have to pick my argument carefully. "Look. Mom. I get that it's 'inconvenient' to deal with Loretta going to the compound. But it's not fair to fire her just because she's a wulf."

Jessica's laughing and shaking her head. "So, what? Now you're a wulf-rights activist? Little Huey Seele? Since when do you care about wulves so much?"

"I'm not an activist and I'm not talking about wulf rights. I'm talking about Loretta, not some random wulf. She's practically family."

Jessica snorts and tosses her hair. "I'd kill myself if I was related to her."

"Why not do it anyway?" I suggest.

Mom slaps her hand on the table. Her jewelry rattles. "That is a horrifying thing to say, Dante. What is *wrong* with you?" she hisses.

"What's wrong with *me*? How about your daughter there, who's acting like a complete b—"

"Easy, now," Troy interrupts loudly. "Let's not have a squabble. Let's all just remain arctic."

I look at him. He gives me a big smile. Maybe he didn't mean any harm, but it just makes me madder. So now I take on an upper-crust British accent. "Yes, let's do. We are not barbarians. And those nasty emotions are so . . . *wulven*."

Mom hits the table again. "That's enough out of you, Dante. I don't care for that tone. And Troy did not bring up wulven issues. You did. You're lashing out at everyone, behaving like a complete . . . bear. So I strongly suggest you put this attitude aside."

She was going to say I was acting like a complete wulf. I know she was.

"Sorry, Troy," I mumble.

"Ah, don't worry about it, chilidog," Troy says.

Mom shakes her head at me. She sits back in her chair and picks imaginary lint off her (or make that Jessica's) hundred-dollar sweatpants.

I move the food around my plate for a minute or so. "May I be excused?"

"Please," she says, adjusting her jewelry, which was perfectly straight already.

I take my plate and unused glass to the kitchen.

Upstairs in my room, I turn on the monitor and choose the display from camera two, which faces east. The sun is hitting the woods in the nature preserve behind our house.

I switch my computer on. Troy installed an Internet window that runs continuously, day and night. He says it's important to be up on current events if you want to get anywhere in this world. I hate that he messes with my computer.

There's a video of Congress in session, with a reporter speaking over the image.

"The Senate vote was split along vampyre-human-wulf partisan lines, in a landslide veto of the proposed National Lycanthrope Rights Hearing Committee—the third such veto this year. Senate Majority Leader Elinor Reid, a vampyre Neo-Republicrat from Texas, had this to say . . ."

The camera cuts to an attractive blond woman who looks about forty, but at 167, is actually the oldest member of Congress. "The bill is dead. We can finally stop wasting time and federal funds on this foolishness." The picture switches to the reporter, a handsome vampyre, who says, "Wulf activist Huey Seele vows to take this issue to the U.S. Supreme

Court. But with a vampyre-packed legislature, he's unlikely to find any—"

I turn the sound off. I'm tired of hearing the same old wulf-rights stories, the constant fighting against a system that won't change. I still have a headache.

Too bad for the wulves, but I've got problems of my own.

2
EVERYTHING I'M NOT

How cool is this? Mixed grade levels in Gym could have turned out to be a nightmare, with freshmen getting destroyed by the older kids. But that's not what happened. Not to me, anyway. Somehow *I* got on the good side of the most popular kid in school.

Gunther Hoering's a senior, and is basically the school's biggest celebrity. He's smart, he's rich, and girls love him. He keeps his nearly white hair very short on the sides and back, and long, like way over his eyes, in the front. He's constantly tossing it out of his face. I wouldn't notice this kind of thing, except that all the girls talk about him and his hair and how *cute* he is. And if that's not enough, he's an athlete—a runner and an ATA-ranked tennis player. I've never heard anyone say a bad word about him. He's everything I'm not.

So it's crazy that he would even acknowledge my existence, and even more unbelievable that he seems to *like* me, too. I was paired up with him for the Presidential Whatever test three weeks ago and held his feet down while he did sit-ups. Gunther was competing with a friend of his; they'd bet a hundred bucks on who could do more crunches in the the allotted time. So when the other kid passed seventy and Gunther was only up to fifty-five, I did the sensible thing: I started counting by twos. Mr. Carver didn't believe the final number Gunther reported, which was twenty-four more than his friend, but I vouched for the count. Gunther won the hundred bucks, so here I am, listening to his commentary as each kid climbs the rope.

"Watch this, watch him slide down," Gunther says, looking up and elbowing me. "That rope is the closest he's ever been to true love."

"Yeah, and good luck getting his underwear unstuck from his butt after that," I say.

Gunther laughs. I'm like his court jester, which has benefits. One time in the locker room, he stopped another senior from snapping me with a wet towel. And last week, Gunther said hi to me while he was walking down the hall with his buddies. The best part was that Jessica happened to be nearby, and I thought she was going to drop dead from shock. She *never* acknowledges me at school, and I could tell she was trying to figure out how her uncool little brother got in Gunther Hoering's good graces.

"What's up with *that* kid?" Gunther asks. He nods at Craig Lewczyk, who was sitting by himself on the floor until Mr. Carver pointed at him to climb. He limps toward the rope.

"That's Craig Lewczyk."

"You know him?"

"Kind of. A little," I say.

Actually, we used to play war games in the nature preserve behind my house when we were in elementary school. But after he turned twelve and registered, Craig went through the Change and started hanging out with wulf kids. He doesn't talk much anymore, and he doesn't talk to me at all.

Now Craig has lycanthropic arthritis. His joints are all messed up from the Change.

He struggles to get up the rope.

Gunther shakes his head. "Look at him. Why would they put a kid like that in our gym class?"

I shrug. It's not like I owe Craig loyalty or anything. After all, *he's* the one who cut *me* off. Maybe for him it's like how cops have a hard time relating to civilians, because they don't think regular people can understand what the job does to them.

I don't feel anything for him except maybe pity as he works his way back down the rope. He didn't even make it to the top.

"Mr. Hoering, you're up," Mr. Carver says.

Gunther leans over me. "Watch me rocket up this thing. I'll be the fastest one in class. Guaranteed. And this'll be for real. No counting by twos necessary."

He gets up and walks to the rope, then turns to all of us watching. "Don't blink, boys, or you'll miss the fastest trip up the rope in school history." Mr. Carver blows his whistle. Gunther throws up his arms and takes off. He has a good vertical jump and his hands grab on about ten feet from the floor. He entwines the rope around his feet and shimmies up like a snake. Before I know it, he's at the top.

"Seventeen seconds," Mr. Carver calls.

Gunther's almost a blur as he slides down.

"Next," Mr. Carver says.

That's me. I get up and go to the rope. After Gunther's lightning-fast climb, this is going to be embarrassing. Mr. Carver gives a short blast from the whistle, and I jump.

I pull myself up, trying to get the rope around my feet, but I can't get it hooked right. Better to forget about using my legs. I pull with my right arm, and it feels way too easy. Now left. Now right, and it's like I weigh ten pounds.

Hand over hand, I move up the rope, my feet hanging loose. I bang my head on the ceiling of the gym.

I hear Mr. Carver shout, "Thirty seconds!"

Totally humiliating. I thought I was faster than that, maybe twenty-five. But *thirty*?

When I get to the bottom, Mr. Carver is staring at me, his ridged and scarred brow raised.

"Not even twenty-nine?" I say.

"What are you talking about? It was thirteen seconds."

"Thir*teen*? I thought you said *thirty*."

"Thirty? You flew up that rope. I never saw you move so quick. Nice job." He claps me on the shoulder, a little wulf-to-wulf solidarity, which I don't need or want.

Everyone's shouting at Gunther Hoering. A lot of woo-hoos, some whistles. There are also a few comments, like: "Gunther, dusted," and "Gunth, man, you just got blasted by a freshman. How bad do *you* suck?"

Thirteen seconds. Thirteen. That's even faster than the wulf jocks.

I go back to my spot against the wall. Gunther is not smiling.

"That was fast," he says.

"Yeah, I'm surprised."

"Are you?" He turns away from me and watches the next kid climb. Getting beaten by a freshman does not make him happy. It's probably best to leave it alone, so I stay quiet and wait for the bell to ring.

"Another weapon that Confederate soldiers used is believed to have been invented by General Thomas 'Stonewall' Jackson," Mr. Morrison says.

I'm only half listening. I'm looking at Juliet Walker, trying to think of a casual way to talk to her.

"Danny? Are you with us?" Mr. Morrison asks, rapping his knuckles on my desk.

"Huh? Yes, I am. Stonewall Jackson."

"Right. Stonewall Jackson is credited with inventing the 'rebel yell,' which makes sense, coming from a wulf. It has a primal, feral quality that makes the blood run cold. Jackson himself caused it to be introduced to the Union army. At the Battle of Manassas, he ordered his soldiers to 'Charge, men, and yell like the furies!' And then they attacked."

Suddenly the air is filled with an astonishingly loud, high-pitched shriek, like a cross between a scream and a fire engine siren, which is why I'm on my ass with my chair and desk knocked over, my heart going a mile a minute.

Of course, the class goes wild. Even Mr. Morrison is smiling. "And Danny Gray was kind enough to demonstrate the effect the rebel yell had on the Union soldiers."

"Oh, happy to be of service," I say, my ears still ringing. I get up and right my desk and chair. Looking to the side, I see that Juliet Walker is smiling.

Way to go. Could I have made a bigger fool of myself in front of her?

The period bell does its *ping-ping-ping*, and we all gather our books and head out.

"Hey." A female voice.

I turn. It's Juliet Walker. It's *her*. Talking to me. Completely out of the blue. Talk, say something. "Uh . . ."

I've never been this close to her. Now I can see a spray of freckles on the bridge of her nose. No vamp kids have freckles, of course. But she does. It's so . . . exotic.

"Are you okay?" she asks. And her eyes are green. I love that. "You *can* talk, right? Or are you still feeling the after-effects of Mr. Morrison's rebel yell?" she asks.

"No. I mean, yeah. Oh, man. He totally startled me. It was, like, so sudden and loud."

"I know. I almost peed my pants," she says.

"I almost did a lot worse." Her locker is down at the other end of the hall, which means she came here on purpose. To talk to me.

"Oh. I thought you fell off your chair for a laugh." She leans against the locker.

"Well, in that case," I say, "yes. That was my plan." Keep it cool, stay relaxed. Or at least pretend to be.

She laughs. "Nice try. We were *all* pretty startled, I'd say."

"I think I'll get revenge by giving *Mr. Morrison* a rebel yell when his back is turned. See how he likes it."

"Um, he's not exactly young. You'd probably give him a heart attack."

"Probably." This is a conversation. We're having a conversation.

"What?"

Don't let it stop. Keep going. "I guess I'll have to pay attention in there from now on. I can't say I was, you know, riveted by the lesson."

"Me, neither," she says. "I was half asleep. I do the afternoon schedule here. Then I go home, eat, and come back for Carpathia classes, eight to midnight. And after that, homework."

"That's brutal," I say. "I'm impressed. I mean, seriously. Two schools, plus advanced classes here, and you still do great."

She shakes her head and smiles shyly. "I don't know about *great*."

"You do. I mean, I notice in class, you always have the right answers. You're smart." Easy, boy. Don't embarrass her. "But it must suck to have to be all about school every minute of the day and night."

She smiles. She smiles at *me*. "Well, I have *some* free time."

Okay, now that's interesting. Is she trying to tell me something? "Sure. Of course," I say.

"I mean, I need to have fun, too. Right?" she says.

Oh, man. There's no way I'm misreading her. I'm sure. No, no. Not sure. But there may not be another chance. Just say it. "Well, maybe we can do something. Go out and do something sometime. I can't promise it'll be fun. . . ." Shut up, just shut up right now. "But we can give it a good try." Idiot!

She pulls the ends of her sweater sleeves over her hands. "Sure."

Did she just say what I think she said? "Huh? Sure?" I repeat, like a dim-witted parrot.

"Yeah. Saturday night, I usually hang outside Bartlow's Market, in the parking lot. You know where that is?"

"Bartlow's? Sure. So, what, you just go and stand there in the parking lot? Just, like, stand there?"

"That's where we hang out."

"Great. Saturday night? Great." Say *great* one more time. Impress her with that wide-ranging vocabulary.

"Okay. I have to go. My dad is probably waiting for me out front."

"Okay. Well, see you tomorrow."

She smiles again and I watch her leave.

"So what do you think that means?" I ask Claire.

"I told you, I don't know. But keep asking me. Maybe after the twentieth time I'll have an answer."

We're walking down the crowded hall after third period. Oliver is walking with us, twisting his gelled blond hair into spikes.

"If you ask me," Oliver says, "it means you're in. Definitely. It's code."

"That's idiotic," Claire says, throwing him a look. "Which is why nobody *is* asking you."

"I'm almost positive she said 'that's where we hang out.' *We*. So does she mean that's where we—meaning her friends and *she*—hang out, or does she mean *we* like the two of us?"

"How could she mean the two of you, if you've never hung out with her?" Oliver asks.

"I don't know. That's what I'm trying to figure out."

"You know what?" Claire says. "We're getting sick of this conversation."

"I'm not," Oliver says.

Claire narrows her eyes at him. "Then I'm using the royal *we*." Then, back to me. "We, that is, *I*, am done talking about this. You'll find out what she means on Saturday."

"I just want to know what to expect," I say, more to myself than to them. "Hey, look who it is." I raise my chin, directing their attention down the hall.

"Who?" Oliver asks. "Gunther Hoering?"

"My *pal* Gunther Hoering."

Claire shakes her head. "Yeah, so you've been saying. For three weeks."

"Because it's true."

Claire laughs. "In your dreams."

"Seriously. Watch." As we get close to passing, I call to him. "Hey, Gunther. How's it going?"

I'm pretty sure he glances at me before turning back to the girl he was talking to.

"I see what you mean. That's a really tight bond you two have," Claire says.

"He just didn't hear me."

Oliver laughs. "He didn't see you, either. Give it up, Danny. We are so under his radar, he doesn't even know we're alive."

He turns and looks at Gunther. "I'd love to get my hair cut like his, though."

I could argue with them, tell them how Gunther jokes around with me in gym, but they're not going to believe it, so why waste my breath? Then I notice. "Pot roast for lunch."

"You saw the menu?" Oliver is always interested in what's for lunch.

"No, I smell it."

Claire laughs at me. "How can you smell it? The caf is on the other end of the building."

"How can you *not* smell it? The whole school stinks of it."

She gives me a look, like, *You're a wacko*, but she has to be kidding: the hallway reeks of meat. Now that I think of it, it reeks of a lot of smells. Sweat. Laundry detergent. Someone with totally rank body odor. Paint. Fertilizer someone must have walked through on the way to school. Deodorant. The urinal cakes in the boys' room. Perfume. Cherry lip gloss. And I can pick out at least fifteen different types of shampoo.

I've never had an unusually good sense of smell, so this is a little weird. I don't know what to make of it.

But what do I care? The important thing is that Juliet Walker is going to hang out with me. Or with me and her friends, but whatever. Either way, she said yes. Which makes this a very, very good night.

3
SPECISTS

I'm walking home with Claire after school when headlights shine past us and a new Porsche rolls up to the curb.

Gunther's car.

His window goes down. "Come here."

Claire and I glance at each other. She looks confused. "*See*? I told you," I say. We start toward the car.

Gunther shakes his head. "No, not you. Just him."

We look at each other again. "Don't worry. If he's giving me a ride home, I'll make sure you can come, too."

Claire raises her eyebrow at me, but doesn't say anything.

I go over to Gunther's window to see what he wants. He's alone in the car, wearing a black cable-knit cardigan and an ivory fedora with a red band. I wish I had the confidence to dress like that. I'm always in browns and greens.

"Hey. What's up?" I ask.

He looks ahead through the windshield. "That whole thing in Gym. With the rope. How'd you do it so fast?"

"Oh. Well. I don't know. It's no big deal. Really. You were fast, too."

"I know you're half-vamp, that's obvious. But that only accounts for speed and coordination." He looks at me. "You didn't even use your legs. And strength like you had this morning? That's not human." His eyes narrow. "So it makes me wonder about your other half."

I hate when this comes up. "Well, I'm half-wulf."

Gunther's lips tighten. "Half-wulf. Funny you never mentioned it."

"Why would I? I mean, you can see that I'm not totally vamp, so that means either part-human or—"

"But isn't Jessica Gray your sister?"

I put on a face and voice like a guilty man confessing. "Okay, I'll admit it. She is." I cross my hands at the wrists like they're handcuffed and hold them out to him.

He pulls back in his seat, away from my hands. He's not smiling. "Well, she's all-vamp, right? She looks like she is."

Okay, if I tell the truth, Jess is going to murder me. Literally. "Um, yeah." Not a lie, strictly speaking.

"Right. So I had no reason to think you were wulf."

"I guess not." This is so disappointing. Well, maybe I can fix this. Make him laugh. "I guess I should probably wear a shirt—or wait, a sandwich sign—with 'I'm one-half wulf!' on it."

"Yeah, that's funny." He didn't smile. "Don't you think you should warn people? You think it's honest to deliberately make people believe you're human?"

"I never said I was human."

"Yeah, well, you don't seem like one of . . . them. A wulf."

"But I'm not. I mean, I had the genetic treatments." Which is true. I don't have to go into the details about how I had a Recombinant DNA-mRNA Mutation reaction, the anadiploidy shock, or how that meant they couldn't finish the series of treatments. It doesn't matter. "It's not like I'm a *wulf*-wulf. Those genes were deactivated."

"Yeah, but you were born with wulf genes. So you're part-wulf. Right or wrong?"

"I guess so, if you put it like that. My dad was a wulf."

"Was?"

"I mean, my dad when I was born. He and my mom split up. I don't see him much anymore."

"Oh, so it's not that he's dead."

"What? Oh, no. Not at all. He's totally fine."

"Huh. Too bad."

Then Gunther revs the engine, throws the car into gear, and nearly runs over my toes as he roars away.

When we're one block from where Claire goes left and I go right, Claire says, "He's a total specist. I could have told you that."

"So why didn't you?"

"Because you thought he was the best guy on the planet, and you had this bizarre fantasy that he was your friend. Besides, with your little hero-worship thing going, you wouldn't have believed me anyway."

I don't know if it's her raised eyebrow or the fact that

she's right that makes me want to shake her. "Probably not. He didn't seem that way."

Claire shrugs. "They never do. Look at his father."

"His father? Come on—he's, like, a pillar of the community. I heard he worked as an advisor to the president once."

"He's also in the Knights of the Brotherhood."

"So? He *is* a vampyre. What's so bad about a vamp being in a vampyre social club?"

"Oh, nothing, except the Knights of the Brotherhood is one step short of being the KKK. If it were up to them, they'd have every wulf in the country exiled or lynched."

"I think that's a myth."

"Look it up. Anyway, the point is, Gunther Hoering and his family hate wulves."

We get to her house and she checks the mailbox.

This whole thing is really depressing. "I just don't get why Gunther feels like I tricked him. So, what? I'm supposed to say, 'Hi, I'm Danny Gray and just so you know, I'm half-wulf,' to everyone I meet?"

"Not everyone. But use your judgment, dummy."

"How was I supposed to know he was a specist?"

"My approach? If in doubt, assume someone is evil."

"What a refreshing and optimistic view of life."

"It's a cold, cruel world, baby. Get used to it." She squeezes my cheek like an obnoxious relative pinching a baby. "I'm going in. You staying or going?"

"I better go home. It's going to be light soon."

"Okay. See you tomorrow."

Walking home, I think about how Gunther turned out to be a specist scumbag. How I actually thought we were friends.

As far as I'm concerned, I couldn't care less if I never talk to him again.

"What did you say to Gunther Hoering?" Jessica shouts at me the second I walk in the house.

"Can you speak up? I didn't hear you." I drop my book bag and shut the door. The Sol-Blok shades on the windows are already down and sealed.

"Did you tell Gunther Hoering that I'm part-wulf?" Maybe not a scream, but a bellow for sure.

"I'm sorry. I seem to have gone deaf because of a piercing shrieking sound. I don't know sign language, so maybe I'll understand you better if you talk softly and slowly."

Jessica's normally white face is now dark red, moving toward purple. She's breathing loudly through her nose. She knows I'll walk away if she keeps shouting, so she's working hard to control herself. "What. Did. You. Say. About. Me. To. Gunther. Hoering."

"Oh, that's what you wanted to know? Well, it's like this." I walk into the kitchen. Partly because I'm hungry, partly because I'm going to make Jess pay for screaming at me. She follows me in.

"Tell me," she demands.

"Hi, Loretta," I say. "How's your day been?"

"Not too bad. I got some nice Cornish game hens for your supper tonight, and I made that string-bean dish your mom likes."

"Sounds good," I say, picking a pear from the bowl on the granite counter. "Does that take a lot of work, cooking those hens?"

Jessica actually stamps her foot. "Dante! If you don't just . . ." She stops herself and closes her eyes tightly.

Loretta looks at her. "You be careful before you burst a blood vessel or something."

"I just want my darling brother to stop . . . fooling around and to answer my question before I have to open the knife drawer."

"It's touching when you call me *darling* with so much affection. Really."

I brush past her as I leave the kitchen and go into the living room. Of course, she follows me.

"Can you *please* just tell me what you said to Gunther?"

I sit on the couch and bite into the pear. "Why, did he say something to you?"

"He asked me if you're my brother. I told him: unfortunately, yes. Then he asked if I dyed my hair or used DermaWhite. When I said no, he said that that's what he thought, and then he asked what your deal was. I asked him what he meant, but he told me to forget it."

"Then what?"

"Then he left. I want to know why he's asking about me and you in the same conversation."

"Maybe because we're related and have the same last name."

Jess adjusts her T-shirt dress so it hangs perfectly over her black-and-gold tights. She checks the clasp on her Tiffany bracelet and rearranges the long necklaces that loop down to her waist. "How does he know you?" she asks.

"We hang out in Gym. Joking and stuff. Or we used to."

"Right."

"Seriously." I put my feet against the edge of the glass table, which Mom would kill me for doing. "Hey, I was surprised, too, believe me. Then today he asked me if I was part-wulf."

"He what? Why?"

I shrug. "I don't know. I climbed the rope faster than him, and he got all weird."

"Well, what did you say?" I can see the tension in her jaw. It's kind of funny.

"I said I was."

"Unbelievable. Thanks a lot!" she says, starting to turn that purple color again.

"Well, sorry, but it's the truth. I can't help it." I finish my pear and put the core on the table, careful to stand it up so only the dry skin on the bottom touches the glass. Mom doesn't like smudges. I turn back to Jessica: "Why are you all psycho about it, anyway? I mean, yeah, Gunther Hoering is a big shot at school, but did you know he's a complete specist? Like, *viciously* specist?"

"So?" Jessica is pacing back and forth across the living room, holding her head in both hands. She adjusts her tartan headband.

I shake my head. "He's a jerk. What do you care what he thinks about you?"

"See, this is why I don't want you even *talk*ing to my friends when they're here. You're a social moron. You don't get it. Why do I care? *Everyone* cares what Gunther Hoering thinks."

"No, I do get it. But then when I saw what he's really like—"

Jess looks at the ceiling and actually growls, then grabs her own hair and pulls at it like she might tear it out of her head. "Why am I even talking to you?" She glares at me. "*Don't* talk about me again. Ever. To anyone. We're not related. I have nothing to do with you. Understand me?"

"Yeah. I shouldn't talk about you to anyone. Except seniors. And really popular people. And only to let them know that you're half-wulf. That's what you mean, right?"

She smacks me on the back of my head as she storms off.

For some reason, my ears are ringing, even though she didn't hit me hard. And here comes that headache again.

I reach for the pear core on the table, and . . . now, this is weird. My right hand won't close. I can only bend my fingers about halfway; then they get tight. I open my hand and flex the fingers straight, but when I try to close them to make a fist I only get about halfway again. Trying to force them with my other hand only makes it hurt more.

The knuckles on the fingers of my right hand are kind of swollen. They look like an old human's arthritic hands. Or like Loretta's hands, though not nearly as bad.

I pick up the pear core with my left hand and go to the kitchen to throw it away. I'm not going to worry about this anymore. It's probably just some kind of flu. No big deal.

Except for one thing.

Vampyres don't get the flu.

They don't get sick.

Ever.

4
REVERBERATIONS

Health class is so stupid. Like we haven't heard this stuff a million times already. But Ms. Vaughn doesn't seem like she's about to stop, so I guess it's going to be a million and one times.

"Okay, trade quizzes with your partner so we can mark them. Let's go. Number one: ISTD stands for? Michael?"

"Um, A: Interspecies Sexually Transmitted Disorder."

"Close. It's D: Interspecies Sexually Transmitted *Disease*. Put an X through the number if it's wrong. Two, true or false: a human can be turned into a vampyre through sexual contact. Elyse?"

"False."

"Correct. This isn't on the quiz, but can a human be turned into a vampyre from a bite?"

We all say no, in completely bored voices. Like anyone still believes that idiotic myth.

"What are the ways a human can be turned into a vampyre. Danny?"

This is like third grade stuff. What a waste of time. "They can't. The only way to be a vampyre is through genetics. If your parents are vamps."

"Absolutely correct. Next question, three: a human can sexually transmit HIV to a vampyre, true or false. Sydney?"

"False. Vamps are immune to all human diseases."

"Correct. Next: if a male vampyre mates with a human female, she can become pregnant, true or false? Tomas?"

"If he's stupid and doesn't use protection, sure. But if he's smart, he'll deny it's his."

Not so many people laugh. We've heard all his jokes before, and we just want the period to end.

"That's very honorable, Tomas. Now, moving on: if a female vampyre mates with a male wulf—"

"Eww," Tiffany Welsh says, loudly enough to make sure everyone hears her.

"Tiffany . . ."

"No, seriously, Ms. Vaughn. Why would a vamp girl do it with a howler?"

"How about, like, *really* low self-esteem?" Elyse says.

A bunch of the girls laugh. The vamp boys look at each other and grin smugly.

Ms. Vaughn folds her arms over her chest, making herself look smaller, which she does whenever she gets uncomfortable. "First of all, let's start with you not using derogatory terms."

"So we can't say face-case or moondog or crumpskull or lunabitch, either?" Tomas asks.

"It's not like there're any wulves in here anyway. The only one in this class is Craig Lewczyk, and he's still out sick."

I keep my mouth shut.

"Regardless," Ms. Vaughn says, "I don't want those kinds of expressions used here."

"Sor-reee," Tiffany says. "But seriously, why would any self-respecting vamp girl want to have *sexual relations* with a lycanthrope?"

She is so obnoxious.

Vocabulary quiz from Constance, eighth grade: Natatorium. Nobody knew; she told us it was an indoor swimming pool building.

I hate the smell of chlorine. And I hate this heavy, humid air. Faded MILLBROOK HIGH SCHOOL CHAMPION banners hang from the ceiling; we don't have our own team name because we're technically part of Millbrook.

"What's the point of making it mandatory to go to ten school events if we don't want to be here?" I ask Claire.

"To keep attendance up, I guess."

"Nothing like fake school spirit, huh?"

"Stop your whining. It'll be over soon. At least it's Friday."

It *is* Friday. Which means tomorrow night is my date—or hangout or whatever it is—with Juliet Walker. Emphasis on *whatever it is*.

"What if I'm reading her wrong?" I ask Claire.

She tilts her head back and turns her eyes to the ceiling. "Please, not again."

"I trust your opinion."

She looks at me, a half-smile on her face. "That's the best you can come up with?"

"It's true." There's the eardrum-piercing shriek of a whistle, followed by a splash as the swimmers hit the water. My ears are ringing from the whistle, which is amplified by the tile and the high ceiling. "Seriously. I need to know if she likes me, and I trust you."

Claire turns back to the pool. "First, you're making me sick, so don't bother trying to act all sincere with me. You're not good at it. Second, you're asking the wrong girl. I don't have a whole lot of experience with . . . relationships, or whatever. As you know."

I look back down the pool, watching the girls slice through the water. Gunther's current girlfriend, Alana Gibson, is swimming in practically every race. Gunther and his crew are a few rows in front of us.

There's a pack of wulf kids sitting at the very end of the bleachers, near the starting blocks. There's at least five yards between them and everyone else. They're obviously here just to get their extracurricular cards stamped.

When Alana wins the 100-meter butterfly by two-and-a-half body lengths, Gunther and his guys go wild.

One of the referees taps the microphone, setting off a squeal that reverberates through the pool house. "Once again, the winner is Carpathia's Alana Gibson."

Gunther and his buddies whoop and whistle over the referee's announcement of the names of the vamp girl who finished second and the human girl who finished third.

The wulf kids cheer and shout, too, but there's a different tone to it.

"Why don't you mutts shut the hell up?" Gunther shouts at them.

One of them, a kid named Charlie Hogan, grins at Gunther. "Hey, man. We're just cheering for our girl."

"She's not your girl," Gunther calls. "Notice that she walks upright."

Alana Gibson pulls herself up out of the pool. Her slick red bathing suit hugs every curve, and water streams down her long legs.

I turn to Claire, who's staring at her.

"Easy, now," I say.

"Yeah, same to you."

Alana has to pass right in front of the wulf kids to get back to the swimmers' bench. They watch her, all of them grinning as she comes close. She slips her thumbs under the straps on her shoulders and pulls the bathing suit up a bit.

The wulf kids yell, "Hey, Alana!" and "Nice strokes!" when she passes by. I'm watching her face as the guys call out to her. She rolls her eyes, but there's definitely a hint of a smile.

"Hey, can't you do something about that smell?" Alex Fourier calls to the wulves. "The whole place stinks like wet dog."

"Go chase cars or something," Gunther yells.

The wulf kids shout back at them, mostly curses. Since wulves don't have the same bleeding problems that vamps have, they don't worry much about avoiding fights.

The assistant swim coach, Mr. Wentworth, walks over to the wulf kids. "If you boys can't act civilized—"

"Try housebroken!" Gunther yells.

A bunch of people around us laugh, but I don't. Claire doesn't, either.

"You're going to be removed," Mr. Wentworth finishes.

"*We're* going to be removed?" Charlie Hogan says, his eyes wide. "What about what *they* said?" He points his thumb over his shoulder at Gunther's crew.

"I didn't hear anything from them." Wentworth raises his voice, loud enough for a lot of people to hear. "You, boy, on the other hand, were rude, obnoxious, and disgusting. Any more trouble from you, and you're all suspended."

Gunther claps his hands. "Yeah, suspend him," he says cheerily. "By his *neck*, from a *lamp*post!"

Hogan gets to his feet, yanks off his varsity wrestling jacket, and glares at Gunther, but John Fusco elbows him and shakes his head. Hogan sits back down.

"We're just showing school spirit," Fusco says to the assistant coach. "Go, Carpathia. Rah-rah." His voice is monotone.

Mr. Wentworth walks away. The swimmers for the next race are standing on the starting blocks, watching the show. The starter is also watching, the whistle dead between her lips.

"I'm so glad we didn't get thrown out," Hogan says loudly. Then, even louder, he shouts, "Because we're really pumped to watch this intense sport."

"It's *way* cooler than mixed martial arts. Or football," Fusco says. "All the action of . . . watching. Grass. Grow."

"That's because you mongrels can't swim," Gunther calls back.

"Yeah, they can," Taylor Lattimore says. "They can doggie-paddle."

Gunther's boys laugh.

"You roasters aren't athletes," Hogan shouts. "You can't wrestle or play football, because one little boo-boo and you'll have a blood flood."

Gunther strides over to where the wulf kids are sitting. His guys follow.

The wulves stand up. Deadlock.

Gunther is a full head taller than Charlie Hogan, but Hogan is built like a fire hydrant.

"We stick to *refined* sports," Gunther says. "All you moon-dogs know how to do is smash and bash. Limited animal brains, lower form of life."

Hogan's nostrils flare and he balls his hands into fists.

Mr. Wentworth gets up again and moves toward them.

"Do it, troglodyte," Gunther says.

But Hogan doesn't hit him. He grabs Gunther by the front of his shirt and shoves him hard. Gunther goes into the pool, hitting the water with a big splash.

The crowd roars.

Gunther heaves himself out of the water. His expensive clothes drip heavily. Two teachers have come to walk Charlie Hogan out. He's laughing.

"This is a Rolex, face-case!" Gunther screams at Hogan. "If it's ruined, you're paying for it."

"Sue me," Hogan calls over his shoulder.

"You couldn't afford it. I could buy and sell your whole family."

Mr. Wentworth and two custodians escort Charlie Hogan

to the doors of the pool house. The vamp kids cheer, while Gunther looks up into the bleachers and clasps his hands over his head in a champion gesture. Then he tosses his blond hair, sending a spray of water onto some vamp girls, who squeal with delight.

The rest of the meet can't match the excitement of the floor show. Carpathia wins, mainly due to Alana Gibson.

"Well, that turned out to be a decent meet after all," Claire says to me as we climb down the bleachers.

"That was an *outstanding* meet," I say while pulling on my leather jacket. "Did you hear Gunther scream about his stupid watch?"

We shuffle along with the crowd toward the exit. I lean into Claire. "Oh. I came up with a really good solution to our problem."

"What problem is that?"

"About how to tell if Juliet Walker likes me or not."

"Right, see, that's not *our* problem, that's *your* problem," Claire says, staring hard at the back of Tiffany Welsh's head, impatient because Tiffany is yakking instead of trying to move forward.

"Whatever. Anyway, I figure the simplest way to do this is for you to come tomorrow night so you can watch and give me your opinion."

"Gee, really? I can? What an honor!" She sneers at the back of Tiffany's head and mimes punching it. "Thanks, but I'll pass."

"I'll be forever in your debt."

"You're already forever in my debt. And anyway, it's a stupid idea. You're trying to figure out if she likes you so you show up with another girl?"

"You're not another girl."

She jams the point of her elbow into my solar plexus, half knocking the wind out of me. I should have seen it coming.

"Good luck getting me to help you with *any*thing after that," she says.

"You know what I meant. I'm saying, you're not a girl-*friend*. We couldn't pretend to be together even if we wanted to. Just come. I know you don't have any plans."

"How do you know?"

"Because it's Saturday night. What plans would you have besides hanging out with me?"

She rolls her eyes. "Fine. It'll be fun watching you try to flirt." She stands on her toes, trying to see what's holding things up. "Would you guys move?" she shouts.

We finally get outside, and the crowd spreads out. Claire's dad is supposed to pick us up. "He said to wait for him there," Claire says, pointing to a far corner.

Just as we head in that direction, we hear the voice of our school's golden boy. "Nope, not this weekend," Gunther says. "I'm going hunting with my father."

"Yeah? For deer, or elk?" Victor Harmon asks.

"An elk is a type of deer, dumbass," Gunther says. He's still wet and his shirt is clinging to him. "Anyway, I don't care what I shoot as long as I get a good kill. Maybe I'll accidentally shoot a wulf. Now, that would be a tragedy." He turns to the side, raises an imaginary rifle to his shoulder, squints into an invisible scope and makes a *ka-pow* sound.

I can't tell if he knows I'm behind him or not.

"And maybe he'll accidentally shoot him*self*," I say to Claire. "Golden Boy? More like a dirtbag poser."

"Wow. I guess he's fallen off his pedestal," Claire says, shaking her head.

We take maybe five more steps before I hear Gunther shout.

"Hey, wulf boy." Gunther's holding open the passenger door of his Porsche for Alana Gibson. "Did you just call me a poser?"

I turn to Claire, who looks as surprised as I feel. I didn't think Gunther could hear me.

He shuts the door. "That's pretty funny coming from you, since *you're* the one trying to pass as a vamp." His smile is big. His friends think he's hilarious. He puts on a confused face. "Did you also say you wished I'd shoot myself?"

"I didn't say that I *wished* you would." Not out loud, anyway.

He walks around to the driver's side and opens the door. "You don't have to be scared. See, I don't care if you want me dead. I feel the same way about you. And by *you* I mean all your kind, but you especially. You don't even have to be dead. As long as you're gone." He smiles big, his perfect white teeth gleaming.

"Is that a threat?" Claire asks him. "Did you just threaten to kill him?"

Gunther laughs. His idiot friends join in. "No," he says. "I'm not threatening him or anyone else. I'm just saying how I feel. What I wish." His eyes have held mine the whole time he's been talking.

Obviously, I need to ignore him and walk away. "Well, I

guess it's a good thing for me—and 'my kind'—that you're *not* in charge. Even though you think you're the king of this school, you don't actually have any power over what happens or doesn't happen to any of us."

Gunther raises his eyebrows in mock surprise. "Okay, wulf boy. We'll see." He pops the collar of his shirt, still wet and still expensive.

I look at him. Claire squeezes my arm, but I'm determined not to lose this stare-down.

Gunther raises his imaginary rifle at me, squints, and pulls the invisible trigger. His lips form another *ka-pow*, but he doesn't make a sound. He lowers his "gun," then winks at me as he gets in the car.

Claire rolls her eyes. "That was just so cool and fun. Thanks for the experience. Now can we get out of here?"

But I'm not going to leave before he does. It would be like giving up.

Gunther starts the engine, then the car takes off.

I'm not sure what just happened, but I have a feeling I didn't come out on top.

5
HEARTBEATS

Saturday night. It's 9:40 p.m., and Juliet is late. Claire and I are standing in the shadows of Bartlow's Market. For thirty-five minutes we've been watching a bunch of kids hanging out at the far end of the parking lot. I'm nervous; Claire's annoyed.

"I'm thinking she might not show," I say. "Are you thinking that?"

"I'm thinking I should never have said yes to you. I have better things to do with my time."

"No you don't."

"Okay, but still."

I'm wondering if it's possible that one of those kids is Juliet and she's been there all along. No. I've been checking constantly, and my vision is sharp. Sharper than usual, even. Juliet isn't there. "Do I look okay?" I ask Claire.

"Not really."

"What?" I'm wearing jeans, a new green Oxford shirt over a GOT HEME? T-shirt, and my leather jacket. "What's the matter?"

"Well, you look like you always do, and that's not so good. No offense."

"Thanks. If you're trying to make sure I don't get over-confident, it's working."

Claire takes a look at me. I step back for inspection. "It wouldn't have killed you to shave," she says.

"Yeah, right. I just did, like two days ago."

"Well, maybe you're extra manly, but whatever; get rid of that stuff. It's gross."

I touch my face—she's not kidding. My chin and jaw have stubble. Impossible. Vamp facial hair doesn't grow that fast; I usually shave three or four times a year, but lately it seems like I've done it nearly every other week. Now it's every few days? What's that about?

Claire pulls back the sleeve of her vintage green army jacket, the one she keeps in her locker because her mother won't let her wear it, and looks at her Tiffany watch. "How long are we going to wait? We've been here over half an hour."

"I'm ignoring that, because you sound like a child. Anyway, you remember the signal, right?"

Claire laughs. "Wait, you're talking about a secret signal, but you say *I'm* acting childish?"

"I'm serious. When I put my hands behind my neck, then raise them up to stretch, that's the signal. I'll go into the store, then you wait at least one full minute before coming in after me. That way you can tell me how you think it's going."

"Why don't I just go into the store a few minutes after you do? Why do we need a signal?"

"It's just better that way. What if I go in the store to use the bathroom or something before you've had enough time to evaluate the situation completely? Then what? No, we're using the signal."

Claire shakes her head. "There's something wrong with you. Seriously."

"Hey," says a voice from behind us.

I jump. It's Juliet. And she looks really good.

"Sorry I'm late," she adds. "I had a whole big thing with my parents."

I knew it. I knew there'd be a good reason she was late. "Everything okay?" I ask.

"Yeah, it's fine. They wanted me to stay home and sleep. But I told them that I could sleep in tomorrow. So."

"So," I say. Juliet turns her head a little and smiles at the space to my left. Which I remember isn't just a space. "Oh, right. This is Claire. My friend, Claire."

They say hi to each other. "Yeah, I've seen you with Danny at school," Juliet says.

No, no, no! "Right. You've seen us together. That's because she's my friend," I say. "Claire, she's my good friend. Best buddy, really. I mean just . . . you know, we're *good friends*."

Both of them are looking at me. Juliet is smiling, but Claire is staring like she's watching a car crash.

"Friends are welcome," Juliet says. "Come on."

We walk across the parking lot toward the bunch of kids. They're all human, I'm guessing. She introduces us to everyone—Matt, Emily, Victoria, Stefan, Jamie, and Michael.

Stefan finishes a story he was telling about a kid who got caught in his parents' basement, passed out with an empty bottle of vodka next to him. "They pumped his stomach."

"I heard he was in a coma," Jamie says.

"No. He had alcohol poisoning. They said his heart stopped for, like, ten minutes."

"He'd be dead," Juliet says.

"Maybe he's actually a vamp. Then he wouldn't die from it," says Emily.

I notice a couple of them looking my way, obviously trying to figure out what I am. My blue eyes say one thing, my coloring and build say another. Some of the guys are sneaking looks at Claire. They probably don't hang around with vamp girls too often, and I always forget how pretty she is. To me, she's just Claire, so it's kind of funny to see guys checking her out. Not to mention that none of these guys is her type, due to their being guys.

They argue for a while about whether the kid's heart stopped or if something else happened. Then the subject changes to classmates from Millbrook. Of course, I have no idea who they're talking about, but that doesn't matter. I'm here with Juliet Walker.

She's smiling at me a lot, but not so much that it seems fake, so that's good. She includes me when she's talking, and looks at me, which is another good sign. But every time I look at Claire to get a sense of how she thinks it's going, she's talking to that girl Victoria.

I'm trying not to stare at Juliet while she talks. Just keep it cool. At one point she tosses her hair and I see that she's wearing earrings, hoops in hoops. I'm not used to that. Vamp girls don't usually bother with earrings, since the holes would close up the second they're taken out.

When the conversation turns to movies, Michael goes on about how bad the new Kurt Helsingermann movie is. "The action was lame. And that guy is too old now."

This is my chance. "Helsingermann is the finest actor alive," I say. I push my hair up like his. Claire catches my eye and shakes her head tightly, like, *don't do it*. But this is a specialty of mine. I point at each kid while I put on the famous Bavarian accent. "You, go get zee veapons! You, get zat antenna vorking again! Und you, take ze girl und take cover. Und me? I vill disable zat varhead, und zen . . . I'll come *back*!"

It gets a pretty good laugh. Claire is looking at the pavement, shaking her head, but what does she know about brilliant impersonations?

Juliet is laughing. She bumps her shoulder against mine. That means something. I'm sure of it.

She's not paying more attention to me than she is to the other guys. I don't know if it's because she doesn't like me more than them or because she doesn't want to be obvious. I look over to Claire, who's still talking to that Victoria. Thanks, Claire. Big help. You're supposed to be watching me. I put my hands behind my head and stretch, but she's not looking this way, and totally misses the signal.

I'm tense and forget not to grind my teeth. A white-hot arrow of pain shoots through my jaw and electrifies every nerve in my body. I yelp, in a less than manly way.

Everybody goes silent and looks at me. "Are you all right?" Juliet asks.

"Yeah, sorry. Bit my tongue."

"Oh, I hate when that happens," she says. Fortunately, the conversation starts up again. I do the secret signal twice in a row, and as I walk across the parking lot to the store, I'm still not sure Claire even noticed.

It feels like I've been standing next to the frozen food cases forever. I'm frustrated and I'm cold. If Claire doesn't get here in the next thirty seconds, I'm going to kill her. And what is up with that pain in my tooth? It doesn't hurt if I push on it with my finger, but it kills when I clench my teeth.

"Why are you hiding in the back of the market?" Claire asks.

"Where were you?" I say to her. "I've been waiting here for, like, half an hour!"

"You were waiting maybe two minutes. I was talking to Victoria. Sorry if I didn't stop her in the middle of a sentence so I could rush across the parking lot and into the store. That wouldn't have been *too* random."

"Well, I was worried that you didn't see the signal."

"Didn't see it? It looked like you were bringing a plane in for landing. Who wouldn't see it?" She looks through the glass freezer door, opens it, and peers inside.

"Claire! Come on. You're here on a mission and you haven't even been paying attention."

"I've been paying attention. Just not every second." She reaches into the freezer and takes out a bag of peas. It makes an annoying crunching sound as she kneads it back and forth in her hands. "How old do you think Victoria is? Guess."

"We're not talking about Victoria. We're talking about Juliet." I pull open the freezer door, take the bag of peas from her, and toss it back inside.

"She's a senior," Claire says. "Doesn't she look younger?" She draws a smiley face in the fog on the glass.

I wipe it away and shut the door. "Would you please focus for one minute? Come on! You came here to help me read the signals. What do you think?"

"I think maybe she likes me," she says.

"Juliet?"

"No. Victoria." She opens the next freezer door and watches the glass fog up. She starts to draw another smiley face, but I grab her finger and hold it.

"Okay," I say. "You don't even know if Victoria likes girls. Do you?"

"Not for sure, no. But I get that feeling." She starts to draw with her other hand, still not looking at me. "She's cute, isn't she?"

I let go of her finger and give up. "Yes. She's cute. And I don't know how to tell if she likes you, so don't ask me."

She draws a big smile on the face, and then adds horns, for no reason I can imagine. Trying to talk to her about Juliet is pointless. Suddenly I hear the quick, steady pulse of a heartbeat, right in my ears. But my heart doesn't feel like it's going that fast.

Claire looks upset. "I wish I'd worn my black lamé pants instead of this dorky skirt, which I don't even know why I bought in the first place. It's a bad look. The lamé would have been much cooler, right?"

"No. And I can't believe I'm saying this to you, but you

look great," I tell her. This night is so derailed it's not even funny.

Claire erases the face on the glass and starts another. "I think Juliet likes you."

"Really? Why do you say that?"

Claire shrugs. "She had this look on her face when she was laughing at your Helsingermann impersonation. Which, by the way, was mortifyingly bad and is something you should never repeat in public."

"What kind of look?"

"The right kind." She shuts the freezer door. "I think it's time to stop being a coward, put a signal out there, and see what she does."

I like the idea, even if I don't know whether she's talking about Juliet and me, or about herself and Victoria.

It's been light for hours and I still can't sleep. I keep thinking about what happened last night.

Whether Claire's advice to be brave and put out a signal was meant for me or for herself, she was right; on the bus ride home, she told me that she'd gotten Victoria's phone number.

After at least half an hour of agonizing, I finally got up the nerve to put my hand on Juliet's elbow, and she didn't move it. After I let go, I tortured myself wondering if she was just being polite, but then she put her hand on my back and kept it there.

Which was better than I dreamed—I should have been ecstatic. But then there was that surprise last night, and it's been giving me a nagging, dark-cloud feeling ever since.

Claire left the store a few minutes before I did, so it wouldn't look like we'd had a little strategy meeting. And I kept hearing that beating sound. Throbbing, like a racing heart. But when I put my hand on my chest, my heart was beating much slower than the sound. I had to be imagining it.

Except that it was just too clear, too real. I was definitely hearing it, and it was coming from somewhere in the store. I looked around, and then in the convex security mirror, I saw. On the other side of the store there was a guy, maybe in his early twenties, standing in front of the candy rack. He had a magazine open in one hand, his head tilted down as if he was reading, and with his other hand he was stuffing candy bars into his pocket, one after another. He was looking back and forth, up and down the aisle. Nervous. Jacked up.

And I knew. I walked toward him, just to make sure, and as I got closer the sound grew louder.

I was hearing the shoplifter's heartbeat.

I'd heard it from across the store. I don't know what that means, but one thing I do know: it's definitely not normal.

6
IDEOPATHIC

Maybe getting to school half an hour early is overkill, but
I don't want to miss Juliet before class. I wonder if staking
out a girl's locker is considered stalking. It's probably not
stalking if she likes you.

At least I feel better now. When Mom woke me up after
midnight on Sunday, asking if I was planning to sleep the
whole night away, it sounded pretty good to me. I'd been
up all day, thinking, and I'm no good without a decent day's
sleep. Mom could see that I didn't look great, so I told her
my crit was low, and luckily the hemometer backed me up
when she checked. After I finished a liter of SynHeme, which
I barely got down, she let me go back to sleep, and I spent
almost all of last night and today dozing in bed under my
Sol-Blok canopy.

Which is why I had no trouble getting up before sunset
tonight so I could get to school early. And here come the kids.
It takes less than a minute for the halls to fill with students.

There she is. Juliet smiles when she sees me waiting at her locker. Her teeth aren't picket-fence perfect like vamps' teeth. She has this one on the bottom, next to the middle ones, that's just a tiny bit crooked. I love that tooth.

"Nice way to start the week," she says.

"I had a good time Saturday night."

"Me, too." She makes a shooing motion to move me away from in front of her locker. She spins the dial. Her fingernails are short, and each one is painted with different nail polish, all deep blues running into green. I'm surprised I never noticed it before, but it's cool. Something a vamp girl would never have the nerve to do. "We should do it again," she says. "Go out, I mean."

"When?" I say, too quickly.

She laughs. "Whenever you want to."

Whenever I want to. Well, that would be every day of the week. We could drop out of school, too. But that's probably the answer a completely obsessed psycho would give. Not the impression I want to make. "So, you guys do that every Saturday night?"

"Most of the time, yeah." She's got her notebooks, but keeps rooting through her locker. "But it doesn't have to be with them. We could do something, just us. If you want."

Just us? Did I hear her right? "Well, I don't know. I don't usually hang around alone with a girl until I'm sure she's not going to try to take advantage of me." Oh, man! Did I really just say that?

But she laughs. In a really good way. "Maybe it's worth taking a chance. Live dangerously." She closes her locker and gives me a sly smile.

"I'll have to think about it," I say. I try to smile the same way she is, but I probably just look demented.

It doesn't seem to bother her, though. "I have to go to the girls' room," she says. "Go on ahead. I'll see you in class."

"Sure. I'll English in see you. Wait. See you in English. I meant to say it that way the first time."

She laughs and shakes her head, then gives me a little wave as she starts down the hall.

We could do something, just us. It's going to be hard to think about anything else today.

The problem is right in front of me, but I just can't pull myself together to solve it.

$$y(x+h) = y(x) = \frac{k_1}{6} + \frac{k_2}{3} + \frac{k_3}{3} + \frac{k_4}{6} + O(h^5)$$

Between the good news of Juliet wanting to go out with me again and this distracting feeling that the bone marrow in my arms and legs has turned to molten lava, it's a little hard to concentrate.

Mr. Wells is watching us take the test, his eyes wandering from student to student. He looks kind of sad, which I guess I can understand. Being a human, he probably didn't take this level of math until graduate school.

He has tiny capillaries in the whites of his eyes, like little brooks branching out from streams. He also has big pores on his cheeks. And there's a little spot next to his mouth where he didn't shave as closely as the rest of his face; most of it is regular stubble you'd see at eleven o'clock, but in that spot, it's maybe a tenth of a millimeter longer.

Wait: I'm in the back row and he's sitting at the front of the room. I must be hallucinating.

I snap out of it when I notice Mr. Wells looking at me right in the eye. He taps his watch and I go back to the test in front of me.

"How can you say that?" Bertrand is beside himself as we walk down the hall. "It was the easiest test we've had all year!"

"I don't know. I just couldn't focus," I say. The hall is crowded and everything seems too loud.

Two arms drop heavily on our shoulders and then Hugh is between us. "Boys, get ready for this. Tickets for the Rubber Crutches go on sale tomorrow."

"They suck," I say.

"Plus they'll sell out in about ten seconds," Bertrand adds.

"True, but my dad knows the guy who owns their label, and he could probably get us tix. Good ones."

"That's what you said for the Mad Scientists concert, and you came up with nothing," Bertrand says. "Your father's connection is . . ."

"Disconnected," I say.

"Danny Gray!" calls a female voice, high and squeaky. I stop walking, turn, and see Alexis Bouchon, one of my sister's friends. She waves me over. I tell the guys to wait for me, and I go to her. She looks like a near clone of Jessica, but with slightly less attractive features. "So, Jess wanted me to tell you something." Of course she did, because Jessica would never talk to me in public. "She said, 'Turn your phone on, stupid. Mom's been trying to call you all evening. She's picking you up after school for a dentist appointment.' Oh, and, 'Wait for her in the back parking lot.' That's it, I think."

"Thanks."

Alexis shrugs and heads back to my sister.

"Alexis. One thing."

She turns to listen.

"It doesn't bother you to deliver messages for my sister?"

"Why would it? Jess gives messages to my little brother for me so I don't have to talk to him, either. It's what we do." She walks away like what she just said is the most sensible thing in the world.

Ah, a trip to the dentist to make the day even better.

"Didn't I just go, like, two months ago?" I ask Mom in the car.

"You went nine months ago, and it's my fault for not getting you there for your six-month filing. Your teeth must be quite sharp. I had to schedule a double appointment so he could get all the work done."

"Sounds super."

Dr. Loeb takes me in almost as soon as we get to the waiting room. He asks how school is going while he gets me set up in the chair and starts checking around in my mouth. Then he furrows his brow and he says *hmmm* a few times. He wheels backward on his little stool and looks at my patient file. "That's strange," he says.

"What?"

"It's been almost ten months since you were here, but I'm

looking at your teeth now, and they don't need filing. They haven't grown at all."

"That's weird. What does it mean?"

"I'm not sure," he says. "Open, please."

I open wide, and he pokes around with a little hook instrument. "Any problems with your other teeth? Anything bothering you?"

"Ackshully, 'esh," I gurgle around his gloved fingers. He takes his hands out of my mouth.

"What's up?"

"Well, the other night I guess I was grinding, and I got a sharp pain in this tooth here," I say, pointing.

He examines the tooth, pokes some more, then tells me he's going to take some X-rays. A few minutes later, he's looking at the pictures on a big monitor, going *hmmm* again a bunch more times, and checking my file again.

"Did you find what caused that toothache?" I ask.

"I think so. You don't mind if I have your mother come in for a moment?"

I told him it was fine, and he brings her in from the waiting room. "Is everything all right?" she asks.

"Yes, I think so. Danny mentioned a toothache, so I took some X-rays and found something a bit unusual."

"Unusual is usually bad," I say.

"Not necessarily." He turns to Mom. "His genetic treatments were discontinued before completion, is that right?"

"Yes. He had seven rounds, but the doctors couldn't finish the last three. Why do you ask?"

"I'll show you." He moves the monitor so I can look, too. I see the whitish teeth and light gray gums. Looks fine to me.

Dr. Loeb uses a sharp instrument from his tray to point things out on the image. "These are your permanent teeth, all of which look perfectly fine. I'm not sure why your fang-teeth don't need filing, but that's another matter. Now take a look here." He points at white shadows beneath my regular teeth. "See these? Because you're bi-specian, you were born with a set of wulf teeth deep in your jaws, underneath your vamp teeth. When genetic treatments are successful, the wulf teeth shrink down to tiny, calcified nubs that stay dormant. But something else is going on here."

I'm not sure I like the sound of that, and I get this bad feeling he's about to start talking about pulling a bunch of teeth. "What *is* going on?" I ask.

"The wulf teeth didn't shrink. They're almost full size."

Looking at the X-rays, I have to agree. And the wulf teeth are kind of nasty looking, some with a bunch of sharp little peaks. "What does that mean?" I ask.

"Well, right here, you can see what caused that tooth-ache you mentioned. This wulf tooth is a little higher—that is, closer to the surface—than the others. Which means it's closer to the root of the vamp tooth above it. The other wulf teeth I assume are stable, but a good deal bigger than I had expected them to be."

"Why do I have them?"

"My best guess is because the treatments were discontinued. The last of the treatments would have essentially killed the wulf-teeth structures and roots. But instead, they developed."

He looked at the screen, obviously fascinated.

"What can we do about it?" Mom asks.

Here it comes, the part about me having to get thirty teeth pulled.

Dr. Loeb shakes his head. "As long as they don't erupt or push against the other teeth, I think we should leave them as they are."

"Do you think they'll become a problem?" I ask.

"There's really no way to tell." He turns off the monitor. "We'll just have to wait and see."

I don't know. In the bathroom mirror, I look exactly the same as I always have. But there are too many things happening with my body—too many things to be coincidence. I don't think I can ignore it anymore.

I put on my shirt and go back to my room. It's almost noon, and the house is totally quiet. Everyone's asleep.

The piece of paper is in the back of my desk drawer. I take it out and look at it. I had to write it down, because I used it so rarely that I couldn't remember it.

I open my phone and dial the number.

The phone rings, and then I hear his voice. "Hello?"

"Hi. It's Danny. I know this is out of the blue, but if you can, I need to see you. Dad."

7
LIKE FATHER

It's been a while since I took the train into the city. The 7:34 p.m. train—the first one after sunset—is almost empty, which makes sense, because people who work in the city but live in the suburbs will be going home, in the opposite direction. Before going to bed I told Mom I'd be leaving for school early because I had to work on a social studies project with some kids from my class.

It's only a twenty-seven-minute ride downtown. The train leaves the suburbs and enters an industrial area, then a neighborhood of run-down tenements at the city's edge, where the poorer wulves and humans live. I'll be getting off at the next stop.

I'm nervous. I haven't seen him since I was twelve. I was in a play at Murnau Night Middle School, a shortened version of *Our Town*. I was Howie the milkman. Mom was there with Troy, who she was dating at the time. I invited Dad, but he told me he couldn't make it because of a house that needed emergency roofing work.

My hair was still dirty blond then. At that point, my skin was just slightly darker than the average vamp's. I could still pass.

When the play was over and we were taking our curtain calls, there was plenty of polite applause from the audience. Then came shouting from the back of the auditorium: "Yeah, Danny! Nice job, kid! That's my son, there!"

I never found out if he was loaded or just really proud of me. But everyone in the auditorium looked back at the wulf, who was cheering and whistling. I could see Mom and Jess turn to face forward, their features like stone. They made sure to steer clear of him on the way out.

But he was really whooping it up at that curtain call. There was no ignoring him. "Is that your dad?" Tiffany Welsh asked.

A vocabulary word we had learned earlier in the week came to mind. I was *mortified*.

"I don't know *who* that is," I lied.

Word got out after that night: Danny Gray's father is a wulf.

I never said anything to him about being embarrassed. But I resented him for letting the cub out of the bag, and I started to be busy on the weekends. Then, for some reason, I kept forgetting to return his phone calls.

It would have happened soon enough anyway, even without the play incident. That summer, my hair darkened and my growth slowed down, while all the other vamp kids got taller. Nobody, even people meeting me for the first time, could mistake me for a full vamp anymore. By then, things had already settled with my friends: the ones who were going to drop me because of my background had dropped me. The ones who could tolerate it were still around. But by that point, I wasn't seeing Dad anymore.

Jessica dumped him suddenly and completely, though. I thought it was horrible, but I had no right to judge her: not too much later, I abandoned Dad, too. Only I'd been a lot closer with him than she had, so my betrayal was worse.

A lot of vamps would be nervous walking in this neighborhood. The buildings are run-down, and it's not clean and sparkly like the North Side, but surprisingly, there's not a lot of crime.

Looking around really brings back memories. I'd totally forgotten the huge ad painted on the side of the building next to the vacant lot. It's a picture of a very serious-looking woman—whether it was human or wulf was left ambiguous—whose eyes seemed to follow you when you walked by. Even though the paint is faded now, I can still make out the words:

If You Know About a Wulf
Who Hasn't Registered—Make a Report.
It's the Right Thing to Do . . . And It's the Law!

I have to stop to get my bearings at the corner. I haven't been here in a while, and I'm not sure whether to go left here or the block after.

Across the street are two men wearing dark jackets with LPCB PATROL printed on the backs and down the sleeves, just

74

in case anyone couldn't tell from all their gear that they're with the Lycanthrope Protection & Control Bureau. They have helmets and bulletproof vests, holstered pistols on their belts, and assault rifles slung over their shoulders. The shorter one keeps checking a small handheld computer in his palm. The taller guy is watching the pedestrians. Obviously, they're looking for a moonrunner. If they find him, they'll lock him up in the armored LPCB truck parked down the block. That is, if he doesn't try to escape. If he tries and fails, he'll leave in the coroner's truck.

The Last Chance Diner has good food and is open twenty-four hours, so you get a mix of humans, wulves, and even a few vamps. A wulf in a raincoat is sitting at the counter, hunched over a mug of coffee. His white hair is short, and his head is knotted with the worst cranial ridges and scars I've ever seen. I have to turn away.

Dad is sitting in a booth across from the counter. He stands up when I get there.

Awkward: handshake or hug? I put out my hand, and he does the same, then we both take a half step toward each other. It's like a dance as we try to figure out what we're going to do. I move closer, and we end up hugging with our clasped hands pressed between us. I remember that after-shave. Sandalwood. He pats me on the back, and we take seats across from each other.

He looks me over, smiling. There are little crinkles at the corners of his eyes that I don't remember him having. "You grew some," he says.

"Yeah. A *lot* of people think I'm gruesome."

He laughs at the lame pun, then combs his fingers through his still-thick hair. There's gray in there that I haven't seen before.

"Well, you look good," I say. "You hitting the gym or what?"

"Me? Are you kidding?" He pats his belly. "No gym for me. I've been trying to eat better, though. Cut out the steak and the beer. And I'm doing more work on the jobs, instead of playing foreman. Hard work; keeps me in *some* kind of shape."

"It shows."

"How you boys doing?" the waitress asks, appearing out of nowhere. She puts menus on the table. Her nose is flattened like a boxer's. Wulf.

"You know what you want?" Dad asks.

"Um. Do you?"

"I'll have a turkey club," he says. "No fries, mashed if you got 'em. Thanks."

"And you?" she says. She smiles at me and I notice a finger-wide scar running from the edge of her mouth all the way down her neck.

"Oh. I'll have the same as him. Thanks."

"SynHeme?" she asks. It sounds like there's a little bit of extra politeness in there, but I could be imagining it.

"Sure. Thanks."

"Ted?" the waitress asks.

"Just water for me. Thanks, Jeannie," he says.

I nod a few times for no reason and take a look around the diner, mainly so I don't have to look Dad in the eye. "Place looks exactly the same," I say.

"Probably hasn't changed in fifty years."

"Huh. That's good, I guess."

"So . . ." he says.

"So."

He drums his fingers on the top of the table. "How's Jessica?"

"She's fine. Thinks she's the greatest thing since SynHemesicles."

He laughs and cracks his knuckles. I forgot about those thick strong hands and his wide, square fingernails. "And your mother? Everyone else?"

"Mom is fine. And Paige, I think you met her once, she's good. And you know, everyone else. Everyone is fine."

"How about Troy? He treating you all right?"

"Troy's just fine." That might be hurtful to him, I realize too late. "I mean, we're not close or anything. He's just . . . kind of there. But he's not a problem."

"Good. Good."

The rest of the conversation doesn't get any less awkward. We talk about how I'm doing in school and about his business. Then we do the talk about sports and movies. The food arrives, and I think we're both relieved to have something to do other than work so hard to make conversation.

"Was that enough for you?" he asks when he puts his fork down on his empty plate.

"Oh, yeah. Plenty. And very good."

The waitress comes to the table to get our plates. "How about dessert?"

Dad looks at me, the hint of a smile showing at the corner of his mouth. "You up for it?"

This is from back when we spent time together. It should feel familiar and warm, but I still feel awkward. Maybe we just need to get back into it. "Of course."

"Jeannie, do you have two nice big wedges of the banana cream for us?" he asks.

"Good choice." She smiles at him as she takes our plates away.

He moves his napkin to the right, then back to the left. "Okay, let's just get to it. Why did you need to see me?"

I feel like a little kid who's been rude to his parent all day, then asks for a present the same night. "Well. There's something I need to talk to you about, if it's okay."

"You can't possibly be asking for money. I mean, if you are, I'll do what I can, but I thought that Troy guy was loaded."

"It's not money." I look around. The place is mostly full, and the tables are close together. That old wulf at the counter hasn't moved an inch since I came in. "But the thing is, it's kind of personal. Maybe we could go somewhere else, so we can talk in private?"

He nods and looks out the window. "We can go around the corner to my place, if you want."

"Sure. After the pie?"

"Hell, yeah, after the pie. It's already got our names on it."

Of course I know his apartment, but it looks a lot darker and more run-down than I remember. Books and magazines on all the surfaces, including the floor. He still has the couch he's had since the divorce. And it looked worn out back then. The only nice thing in the place is the big-screen TV.

"Have a seat," he says. "Just push that crap over, or dump it on the floor."

He goes into the kitchen. I clear a spot on the couch and sit. I'm feeling all jangly and nervous. I don't even know how I'm going to say it to him.

He comes back in with some glasses and plastic bottles of Coke. "I was going to get you some SynHeme, but then I figured we wouldn't end up coming here. Sorry."

"That's okay. I don't need any right now anyhow."

"Twenty bucks for a sixteen-ounce bottle. Unbelievable."

"It's a little cheaper when you have it delivered by the case. That's what we do."

"Right. Of course." He puts the Cokes and glasses on the table and sits across from me in his easy chair. How am I going to do this?

"Okay," he says. "What's the big personal thing you want to talk about? I'm figuring it's about a girl."

"Oh, no. It's not that."

"No girlfriend?"

"Kind of. There's a girl I like. I'm pretty sure she likes me."

"Vampyre girl?"

"Actually, no. She's human, but she goes to my school."

He nods. I wonder if he's secretly happy that it's not a vamp girl. "Must be smart."

"She's very smart. Nice. Funny. Good-looking."

"Sounds like the whole package." My dad was always cool that way. That's probably one of the reasons he and my mom split up. That, and her parents, who more or less dis-owned her when she married him, then ten years later offered her a big house and a ton of money if she would leave him. I guess she and my father were already fighting a lot, so they decided to call it quits. We moved into the big house in the Hills. And that was that.

Anyway, I don't believe my father was interested in Mom just because she was beautiful and a vampyre and it was sort of moving up socially for him. He never cared about any of that. From what he's told me, she was a lot of fun back then, and there weren't any species issues between them. Not for him, anyhow.

"Okay, so it's not girl trouble," he says. "Let's hear it."

"I was just wondering." Keep that voice steady and casual. "And you don't have to answer if you don't want, but how old were you when you had your first Change?"

"The first full one? I guess eleven, almost twelve. On schedule. Why?"

I don't say anything for a couple of seconds. "What was it like?"

"You came to ask me what *primitis* is like? When you can find out all the details you want from a book or the Internet? Come on, now. What's this really about?"

I haven't said it out loud to anybody yet. "I think something's happening to me."

He takes a Coke and pours some into one of the glasses, then sits back and watches the foam dissolve. "You had treatments. Almost all of them."

"I know."

"So why would you think it has anything to do with the Change?"

"Because. I know it sounds impossible, but what's

80

happening sure seems to me like *primitis-Lycan*-whatever."

"*Primitis Lycan–metamorphosis.* No. You're howling up the wrong tree. It's got to be something else."

I don't say anything. He drinks.

But the subject is open now, so I can't let it stop there. "They had to stop the treatments, though. Because I got sick."

"Yeah, but you were almost done. Except for your hair and skin tone, you're practically all vamp. You have the blue eyes, you got the smarts, and you have the Thirst. Oh, sorry. I don't know what the politically correct expression is now. What makes you think you're having a *primitis*?"

"One thing is that SynHeme is making me kind of sick. I sometimes feel like puking when I drink it."

"That's how I always felt when I tried it."

"But you're not a vampyre. That's normal for you. I still have the Thirst, so it shouldn't make me sick."

He shakes his head. "I don't know what would cause that, but having a stomach ache doesn't mean you're going to Change."

"I've been getting headaches," I tell him. "I have aches in my muscles and bones. And joints."

"Big deal. Flu." I give him a look. "Oh. Right. Okay, so it's not a flu. But it could be a thousand other things."

"My teeth haven't needed to be filed down for over eight months. Yesterday the dentist said that my wulf teeth never shrank. He said it was probably because the genetic treatments weren't complete."

He shakes his head and brushes his hair back with his fingers. There's one small ridge on his temple. Other than that, his facial plates are perfectly aligned. "Okay, so the teeth business is strange. And the dentist could be right about the reason."

"I'm stronger than I used to be."

"Well, sure. You're getting older and bigger."

"No, I mean *way* stronger. Like *weird* strong."

He nods, and I can see his jaw muscles working. He rolls his flannel sleeves down, then rolls them back up. After a minute, he gets up and turns on the table lamp next to the couch. He looks at my face. "Your eyes are still vampyre blue. When you look at the moon, do you notice anything . . . different?"

"I know what you're asking. No, the moon always looks white. But isn't it only right during the Change—"

"Okay, never mind that." He touches my upper lip, my chin. "How often are you shaving?"

"Three times this week."

He blinks hard, then shakes his head. He goes back to his chair and sits down heavily. He rubs his eyes, purses his lips.

"How long has all this been happening?"

"For the last few months. It's been getting worse each time. And my senses are really sharp. Like, I can smell things really clearly, and see tiny things from far away. I can even hear heartbeats."

He clears his throat. He's got a little smile on his face, but it's not in his eyes. "And this is all when? Around the full moon?"

"No. It's more spread out. It's a lot of the time."

Now he looks happy, not faking it. "See, now that doesn't fit. Most of the things you told me only happen around the Change. Having them all the time doesn't make sense."

"So what do you think is going on?"

"I don't know. But each of the symptoms you described could be completely natural and have nothing to do with lycanthropy."

"I agree, but all of them happening at the same time? I mean, if you put everything together, doesn't that paint a certain picture?"

He gets up and starts to pace in front of the window. "We have to get this checked." There's a tremor in his voice. "But you can't go to a regular doctor."

"Why not?"

"Because, if tests show you *are* going to Change, then by law they have to register you. And then you'll . . ." He clears his throat a few more times. "And then you'll have to go to the compounds." We both think about that for a few seconds before he says, "Damn it."

"Won't I have to do that, sooner or later, if I'm going to Change?"

"Maybe. I don't know. I need to think." He rubs his temples, pacing like a caged tiger.

My head spins with everything this could mean. Will I sit at the wulf table in the cafeteria? Will I lose the advantages of being vampyre? The perfect health, the regen, the intelligence, and agility? Am I going to have to drop down to easier classes? Go to another school? Will I end up working construction with my father?

"I didn't want this for you," he says.

He's got a look of deep sorrow on his face. How messed up is that, that he has to feel guilty about his son being like him? He didn't do anything wrong.

I put my face in my hands and rub my eyes. What a mess.

"Okay," he says. "Your mother thinks you're in school right now?"

"Yeah. I had my friend Claire use my phone to call in, saying she was Mom and that I'd be in late."

"We need some time to think this through." He looks at his watch. "We can't do anything right now, so I'll write you a note and drive you to school. You can finish out the night there."

School. Great. "How am I going to concentrate on schoolwork, knowing all this?"

"First of all, we don't know anything. Second, you're going to have to act like there's nothing wrong. At least until we find out what's what."

He puts his hand on my shoulder, looks at me for a few seconds, then reaches for his jacket.

We're only a few minutes from school. If I'm going to bring it up, which I know is the right thing to do, I have to quit stalling and just come out with it. "Listen. I know it was totally unfair for me to bring all this to you, after what . . . after I haven't been in touch for such a long time."

"Who else could you go to? You didn't have much of a choice."

"That's true, but what I did, when I stopped seeing you and talking to you, it was completely wrong."

He doesn't answer. I was probably hoping somehow that he would say that it's okay, all water under the bridge or something, but he doesn't. He's silent, watching the road lit by streetlamps.

I just have to get it out in the open. He deserves that. "I'm a jerk. I was trying to pass as a vamp and was embarrassed to be part-wulf. I don't blame you if you can never forgive me, but I really am sorry."

Again, he doesn't tell me it's okay or that he understands. But I have no right to expect or want anything like that from him.

"Look," he says. "Right now we have other things we need to deal with. I'm not going to turn my back on you. I'm still your father."

Our eyes meet and I can see he means it. I give him the best smile I can manage, and say, "Lucky for me."

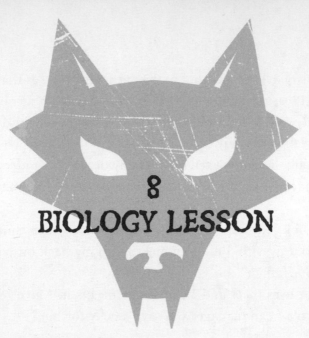

8
BIOLOGY LESSON

It's practically impossible to concentrate on schoolwork with all this going through my mind. At least I have Math, and Mr. Wells has us working on problems. I just can't stop hearing the last part of our conversation before Dad pulled into the school parking lot, under the floodlights.

"There's a doctor I want you to see," he said.

"I thought you said we couldn't go to the doctor."

"This guy is different." He thinks for a second. "You could say he's sympathetic to the situation."

"Is he a real doctor? I mean, like a physician?"

"He's real. He's got a regular practice, but he helps wulves on the side. One day he'll probably get caught, but for now, he's helping as many of us as he can."

I've heard about guys like this, true believers in Wulf Rights. Most of the time they're public figures, wulves like Huey Seele who lead the movement for more wulf representation in Congress, better medical care, all that stuff. But there are also people who work behind the scenes. Subversives, they're called. Some shelter moonrunners. Some are doctors who treat wulves illegally. You see these people on the news, usually with cops on either side of them, walking them past reporters into the police station to get booked.

"I'll find out if he can see us in the next day or two," Dad says.

"That soon?"

"Full moon on Thursday. If this is really pre-Change stuff you're feeling, the full Change could happen any time. If you Change and they catch you . . . well, that would be bad."

"They, meaning the LPCB?" I couldn't believe I was talking about the Lycanthrope Protection & Control Bureau in a way that directly involved me.

"Yeah. And that's not what we want."

"Because I could end up getting shot?"

He didn't answer. You'd have to be living under a rock not to have seen a thousand news clips of bodies lying in the streets, the graphic gunshot wounds blurred by pixilated squares. Last year a photo hit the Internet: four LPCB agents standing with their high-powered HK-422 automatic weapons in front of a dozen wulf corpses stacked like wood. Vamp kids printed the picture and brought it to school. They thought it was cool.

"Look, let's not get ahead of ourselves. We'll see the doctor and make decisions once we know more."

And so I have to go on like there's nothing wrong. Say nothing to my family. Eat. Sleep. Go to school. Take this math test.

On my right hand, which is holding the pencil, I can see

my wulftag, almost invisible under my skin. Stupid to think, but I feel like taking a knife and cutting it out of my flesh. Not that it would change anything.

Luckily, Claire leaves school early, and Juliet needs extra help in math, so I don't have to talk to either of them. In fact, I get through the rest of the night at school without anyone suspecting that something's wrong. Then I make a clean getaway.

The house is quiet. I just need to get to my room and lie down for a while, to pull myself together.

I go upstairs. "Anyone home?"

"In here," Troy calls.

Great. I go into the master bedroom and see him in the adjoining bathroom, a towel around his waist, shaving. "Come on in, my brother," he says in a cheerful tone.

Oh, man. Seriously.

"I have to catch a red-eye to Amsterdam, leaving at ten in the morning. Ouch, huh?" he says. "But come and talk." He has a perfectly toned, pale, lean body: the typical male vampyre build. Totally different from Dad, who's shorter, with squared-off muscular shoulders, chest, and thick arms. If they were dogs, Troy would be a greyhound and Dad would be a boxer. Of course, plenty of people would say my father *is* a dog, or not much better than one.

"So, what's going on?" he asks.

"What do you mean?"

"Well, what's going on in your life?"

"Nothing. There's nothing going on." Easy, now. I look at his reflection in the mirror while he shaves. He looks back at me.

"You okay?" he asks.

"Yeah. Why?"

"You seem a little bummed out." He looks at me again in the mirror.

Please stop. "I'm fine."

"I'm not trying to be your father. You know I would never. But that doesn't mean we can't be buds. Right?"

Right. We can even start a little club: Two Guys Without a Clue. "Thanks, Troy. But really, I'm completely all right."

"Okay, pal. If you say so. But if there's something I can help with, I hope you'll let me know. I'm here to *roll the words* whenever you want."

"Thanks." I try to return the broad grin he gives me.

"Whoops," he says. I smell it before I see it, a big streak of red running down his cheek into the pure white shaving cream, like blood on snow. I turn away, grab a Factor XIV pad from the wall dispenser, and hand it to him, trying not to look at the blood.

"Thanks."

Even turned away from him, I get the coppery taste in my mouth and start salivating, my heart pounding. I make a sound in my throat.

"Yep, this one's a gusher," he says. "You might want to leave."

"I'll see you later. Have a good trip." I get out of there fast.

Just before I pull the bathroom door closed, he says, "Hey, Danny? If you need anything, you can call me while I'm in Amsterdam."

"Thanks." Standing in the bedroom, I take a couple of

breaths to help settle my bloodlust. Then the weirdest thing happens: it passes. Usually it takes as long as half an hour for bloodlust to settle down, but this one faded after—what?—less than two minutes? Very strange.

In the hall I bump into Mom. She's carrying two shopping bags from Lady Abbington's.

"I didn't know you were home," I say.

"I just got back from the mall. How was school?"

"Fine."

She smiles and starts into her bedroom.

"I wouldn't go in there if I were you," I say. "Troy's shaving, and he's got a geyser flowing."

She swallows. Her nostrils flare a little and she closes the bedroom door. She puts her bags down on the hallway carpet.

"Is everything all right?" she asks.

"Yeah. Why?"

"You're just standing here, looking at me. School okay? Anything new?"

Anything new? No, not a thing. "Same old stuff." Fortunately, my cell rings. "That's probably Claire. She needs to get the English homework."

Mom gives me a smile, says, "Okay, then," and goes into her bedroom. I pull out my phone but don't answer it until I get to my room. It's not Claire. It's Dad. I close my door before answering.

"I got us an appointment with the doctor I mentioned," he says. "Tomorrow."

"Tomorrow?" This is moving too fast.

"He's staying in the office for us. Just go off to school like

90

normal, and I'll be parked four blocks north of your house. The corner of Shepard. I'll call the school and tell them that you won't be in. They'll let me do that, right?"

"You're on my emergency card, so, yes, they should." This year Mom actually didn't want to list him on the contacts list, especially since I hadn't seen him in so long. She said that she and Troy were enough contacts. But I said we should keep him on the list. Somehow it seemed too disrespectful to take him off. For once, a good move on my part.

"Great," he says. "I'll be there at the corner. Sundown tomorrow is seven thirteen. How does meeting at seven forty sound?"

"Too early. Mom will get suspicious. I'd say no earlier than eight, or she'll want to know what's up."

"Mm. I hope there's not too much traffic. We'll do our best. You okay?"

"Me? Yeah. Are you?"

"Ask me again this time tomorrow."

The sign on the door says DR. CHARLES J. MELLIN, MD. Below, the word ENDOCRINOLOGY. I reach for the door, but it's locked.

My father shakes his head, takes out his cell phone, and dials a number. He listens, then closes it. After a couple of seconds, the door opens and I see a perfectly average-looking guy in his fifties, with a neat gray beard and glasses.

He motions us inside and locks the door. The waiting room is ordinary; so is the exam room.

"Thanks for seeing us on such short notice," Dad says.

"I understand the circumstances."

"This is Danny. My son."

"Dr. Mellin," he says, and shakes my hand. "You're going to need to undress to your underwear. Do you want your dad to stay or wait outside?"

"What? Oh."

Dad looks at me. The last time he took me to the doctor, I was eight. "You want me to leave?"

"Whatever you want is okay with me."

Dad stays. Dr. Mellin draws four tubes of blood while asking questions about my appetite, aches, sleep, whether I'm sweating more than usual, changes in hearing or seeing. He tells us he'll be right back and leaves the room.

"You hanging in?" Dad asks. I shrug. Am I hanging in? What choice do I have?

The doctor comes back and has me lie on the table. "We'll get preliminary blood results in a few minutes. I'll have to send out for the DNA analysis, but we'll get that back soon."

"What if it comes back positive?" Dad asks. "Won't the lab be legally obligated to register him?"

"I send it out under the name of someone who's already registered. Don't worry about that."

The doctor checks all my joints, then my lungs, eyes, ears, nose, and throat, like with any physical. After he checks my blood pressure and listens to my heart, he raises his eyebrows, which isn't exactly reassuring. He pulls over a small machine on a wheeled stand. "I'm just going to do a quick ultrasound. The gel will be cold. Sorry." He squirts clear gel on my chest and moves a corded blunt instrument about the size of a deck of cards over my chest. He's watching a screen, and when I look at it, it's all a bunch of grays and blacks, but I can see something pumping steadily. Obviously, my heart. Very cool.

He puts the machine away and cleans the gel off me with a scratchy brown paper towel. Then the exam gets a little less typical. He checks my fingernails and toenails. He feels the bones of my face.

"Let's get some pictures," he says. He takes me into the next room. The floor is cold on my bare feet. There he takes digital X-rays of my hands, feet, knees, chest, and front and profile views of my head and face.

"Go ahead and get dressed, son," he says. "Then you and your dad can meet me in the office next door."

I get my T-shirt and jeans on, slip on my sneakers, and walk into the office. Dad sits in one of the chairs by the desk. I sit in another one. He looks at me and starts to say something, but stops when the doctor comes back in.

"Okay, let me show you what we have." He points to a flat-screen monitor mounted on the wall next to the window, then sits at his desk and works the keyboard of his computer.

"Now, let's see how you did in biology. Do you know what's on the screen?" he asks.

"My red blood cells, I guess."

"Right. What types?"

"Well, the oval ones are regular vampyric red blood cells. The five-sided ones are wulf blood cells."

"Yes, technically called lycanthropic penterythrocytes. *Pent* for the five sides."

"Should I even have wulf blood cells?" I ask.

"Of course. Even with the treatments you had as a child, you're still genetically part-wulf. The treatment doesn't *eliminate* wulf DNA. It just deactivates the genes that cause wulf expression, *werewulfism*, if you will. I fully expected to see the wulf blood cells. Completely normal in a hybrid." He moves the cursor and points at a few cells that look like inflated versions of the pentagonal lycanthropic cells. "These are the significant ones. They're meta-lycanthropic penterythrocytes that are going through Metahematosynthesis. Or the Change."

"So that means it's going to happen?" Dad asks.

"I'm afraid so."

My vision swims for a couple of seconds. "Are you sure?" I ask.

"I'm certain. Your heart seemed to be beating quite hard. The echocardiogram confirmed that you have lycardiomegaly. Your heart is thirty-three to forty percent larger than the heart of a vampyre or human your age. It's the size of a wulf's heart."

I try to think of something funny to say about having the mind of a vamp but the heart of a wulf. I come up blank.

"All the other symptoms you mentioned fit the diagnosis." The doctor changes the image on the screen. Now it's an X-ray of my hands. He taps the screen at my finger joints. "Your bones ache because your marrow is working to keep up with the Changing of your blood cells."

The doctor walks over to me, takes my hand, and guides my fingers to the top of my ear. "You feel that sharp little ridge of cartilage there?"

"Uh, yeah, I think."

"That's the base of what will develop into Burr's Ridge. That's where the lycan-cartilage will elongate your ears during your Change. It's what will give you a slightly pointed-ear look when you're not in Change."

He goes back to the computer and switches the image again. It's an X-ray, a front view of my skull. "See these dark areas? Those are your sinuses. They're enlarged to make room for the lycan-metamorphosis. That's the cause of your headaches. These are all very clear symptoms. The only part that is atypical is that wulves don't normally have heightened senses and increased strength *between* periods of the Change. It's odd, but it might have something to do with your incomplete genetic treatments. Nevertheless, it doesn't change my diagnosis."

He lets it sink in, not that I want it to. I look at Dad, and he looks as miserable as I feel.

The doctor clears his throat. "The other symptoms you're having, the ones that feel like flu. That's LMPI. Lycan-Metamorphosis Prodromal Illness. Prodromal means 'first symptoms.' You may also have fever, nausea, rapid heartbeat, and very severe headaches. About half the wulf population gets LMPI every month before the Change. You've seen the TV ads for Lupinox?"

Who hasn't? *Lupinox: to help you feel good when that animal acts up.* I nod.

"It's over-the-counter. It should help with the symptoms."

I'm sure I'll feel just great. Without the crushing headaches and joint pains I'll be able to concentrate on all the fun parts of becoming a werewulf.

"I'll give it to you," Dad says. "You bump into someone you know, how are you going to explain why you're buying Lupinox?" Dad says. His skin looks almost gray.

The image of my skull is still on the screen, and I stare at the dark shapes in my head.

PART II

The average IQ for a human is 90 to 110. In spite of controversy about alleged bias in testing materials, the average wulf IQ is generally believed to be lower than that of humans. However, the average IQ for a vampyre is 165 to 180. If that is not an indication of our superiority, I don't know what is.

—Lord Reginald Bulwyr-Fulton,
Parliamentary Address, London, 1946

Since ancient Rome—earlier, actually—humans hated vampyres, just like they hated us wulves. But in the last fifty years, vampyres have become a partner species with humans, and vampyres have become some of the richest and most powerful people in the world. But what about us wulves? When will it be our turn?

—Huey Seele, Wulf Rights Activist, Interview,
"Big Bad Wulf?" segment, *60 Minutes*, March 16, 2005

See here, mate. I don't write me songs just for wulves. They're for humans and vamps, too. Music is supposed to bring us all together. True, we ain't together yet, but that don't mean I'll quit trying.

—McJahn Le Nin, guitar, the B-Tells,
Billboard interview, May 24, 1968

9
HANG TIGHT

We're parked a couple of blocks from the house, and we haven't said a word for maybe ten minutes. I feel sick. Dad looks wrung out.

I can't take the silence anymore. "I guess it's better that we know," I say.

"We would have found out soon enough, but yeah. It's better that we know. I have to leave for the compound tomorrow, but I'll be back in a few days. We have some time to figure out what to do."

"To do about *what*? We can't stop this. The doctor said it's happening next month."

"There are things to decide. Like whether or not you should register."

I look at him. He's not joking. "What do you mean, 'whether or not I should register'? How can I *not* register?"

"Not everyone does."

"Yeah. Mom will love the idea of me being a moonrunner."

"Easy now," he says. "There are other choices. I'm not ready to talk about any of it, not until I've had some time to think it through."

Looking through the windshield, I can see the lights from our house down the street, glowing in the darkness.

Dad reaches over me and pops the glove box. It's jammed with papers. He digs through them, finds a white plastic bottle of Lupinox, and unscrews the cap. "Hold out your hand," he says. I do and he dumps the pills in my palm. "You don't want the bottle lying around. And keep those hidden."

I let out a breath. I have to say, I'm scared as all hell.

"You should start letting your hair grow a little longer, too. After your first Change, you'll probably want your ears covered."

"Right." I would never have thought of that.

He looks at me. "Okay, better get going."

I pick up my book bag and open the door. He grabs my arm. "We'll get through this," he says. "Don't worry."

I just nod. I'm pretty sure if I say anything out loud, I'll cry.

I close the front door behind me and stand in the foyer. It's almost dawn, and the Sol-Blok shades are sealing themselves. Loretta is getting dinner ready. Mom and the girls are doing whatever upstairs. To them, everything is normal. To me, nothing is.

I'm going to Change. I'm going to turn into a werewulf. It's beyond my worst fear.

Brushing my teeth, I look up into the mirror. Weird. My shoulders and arms look thicker than before. My chest, too.

So, maybe my face won't win me the Sexiest Man Alive Contest, but that's all right. I can hardly believe that it's going to change every month. My nose will break during the first Change, which they say is the worst one. It breaks every time after that, too, but you don't get the black eyes. I hope I don't get the facial ridges. I can't believe I even have to think about this.

I look at my hand as I rinse the toothbrush. After the first Change, my knuckles will swell permanently.

But it's okay. I can deal with this. Lots of people do it every month, and they get through it. It'll be okay.

But it's not just about the Change every month. It's about being someone else now. Being someone, or something, else in the world. It's every day. Wherever you go. Being a wulf is something people won't let you forget.

10
THE SMELL OF BLOOD

I have no interest in the discussion about Hemingway and the question some jerk asks every year about whether he was a human or a wulf. Hemingway's family wouldn't allow DNA tests on his corpse, so it'll be a mystery forever. And what difference does it make? It was all so long ago.

"What about Beethoven?" someone calls out.

"No," Thaddeus Sterling-Willet says. "My father's a conductor at the philharmonic, and he knows. He says the rumor started because Beethoven wore his clothes until they rotted off him. He was nuts and smelly, but he was no wulf."

"What about Van Gogh? He was definitely a wulf," a kid in the back calls out.

"First of all, this is English class, so we're not going to be talking about painters," Ms. O'Conner says. "As far as authors go, there's no clear evidence that Hemingway was a wulf. Same with Walt Whitman, for that matter."

"How about characters, then?" Bernard Laurence asks.

"Like ones who are supposed to really be wulves. Falstaff?"

"Yeah, and Magwitch in *Great Expectations*?" Babette Byer says.

"And Pap in *Huck Finn*," Thaddeus says.

I can't believe this conversation is still going on. It's almost as idiotic as the ones between Paige and Jess about which movie stars are dating, or who's going around the world collecting babies like they're toys.

"Isn't that all just speculation?" Juliet asks. "I mean, we might be reading stuff in that wasn't meant to be there."

"Exactly right," Ms. O'Conner says. "It's fine to have theories. But it's a matter of opinion. And anyway, now is not the time for this." Ms. O'Conner goes to her desk and picks up a stack of papers. "I know this conversation is just a stall to keep us from discussing *Mrs. Dalloway*. In the spirit of helping you remember to do your reading, I'd like to offer you an exciting little pop quiz. Let's clear those desks."

Lots of groans as everyone puts their books under their seats. Juliet looks over at me and I shrug. Yeah, like I was going to start reading Virginia Woolf's book right after finding out that I'm going to Change into a werewulf during the next full moon.

Another thought has been nagging at me: whether Juliet knows that the non-vamp half of me is wulf. I know it's only fair to tell her, but I can't help worrying she'll change her mind about me if I do.

Antony Delacroix is holding a pack of tests over his shoulder, shaking the papers to get my attention. I take them, keep one, then pass the rest back.

Obviously, I can't tell Juliet the whole thing. So, really,

what's the point of telling her any of it?

Nice rationalization. Coward.

I look down at my desk. Someone wrote *You suck!* in purple ink.

No kidding.

I catch up with Juliet just outside the English room. "Hey," I say. The hall is filling up with students.

"Hey. Good thing I read four chapters last night," she says. It seems like every single time I find her, she smiles at me. "Did you do okay?"

"Well, a steady stream of nonsense was flowing out of my pen, but it was pretty well-written nonsense. If she falls for my elaborate doublespeak that says nothing concrete, then maybe I did okay."

When she laughs, her long earrings swing back and forth. "I guess that's one way to do it," she says.

"Yeah, well, it's my fallback. I rely on it when the alternative is doom. But listen. There's something I wanted to check with you."

"Sure. Can you walk with me to my locker?"

"Absolutely. No problem." I don't know if it's the heat from the semi-warm vamp bodies filling the hall, or something else, but sweat breaks out on my forehead and upper lip. There's a nice big drop rolling down my back. I want to back out, but I know it's better to just get it over with.

"So, what's up?" she asks.

"It's not a big deal. I mean, I don't think it is. But I just thought I should make sure, you know, get it out of the way."

She gets her locker open and smiles at me. "Okay, you have my attention."

In the throng, I see Bertrand walking toward us. *Please don't stop to talk.* I try to beam my thought to him. Bertrand puts his hand up high and I slap it when he passes. What a relief.

Juliet bumps her shoulder against mine, shoving me off balance for a second. "So what's this important thing?" she asks.

Just go ahead. Play it casual. "It's just, what do you think I am?"

"What you are? You mean, that you're a freshman?"

"I'm saying . . . what do you think I am in terms of . . . species?"

"Oh. Well, you're in the Carpathia program, smart, and have blue eyes, so that says 'vamp' to me. But then you have dark hair and all that, so I figured maybe you're half-vamp and half-human."

"You're half right."

"Okaaay . . ." she says. She waits for me to get to the point. I just need to go through with it.

"I'm actually half-vamp and half . . . half-wulf."

"Wulf."

"*Half*-wulf."

"Oh." She looks inside her locker and I can't see her expression. "I guess you had the genetic treatments."

"Yeah." Which is true. I did have them. Just not the full series.

She glances at my right hand, looking for the wulftag.

"Yeah, my vampyre immune system rejected most of the

107

ink." I raise my hand to show her. "You can still see it, just a little, when the light hits it a certain way."

She looks at my hand, squinting, then looks back at my face. "I don't see anything."

"Here," I say. I don't know where I find the nerve, but I take a gentle hold of her elbow and shuffle us through the traffic of kids to the window. I spread my thumb out and move my hand back and forth until the moonlight hits just right and the thumbnail-size werewulf-head symbol is clear. I move my head next to hers to make sure she has the same angle. Her hair smells like vanilla and cinnamon.

"I see it," she says. "It looks like it's floating under your skin."

"Yeah. So anyway, I thought I should tell you about my, um, background before . . . well, I thought I should tell you."

"Thanks."

"So, I mean, is it a problem?"

"That you're a wulf?"

"Half," I say, holding a finger up and trying to laugh, though it probably sounds more like I'm choking.

"Not a problem for *me*." And now she grabs my arm to pull me along. She's touching me. She's holding my arm. We stop at her locker.

"Seriously? It doesn't bother you?"

She raises an eyebrow. "Did you think it would?"

"No. I'm not saying that at all, but it's the kind of thing you're supposed to tell someone who you're . . . getting to know. Full disclosure." Okay, maybe not full, but enough. For now, at least.

"It's fine," she says. "So what happened to that idea about us going out somewhere?"

"Well, you still want to, right?

She smiles. "What do *you* think?"

What do I think? I think I love life. I love this world and everything about it. I'm ecstatic.

And suddenly I'm on my knees. The sound of my head hitting the locker reverberates inside my skull.

"Sorry, guy," Gunther Hoering says. "I tripped. You okay?"

He reaches out his hand to help me. Before I can think better of it, I reach up. He grabs my forearm and pulls me to my feet. I hate myself for accepting. Like I'm saying it's okay that he deliberately smashed into me, banged my head into the locker, and completely humiliated me in front of Juliet.

Gunther is staring at my mouth. My upper lip feels warm and I touch it. My hand comes away with a thick smear of crimson blood.

I look back at him. His pupils dilate big as saucers and his nostrils flare. He swallows, and his Adam's apple bobs in his throat.

His buddies turn away. They can smell the blood, too. Every vamp in the hall can smell it.

"Come on, bro," one of the guys says. "We're late for History." They start to pull him away. He stops and takes notice of Juliet.

"I've seen you around," he says. He gives her the smile that all the girls love. "You're pretty cute—for a human. Why you want to hang out with a loser half-breed is beyond me."

He winks at her and leaves. Her upper lip curls in disgust as she watches him walk away.

I told her just in time.

She turns to me. "What was that? Are you okay?"

"Totally fine," I say. My nose is still bleeding and I'm embarrassed as hell.

She reopens her locker, which got slammed shut courtesy of my head, digs inside, then produces a dark blue T-shirt that she moves toward my face. I put up my hand to stop her.

"I'll stain it," I say.

"Don't worry. It's just my gym shirt. If you can stand the smell, you should probably use it."

She pushes my hand away and presses the shirt to my nose. I hold the shirt, too, and our hands touch for a second.

"This is really bleeding," she says.

"Yeah, it's heavy at first, until the regen kicks in, and then it stops and heals really fast. But I'd better get to the nurse before every vamp in the school goes nuts from the smell."

The nurse is at the other end of the building, so the halls are empty and everyone is in class before I'm even halfway there. I'm pinching the bridge of my nose and holding the T-shirt hard against my nostrils, trying not to let any blood drip on the floor.

The boys' room door opens and Craig Lewczyk comes out. He's pushing up the sleeves of the thermal shirt he's wearing under a Rubber Crutches concert T-shirt.

He nods at my face. "What happened to you?"

"Just got bumped into a locker. I'm going to the nurse."

"Yeah, me too."

I notice now that he looks pale, and there's a sheen of sweat on his forehead. "What's wrong?" I ask.

"Nothing. Just a bad stomach and a wicked headache. No big deal."

He looks sick. And he's limping a little. "Is that LMPI?"

"Yeah. I'll live. I just need some Lupinox."

I go through the door first so I can hold it open for him, then I walk next to him.

We haven't talked in so long, I don't know what to say. Maybe a little nostalgia would work. Old times. "So, how's your mom? Still making those great oatmeal cookies?" Brilliant. Very natural topic to bring up.

"Sometimes." It looks like he feels a little awkward, too.

"They were good. I still remember them."

"I guess you do."

He's not working much to keep the conversation alive. But I try again. "You still playing baseball?"

"Lacrosse."

"Very cool." I wish I could play lacrosse. But there's the whole vamp bleeding thing that kind of gets in the way. "You like it?"

"It's okay."

We get to the nurse's office. There are at least eight wulf kids standing in line, and a strong smell of vomit coming from the bathroom. If this is what it's like here at night with the few wulves we have at Carpathia, it must be a total zoo during the day.

The nurse's aide takes a look at me and pulls me out

of line toward a treatment room. I don't know whether I'm getting this privilege because I'm bleeding or because I'm part-vamp.

I hold the gauze against my nose, pressing hard.

"Here, I'll get rid of that T-shirt for you," the nurse says. She reaches for Juliet's shirt.

"No," I say. "It's not mine. I'm going to wash it and give it back."

Which I may not do. Even though Juliet said I wouldn't be able to stand the smell of her shirt, she was wrong. It doesn't smell bad at all. It smells like . . . I don't know, like Juliet. If she doesn't ask for it back, I'm going to keep it.

The nurse takes the bloody gauze from me and stuffs a cotton Hemo-Sealer plug so far up my nose I'm pretty sure she's trying to get it inside my skull.

"Can't have kids smelling this blood. You'll cause a riot." She holds my neck, trying to steady me as she makes the last push. "That's up there," she says.

"I'll say."

"Hmmm. That's strange."

"What?"

"Your pulse," she says. Her fingers happen to be right on my carotid artery. "It's going like a locomotive." She looks at the clock and counts silently.

Think fast. If she gets too worried about my heart rate, she may decide I need to see a doctor, and down that road lies disaster.

"I'm still worked up about getting bumped into the locker," I say.

"No, no. It's about seventy beats per minute. That's as fast as a human heart."

"Right, but I also ran really fast all the way down here. That's why."

"Oh. Well, you shouldn't run when you're bleeding; it only makes you bleed faster. Next thing you know, you'll have the whole school in a frenzy."

"I'll remember that," I say.

11
HOOKED IN

All the noise in the cafeteria is one big annoying buzz that I'm trying to ignore. Constance and the others are debating misheard song lyrics, complete with too-loud singing. Claire is across the table talking to me about something, but I've also given up paying attention to her monologue. She's on her second or third SynHeme Caffeine Plus, and when she has more than one, she becomes a total motormouth.

I keep thinking about Mom. I don't know if I can keep a secret this big for much longer.

"Hey!"

Claire is glaring at me. Those bright blue vamp eyes of hers get icy when she's mad.

"What are you shouting at me for?" I ask.

"Yeah, Claire. Why so shrill?" Selena asks.

Claire ignores her, focusing her annoyance entirely on me. "What's wrong with you?"

"Nothing. Why?"

"You went all catatonic on us."

"You looked like a zombie," Constance adds.

"Sorry. I just spaced out for a second."

"Are you back in the land of the living now?" Claire asks. She flicks a drop of SynHeme from the end of her straw, and it lands on my cheek. I wipe it off.

"Yes, I'm here, and thrilled to be in your company. What were you saying that's so amazingly important?"

"Don't make me slap you," she says. "I was talking about Morgan Wells."

"Who's he?"

She gives me a light smack with the heel of her hand against my forehead, then sighs heavily, making her blond bangs float for a second. "You're really great company these days. You haven't heard a word I said."

"So you want to tell me about this Morgan guy or what?"

"He's right over there. Look. But don't be obvious."

The visual isn't too nice. There's a guy sitting by himself, hunched over the table. The moonlight coming through the window lights up his gritted teeth, which are chattering. His fangs are grown out, one overlapping his lower lip, the other shorter and chipped. He's what people call a blue-tooth—too much SynHeme Caffeine Plus. His blond hair looks unwashed and greasy, his cheeks hollow. I know the guy's a vamp, but his skin isn't pale in the regular vampyre way. It looks dull, waxy.

"What's wrong with him?" I ask.

"Like I just finished saying, he's hooked in."

"What happened?"

"He went into the city, the west side, and got some real blood." I don't know how anyone our age would have the guts to go to that part of town alone. The few times we've had to drive through to get uptown, Mom made Troy lock all the doors. There were crumbling tenements everywhere with weary-looking hookers, a lot of them wulves, milling around in the shadows. Their facial ridging was so bad it was obvious they wouldn't be able to get customers in a better part of town. There were a bunch of shady guys, too, wulf and human, wearing flashy clothing. Pimps or dealers. You couldn't pay me enough to go there on my own. And this kid Morgan went there and got himself some real blood. He didn't get killed, but if he's hooked in, he might have been better off dying that night. It would have been quicker, with less suffering.

"I can't even look at him," Claire says. "It's too disturbing." She shudders and turns away.

"What's he going to do?" I ask.

"It's bad. SynHeme doesn't work for him anymore. I heard he was drinking it like there was no tomorrow, but it didn't help. Then he got, like, twenty units of VeniHeme and that didn't do much good, either."

"Haven't his parents ever heard of rehab?"

"He's supposed to go to Wilton Hills to clean up," Constance chimes in, "but his father is making him come to school for two more days before he leaves."

"Why?" Claire and I both ask.

"His father is L.C. Wells, of Wells and Burkeley Steel. He's big into discipline. Exactly the kind of guy who would make his kid go to school all strung out—just to embarrass him."

I shake my head. "That's great. And dear old Dad really believes *that's* going to help his son?"

"Don't ask me," Claire says. "Some parents have pretty sick ideas about how to help their kids." She shrugs and crunches a celery stick. "So, what's up with all this zoning out? Daydreaming about your honey?" Claire asks with an irritating smile.

"Excuse me, did you just refer to Juliet as my *honey*?"

"Yeah. So?"

"I've never heard you use the word honey in reference to a person. Please don't get sentimental just because you met someone you like. It's scary."

"Wait, what's this?" Bertrand says, turning from his conversation with Constance and Hugh. He has this radar for gossip.

"None of your business. Go back to your pointless conversation." Claire sneers at me. "Thanks a lot. Now he's going to nag me for details."

Bertrand grabs her forearm and shakes it vigorously. "So just *tell* me and I won't have to nag you."

Claire turns her head to glare coldly at his hand until he gets the point and removes it. "I'm not telling you anything, so don't waste your breath."

"What's her name?" Bertrand says. He doesn't let go when gossip's at stake.

"I'm ignoring you now."

Bertrand pulls a sad face and returns to his discussion with Constance, Martina, and Hugh.

Martina sings from a David-Bo E song: "It's, 'As they try to make it in a swirl.' I'm right. That's how it goes."

"You're wrong!" Hugh practically yells. "It goes, 'As they tie a naked squirrel.' Then the next part goes, 'Are a moon to all dedication,' and then it goes on."

Constance laughs. "You are so deaf. 'Are a *man* to your *decoration*, they're unaware where they're going to.' And then it's 'Train to fake the Change' at the chorus."

Now it's Oliver's turn to mangle the lyrics. "That doesn't even make sense. It's, 'Twine, two-faced, you're strange.' Clear as can be."

Claire is going to explode. "Are you guys kidding? Listen." She sings—and pretty well, too—" 'And these wulf-pups that you beat on, as they try to make it in this world, are immune to your degradation. They're all aware what they're going through. . . .'" She nods as she comes to the chorus, and I join in. " 'Ch-Ch-Ch-Ch-Changing . . . Tryin' to face the Change. . . . Ch-Ch-Ch-Changing . . .'"

I trail off as they sing the chorus. Considering that David-Bo E is a vamp, he sure seemed to understand how wulves feel. *They're all aware of what they're going through . . . Changing.*

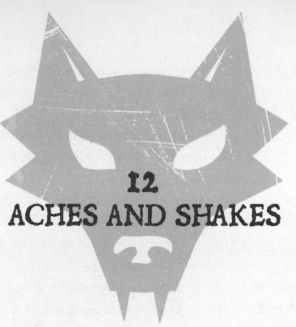

12
ACHES AND SHAKES

Today I keep shaking and getting the chills. Even Mr. Morrison notices in history class and asks if I'm okay. "Too much SynHeme Caffeine Plus," I say.

I've got a headache behind my cheekbones that feels like someone is punching me in the face—from inside my skull. My mouth is dry no matter how much water or SynHeme I drink. And the Lupinox that Dad gave me isn't helping much.

It's not completely unbearable. I'd call Dad to let him know how I'm doing, but he already left for the compound. The thing is, if this gets much worse I'm going to have a hard time making it through the whole school night.

I can see the full moon from the window of every classroom I'm in, it's staring at me. Mocking me.

I'd kill that moon if I could.

• • •

I don't care about Mrs. Dalloway or her stupid party one little bit right now. I just need to get out of this room. Lucky for me, Ms. O'Conner lets me go.

At least it's quiet in the bathroom stall. Every time I open my mouth, the joint of my jaw cracks. My feet are killing me. I take off my sneakers.

That explains it. My toes are all clenched up, locked tight. There's a set of ridges at the top of my feet—joints I never noticed. I can't uncurl them or do anything to ease the pain, so I jam my feet back into my sneakers.

I look out the bathroom window, up into the sky. I don't know if that stuff about the moon looking red to werewulves is true or not, but it still looks white to me. That's good, at least.

I check the mirror to make sure my face is normal. Brow, cheekbones, jaw, nose, ears. Nothing new. I could probably use a shave, but it's not out of control yet.

Wait a minute. I look back in the mirror. My eyes are darker. Not the usual vamp swimming-pool blue: more like a sky about to turn stormy. Maybe it's just the way the moonlight from the window is working with the fluorescent bulbs. I'd better get out of here before I drive myself crazy. I'll just take care of business before heading back to class.

It's bad to be standing at a urinal when someone who hates you comes in.

"Well, well, well."

I zip up fast before looking over to see Gunther Hoering smiling at me, Taylor Lattimore behind him. Taylor is a Hoering-in-training, but without the charm and $250 haircut.

"What are you doing in here?" Gunther asks me.

"Um, what most people do in here." Why couldn't I have come up with a snappier answer?

"Well, I don't think you should be using this facility." His voice is totally serious.

"Why not?"

"Because it stinks like piss now."

"Funny how that happens in a bathroom."

"You don't get my point. See, this is a vamp boys' room. Meaning it's for vampyres. It's supposed to be clean. When your kind come in here, it ends up smelling like the zoo."

I start toward the door. Gunther moves in front of me and pushes me back a few feet, firm fingers against my chest.

"Excuse me, but I'm not finished yet," he says, still sounding almost polite.

"I'm pretty sure I get the gist of what you're saying."

"Is that right? So you know more about this than I do?" He doesn't take his eyes off me when he says, "Taylor, we must be living in the wrong time. My dad told me that in his day, wulves had separate bathrooms, separate water fountains. They couldn't sit in the same part of a restaurant as the normal folks. Doesn't that sound more civilized to you, Taylor?"

Lattimore nods his head, a smile smeared on half his face.

"But I guess those were the good old days. All those dirt-bag radicals like Huey Seele ruined everything for decent people. Now I can't even drink from the water fountain in my own school without having to wonder whether a wulf drank from it right before me."

My heart is going faster, and I'm getting really nervous because there are two of them, both bigger than me. I just need to get out of here in one piece. "Look. I have nothing to do with that. I'm half-vamp myself, remember?"

Gunther laughs, and the sound reverberates off the tile. "You say that like it's a good thing! In my book, being a mongrel is even worse. I don't care if you're one one-*hundredth* wulf. It only takes one drop of wulf blood to contaminate all of it."

"Well, I guess you're entitled to your opinion."

Gunther pulls his head back, giving me a wry smile. Perfect white vampyre teeth. Fangs could use a little filing, though. "That's generous, that you're allowing me to have my own opinion. Very big of you."

"Could you just get out of my way? I really don't need this crap."

"Whoa," Gunther says. He asks Taylor, "You think he's being respectful?"

Lattimore actually sneers at me as if he's in a movie playing the bad guy's henchman. He shakes his head slowly. "Nah. I don't think he's being respectful at all."

I don't like where this is heading; namely, me getting hurt. "Okay. It's been great talking with you, but I *do* have to get back to class." I turn sideways to squeeze between them, but Gunther pushes me back into the middle of the room.

"No, doglet," he says. "You'll leave when I *say* you can leave."

Then Lattimore moves toward my right while Hoering comes at me straight on.

I don't know where it comes from, but I know to move left and dash forward. Gunther makes a grab for me, and he's fast, but I'm faster. I feel his fingertips touch my shirt. I drop low to get past them, but Lattimore's got his arms around me and the momentum of his lunge throws us against the door, slamming it open.

Now we're in the hall, and he's got me in a bear hug, his arms clasped together just below my sternum. This guy is strong. My own arms are pinned to my sides, and when he crouches, pushing me down a couple of inches, I'm all locked up.

I don't know where the strength comes from, but I suddenly push out and break his hold on me. I stagger forward and spin to face him, standing in what I figure is a defensive fighting position.

"Are you kidding me? You can't hold that little guy?" Gunther says to Lattimore.

Lattimore moves toward me, fast, his arms spread wide to trap me. I shove him in the chest, knocking him into Gunther. They both stumble backward.

I'm not waiting for a third try. I turn and tear off down the hall.

Mr. Wells let me study in the library after I told him I had a migraine.

I hope it's okay that I'm taking triple the recommended dose of Lupinox. Anything less than that doesn't seem to help. Now the aches feel only about half as bad as they did before.

I still can't believe how that whole thing ended. Taylor Lattimore has at least eight inches and forty pounds on me. I wish Juliet had been there to see it. Maybe it would've canceled out her seeing Hoering smash me into a locker.

"Danny?"

Juliet's standing next to my chair, giving me that half smile I like so much.

"I was just thinking about you," I say.

"Really?" She doesn't seem disappointed. "Hey, don't you have class now?" she asks.

"Yeah, Math, but I needed to get out for a little while. A bunch of kids were arguing with Mr. Wells about how to solve a problem and I just . . . I don't know. Do you ever feel like you just want some quiet?"

She smiles, then sits at the table with me. "Every day. That's why I come up here sixth period. I mean, what am I supposed to do in the cafeteria for a whole period?"

"Um. Eat?"

"I'm not usually hungry at two thirty in the morning. Anyway, eating takes five minutes. Then what?"

"Well, if you want to hang with some very uncool vamp kids, you can sit with us."

She laughs. "Is that an invitation?"

"I didn't have a chance to get it printed and engraved, but yes, it's an invitation. I didn't even know you had lunch sixth period, or I would've told you to sit with us a long time ago."

We talk about classes for a while. I'm on autopilot, not exactly sure what I'm saying, because I'm thinking about her eyes, her lips, and the shape of her body under that shirt.

Better cut that out or she'll think I'm a perv. "So, what else is up?" I ask.

"Nothing. I'm exhausted."

"Long night?"

"Long day *and* night."

"Don't get me wrong: I love seeing you at night, but wouldn't it be easier for you if you just went to day school?" *I love seeing you at night*? Idiot!

She laughs a little to herself. "Yes. It probably *would* be easier. But I'm sick of being with the same kids since kindergarten. And, not to sound like I'm totally into 'high achievement' and all that, but I really need to get a scholarship if I'm going to go to college."

"I'm not even *thinking* about college yet."

"I *have* to if I'm going to get a scholarship. Nobody else in my family went, and I really, really want to." She stops talking for a second, then smiles, and shakes her head. "I don't know why I'm telling you all this."

She tilts her head a little and looks into my eyes. "That's funny. I thought your eyes were vamp-blue. They're darker than I remember."

I shift my eyes to my book so she can't look directly into them. "Yeah, sometimes they look darker. Depends on the light."

"Anyway," she says. "I have to go. My dad's picking me up." She must see disappointment on my face, because she touches my hand and smiles. "I was actually already on my way out. But I saw you through the glass and wanted to say hi first." She waves and leaves.

She came in to see me. Not by coincidence or because she just happened to be passing the library. She came here *specifically* to see me. That's a good sign. I'm sure of it.

13
PRIVATE EYES

My eyes are much darker now. Not exactly blue, not quite dark gray. Just dark. I stop at the mall on the way home and go to the Vamp-EYEr booth. I have to wait for the guy to finish taking care of a couple of hamps—human girls who dye their hair blond and wear cheap makeup to make their skin pale. A couple of vamp girls walk by and shake their heads. The only thing vamps think is more pathetic than hamps are wamps: wulves who are vampyre-wannabes. Finally, the two girls finish up.

"How you doing today, my friend?" the guy asks.

"Great," I say. "I'm in kind of a hurry, though. I just need some Azure Blues."

"I'll set you right up. Have a seat."

He uses the machine to measure my eyes, and I buy a box with six sets of lenses. I put a pair in, right in the store, and check the mirror. They'll get me by, at least for a while.

During dinner I'm careful not to let Mom or Troy look

me dead in the eye. It's not hard, since they're paying attention—or pretending to pay attention—to Paige's latest review of a celebrity reality show.

"And then they cut to the rehab center where Ian is detoxing from being hooked in. It's so sad that he turned to using blood, but when Marissa moved in with Willem Worthington—who's nowhere near as gorgeous as Ian—and she took the twins with her, it just killed Ian. He started using blood to numb his pain. I feel so bad for him."

"I would've thought he could numb the pain with the twenty million dollars he gets for every bad movie he makes," I say.

Paige stares at me blankly and imitates a deep-voiced announcer. "Got a beast of a headache? Body aches make you feel like a beaten dog? Why suffer when you don't have to? Maximum Strength Lupinox EX. *When you're feeling so bad that your fur stands on end, you can trust Lupinox, your pain-relief friend. Now available without a prescription.*"

"Please, darling," Mom says. "No commercials during dinner. Especially unpleasant commercials."

"There's something wrong with the sound system in my car," Jessica says. "One of the speakers has, like, a buzzing sound. It needs to be fixed."

Troy puts down his glass of Sangre-Vin. "Take my car tomorrow. I'll bring yours to the dealer."

"Great. But could you ask them to have a human mechanic do it? Last time, my car smelled like wulf BO for two weeks."

"Tonight they're interviewing Marissa about why she cheated on Ian," Paige says.

"Is this program appropriate for children your age?" Mom asks.

"Of course, Mom. Everyone watches it. Right, Jess?"

Mom turns to her consultant on all things teen and tween. Jessica shrugs. "It's nothing she hasn't heard before. And I meant to ask you: I need to get my hair cut, so do you want to go to Martine's with me? Then maybe after we could go shopping? I saw the cutest new Manollhos. They're open-toed Mary Janes."

Mom's face lights up. "Yes! Anya Mallory wore them to the benefit luncheon last week. They're adorable."

"On sale, eight-fifty at Annabella's," Jessica says, like it's classified government information.

"Fantastic. Count me in," Mom says.

Like Jessica needs more shoes to add to the fifty billion others in her closet. Usually I'd comment, but I'm trying to keep a low profile because of my eyes. I go upstairs to shower right after dinner.

I've been under the spray for half an hour. I notice water collecting at the bottom of the shower and I check the drain: it's completely clogged up with hair, only it's not thick and wavy like the hair on my head. It's fine, smooth. Like a puppy's.

I reach to touch my back. My fingers come away covered with the downy hair. Same thing with my arms, shoulders, and chest.

After turning off the shower, I use my fingernails to scrape off all the hair I can reach, then pull it from the drain and flush it down the toilet. Now I can dry off. I don't want hair on the towels or anywhere Mom might find it.

I can't deal with another day without sleep. I find Somnambulex in Mom's bathroom. The ads on TV promise "Restful sleep until sundown, because you deserve it!" I dry-swallow two pills.

"Dante, get up," Mom says, shaking me. "It's almost seven and it's already dark out. You're going to be late for school."

Well, the pills sure worked.

I sit up.

"What happened to your canopy?" she asks.

"What do you mean?"

She'd opened the Sol-Blok canopy over my bed to wake me. It has a huge spiderweb crack in it.

"Did you throw something at it?" she asks.

"No. Maybe I was thrashing in my sleep."

She looks at me, one of her brows furrowed. "These canopies are very durable."

"Maybe I had a nightmare and kicked it."

She watches me for a few seconds. I can tell she's not buying it. Finally, she raises both hands and tucks her hair behind her ears, which means she's moving on. "Well, whatever you did, it's broken now. We'll have to order a new one today. It's dangerous to have a cracked one."

"Sorry," I say. I swing my legs over the edge and sit up. I rub my eyes, still tired.

"Dante, I have a question. It's one I never thought I would have to ask my children. Are you doing drugs?"

"What?"

She points at the canopy. "This is very odd. And there's

been something a little . . . off, about you lately. If you're taking drugs—"

"I took some Somnambulex this morning before bed. I've been having trouble sleeping."

"I'm not talking about Somnambulex. I think you know what kind of drugs I mean. Narcotics."

"I'm not doing drugs, Mom. Believe me."

She looks at me. "I want to believe you."

"Good, because I'm telling you the truth."

"All right, then. Please hurry so you won't be late." She leaves me to get dressed.

The Sol-Blok canopy wasn't broken when I went to bed. Judging from the location of the crack, it looks like I punched it while I was sleeping. And like she said, these canopies are practically shatterproof. I must have hit it with a whole lot of force.

I felt okay when I first woke up, but twenty minutes later the aches and shakes came back. Not as bad as yesterday, but not great. Last night was the full moon, so I figure I'm coming out the other side now.

Still, there's no way I can get through another night of school without attracting a lot of unwanted attention.

That's why I'm sitting in this crummy motel room. The wise-guy clerk wanted to know why I wasn't in school, but when I told him I was meeting my girlfriend here and slipped him an extra fifty, he smirked and handed over the key.

I stuff the wrappers from eight burgers into the plastic trash can. Thanks to Claire's help and a call routed through

Mom's cell, the school got word that I was feeling "out of sorts" and wouldn't be coming in tonight.

I have about three weeks to figure out how I'm going to deal with the next full moon, when, without a doubt, I'll experience my first full Change. And then there's Mom. The last thing in the world she'll be able to handle is me turning werewulf.

Two more Somnambulex, washed down with a bottle of SynHeme. With any luck, I'll fall asleep before the nausea hits.

14
QVESTIONS

I feel so much better, I can't even believe it. I can unclench my hands and feet. The headaches and joint pains are gone. My eyes have lightened up to nearly their usual blue. It feels so good to be back to normal—maybe it's what humans feel like when they get well after being sick.

Mom was pissed about my cracked bed canopy, but she called Dial-a-Canopy and got a replacement the same day.

Walking to school in the light of the waning gibbous moon feels good. The air smells clean, the woods have the right damp mossy smell. I can hear animals moving through leaves. An owl is nearby, looking for prey. Everything is good. I'm not thinking about next month. I'm just happy I got through it this time.

My cell rings. It's Dad.

"How'd it go?" he asks. "You okay?"

"I got through it. It hurt. I got my first baby fur. And my

eyes changed, so I got blue contacts and laid low."

"Feet and hands?"

"They started to change."

"How did the moon look to you?"

"Not red. Still totally white."

He sighs, a loud breathy interference on the phone line. "We're going to have to decide on a plan soon."

"Yeah. How'd it go for you?"

"I got a pretty good bite on my back, but nothing thirty stitches couldn't fix."

"Deep?"

"Nah—I'm good. I'll call you later."

I close the phone. Thirty stitches. He says it like it's nothing. I guess you get used to it.

There goes my good mood.

So far, nobody at the table has said anything to embarrass me in front of Juliet. Not that they'd do it on purpose, but with this crew you never know.

"Hey, I have a good one," Constance says. "*Defenestrate.*"

I knew it couldn't last.

"Is that anything like *defecate*?" Bertrand asks.

And here we go. I glance at Juliet and she's already looking at me like, *what is this?*

"Constance likes to give word quizzes," I say. "Come up with the correct definition and you get . . . absolutely nothing."

"No, no," Constance says. "You get my *ut*most respect."

"Which is of absolutely no value whatsoever," Hugh adds.

"Isn't *defenestrate* to throw a person out a window?" Juliet says.

"Right!" Constance yells. She puts a hand up for a high five, which Juliet delivers.

"That's fascinating," Bertrand says. "But I have something better. Guess who got caught shoplifting at Nohrdström's?" Constance, Martina, and Hugh all huddle around to learn this critical information.

Okay, I have no interest in this at all. I take a look toward the serving area, where the wulf table is.

Claire clears her throat. "Uh, Juliet? I've been meaning to ask you. How well do you know Victoria?"

"Pretty well," Juliet says. "What's up?"

I turn back to the table. I'm not sure I've ever seen it, but if I didn't know any better, I'd say that Claire is blushing. "I was just wondering if she's seeing anyone."

"Not that I know of. She's talked about *you* a few times."

"Me? Really? What'd she say?" Claire is trying to act casual, but her eyes are all lit up.

"I think she likes you."

"What, like as a friend?" Claire asks.

Juliet pauses. "If you ask me, more than that. You should go for it."

Claire smiles, eyes down. Sarcastic, tough Claire—with a crush. I can't decide if it's cute or terrifying. But watching her grin to herself is disturbing. I crane my neck to see the wulf table again.

"What do you keep looking at over there?" Juliet asks.

"It's just that this kid I know isn't there, and I'm wondering . . ." I get up. "I'll be right back."

I walk to the wulf table. They're back from the compound, and all of them have cuts and scabs on their faces and hands. They're laughing about something and don't notice me.

"Hey," I say. "Is Craig Lewczyk around?"

Jim O'Conner looks at me. He's one of the not-so-lucky ones: his face is like a fist, lumpy from the bones not realigning right after the Change. "Why do you want to know?"

"I was just wondering where he is."

John Fusco squints at me for at least ten seconds, then says, "What are you?"

"What?"

"I said, what *are* you?"

I should never have come here. He sees. He knows.

"Well, never mind about Craig. I was just asking," I say. Get out of here, like *now*.

I start moving toward the serving area, and Fusco calls out, "Hey, kid. Stop right there."

I turn back to him.

"I asked you a question," he says. "What *are* you?"

"What do you mean?" I ask.

"Just what I said. What are you? What grade?"

Huh? "I'm a freshman. Why?"

"Human-vamp freshmen runts aren't allowed to talk to us or to come near our table without an invitation," he says. "Didn't you know that?"

"Oh. Oh, no. I mean, I didn't know. But I'm not half-human. I'm half-wulf." That should help.

"Whatever," Fusco says, his face stony. "The other half is vampyre."

"Okay. I was just wondering about Craig. I'll leave now."

I start to walk away. Steve Slattery calls out to me. "He got hurt."

"What?"

"We go to the same compound. He wasn't on the bus coming back. I asked, and the monitor said he was injured."

"Is he okay?"

"Well, he's not dead, so that's a good start."

Not dead is a good start. That's reassuring. I head back to our table. As I get closer, I see that Claire and Juliet are talking. Juliet laughs. I'm glad they like each other.

Then, maybe ten yards from the table, I see Gunther striding over, Lattimore and his other obnoxious sidekick, Alex Fourier, a few steps behind him. Gunther stops between me and the table.

"Um. Where you think you're going?" he asks me. I can't read his tone. His face is blank, or if anything, a little happy.

"I'm just going back to my seat."

"I think you're lost," he says.

Juliet, Claire, Hugh, and the others have stopped talking and are watching us. "Nope. I know where I am. I was sitting here just a couple of minutes ago."

He flips his blond hair. "That's funny. I just saw you over at the howler table."

"Well, yeah, I went over for a second, but now I'm back."

"Can't be," Gunther says.

"He was," Juliet says. "He was here, like, two minutes ago."

Claire and the others nod. Gunther barely gives them a glance. "I don't need your input on this. When I want your opinion, I'll give it to you." Lattimore and Fourier laugh. Gunther just looks at me. "No, you belong over there." He nods toward the wulf table. "With your own kind."

I look back at the wulf table, then at Gunther. He makes a motion like he's shooing away a fly. "Now, git."

Fourier and Lattimore smile. Lattimore puts his hands on his hips. Fourier cracks his knuckles.

I'm not going to push him aside and give the three of them an excuse to pound me. But I'm not going to let him humiliate me again in front of Juliet, either. "Excuse me," I say to Gunther. "You're in my way."

"Oh, there's no excuse for you," he says, half smiling at his great wit. "All these vamps are trying to eat, and most of us lose our appetites if there's . . . one of *you* at the table. No. You go sit with the rest of the mutts." He's raised his voice, and now some kids from the tables nearby have turned to see what's going on.

"Why don't you just leave him alone," Juliet says.

"Yeah," Claire agrees. "It's our table."

Gunther completely ignores them, keeps his eyes on me,

and points toward the wulf table. "Get going."

"No."

"You can walk over there yourself, on your own hind legs, or we can escort you," Gunther says in a tone that sounds like a parent reasoning with a difficult child. Lattimore nods, Fourier grins.

"I'm staying here," I say, my voice firm.

Gunther shakes his head. Lattimore and Fourier stroll a few yards to the left and right, so the three of them are in a triangle around me. I'll have to work on whoever grabs me first. If there's enough blood—from them, or more likely, from me—they'll get bloodlust and have to stop. I set my feet, ready for the worst.

"What's the problem?" a school safety officer says from behind me.

"No problem," Gunther says. "We're just helping our friend here. You can go."

"That true?" he asks me. "They're helping you?"

Before I can answer, Lattimore says, "Take a hike, rent-a-cop."

I don't know if there's some kind of signal these guys use, but two more guards appear, hands on their holstered riot batons. "Kid," says the first guard, "you just crossed the line. Now get lost, all of you, before I take the bunch of you to the principal."

Gunther looks the guard in the eye, trying a stare-down. The guard isn't moving, his gray eyes steady.

"All right," Gunther says. "We wasted half the lunch period. Let's get out of here and go out for some food."

He and his pals leave. The guard watches them, then says to me, "Do me a favor. Don't provoke that kid. Just mind your own business."

"I was—" But before I can say anything else, he shakes his head and does his pseudo-tough, slow guard-walk away from me.

I turn to Juliet. "See? I told you you'd like our table."

15
QVARRY

We're parked at an overlook near the quarry in Brockston. I crack the window, but I know the car is going to stink of burgers and fries for days.

"Sorry we're not eating in a restaurant," Dad says, "but we can't risk anybody overhearing us."

"It's fine. I don't mind."

The waning crescent moon is getting low, and I can't see its reflection in the water anymore. Dad has one of his oldies-mix CDs on. It's Dylan Zimmermann: "Wulf in Sheep's Clothes." I've heard this one for as long as I can remember.

> *You call these folks beasts,*
> *from the West to the East,*
> *But they never wanted to harm us.*
> *The Change ain't their fault;*
> *They don't want to assault*
> *Us, and still they seem to alarm us.*

And then that famous chorus:

> *So every month on that day*
> *When they're taken away,*
> *Put your thoughts with the wulven "others."*
> *They are sons and they're daughters*
> *Sent like sheep to the slaughter,*
> *These folks are our sisters and brothers. . . .*

I admire that Dylan's a human fighting for wulf rights, but I just can't stand the guy's nasal voice.

Dad switches off the stereo. "I told the doctor about your pseudo-Change. He wants us to come back for a checkup. Also, there are things he can do to make the first Change a little easier."

It's clear to me from his voice that he's trying to sound cool about this, like he's not worried. I know better.

"He's out of town at a conference, but we'll see him next week," he says. "Right now, we have to start making some decisions. The next full moon is in less than four weeks."

"Twenty-four days, actually."

"Right. Well, the first thing we have to decide is whether we're going to register you."

"If I register, then I go to a compound every month. And I could die there, right?"

"I'd try to get you into one of the easier ones."

"You know people high up enough to get me assigned to an easy compound?"

"Not really, but the people who work at the registration bureau are underpaid government employees who can be bribed." He pulls a pickle slice out of his burger, rolls down the window, and tosses it out.

"You have the money for that?" I ask.

"I'd find a way to get it."

Wow. I believe him. "What do you mean by an easy compound?"

"Maybe one with older wulves, who mainly sleep during their Change. Or at a juvenile compound."

I still don't know exactly what happened to Craig, but I know it happened at a juvenile compound.

"What's it really like?" I ask.

He takes a deep breath. I know he's trying to figure out how much to tell me. He leans his right wrist over the top of the steering wheel. There's his wulftag, dark and way more apparent than mine. I don't know why I never noticed before, but his forearms are massive. I'm not sure if that's from his wulf genes or from years of manual labor. Probably both.

He's still not talking, so I'd better get this going. "I need to know about the compounds," I say. "I mean, I went on the fifth-grade class trip to one, of course."

"Yeah, you got the nicey-nice tour, in between full moons. I'll bet it looked beautiful."

"Sure. Rolling meadows, lots of trees, huge rock formations. Other than the fence and gate we passed through to get in, it looked like the nature preserve behind our house."

"Which is the image the LPCB wants everyone to have. They don't show the less . . . *scenic* parts on the public tours."

"Right. And I'm sure the stuff I've seen in movies isn't exactly accurate, either. Which is why I'm asking you."

"Okay," he says. "Well, we can start with the buses."

"I've seen them." Government buses, army green, run-down and loud. Wulf faces staring out through the windows, expressionless.

"Once you get used to the smell, they're not bad. Ideally, you'd sleep on the way there. It's kind of a long ride, since the compounds are far away from towns."

"Because nobody wants to live near a compound. Just like prisons."

"Right. There's supposed to be a paramedic on every bus, but that only happens if they're due for an inspection."

"Nice. Real concern for safety," I say.

Dad takes his time sipping his soda. "You get there and they open the compound gates for the bus. Two electrical fences are on the outside. The inside one is known as the Shocker. It's got enough voltage to give a jolt you might remember even *after* the Change. Mostly that does the trick and turns back anyone who wandered over or is trying to get out. The outer fence is called the Fryer. That'll turn a werewulf into a smoking furburger." He looks at me, proba-bly realizing that he might have been more graphic than was necessary. "Then there's the compound itself. You have your thirty-foot-high concrete walls and, well, the guard towers."

"The guards are armed."

"Yeah. If the problem is inside the wall, they try tranquil-izer darts."

"If the problem is outside?"

He shakes his head. "It doesn't happen often, but if some-one gets outside the walls, they use hardcore ammunition." He looks at me. "I've never seen that."

I'm pretty sure he's lying.

"When you get off the bus, your ID card and collar are scanned, and that info goes straight to the LPCB in D.C. so they know you've reported. Before nightfall, there are meals in the dining halls. Food's not as bad as you'd think. Anybody who's on medication goes to the compound hospital dispensary."

"What happens in winter? You just stand around in the cold until the full moon comes out?"

"No, no. Until the Change, you stay in barracks. A lot like in the army. When you're . . . when the full moon is out, you wouldn't want to be cooped up inside. You'd go crazy."

"And then there's the full moon, you Change, and the fun begins when you go outside and get attacked by other werewulves," I say.

"You try to keep away from hostile ones."

"How do you know which ones are hostile?"

"You can sense who's dangerous and you just keep away."

"What if you can't avoid them? What if they come after you?"

Dad's left eyelid twitches and his lips go tight. "The hostiles only attack the ones they sense are weak. Weak or threatening. You won't be either of those."

I believe half of that: I definitely won't be threatening.

He goes on. His casual tone sounds forced. "There's lots of room in the fields. There are places you can hide if you think they're after you." He clears his throat and nods a few times. "Some compounds have caves. All of them have man-made half-indoor shelters. The cement floors are heated in winter, cooled in summer. It's not so horrible."

"Yeah. It sounds like a resort. Do they have tennis courts and swimming pools, too?"

"Some of them have lakes. But there's not exactly an activity director. No bingo games, either. You run most of the night and sleep during the day, when your werewulf aggression hormones aren't so revved up by the moon. The truth is, you're not going to remember much of it. Your mind goes into a . . . simpler state. Kind of like when you're half asleep and can't form complete thoughts. Or when you have a high fever."

"I've never *had* a fever."

"Oh, right. I don't know, then. It's hard to explain. Werewulf thinking is more like . . . just sensations, I guess. Hunger. Fear. Anyway, when it's over and you Change back, you get your stuff, scan out, get back on the bus, and you're on your way home."

I don't say anything. The compound sounds like just about the worst thing I can imagine. I'll get torn to pieces there. "Choice two?"

"Well, if you register and have lots of dough—which your mother does, thanks to her parents and her new husband—then you can go the medical route. An LRC."

"Lycanthropic Rest Center? Isn't that just for movie stars?"

"Yeah, there are celebrities. And other rich people who aren't famous. It's expensive. Even though it's staffed by doctors and nurses, medical insurance considers it elective."

"And they put you to sleep for the whole Change?"

"More or less. Basically, they put you in a light coma. But there's a high risk of complications."

"Like what?"

"Like seizures, blowing blood vessels in your brain, permanent coma, and death."

"What are the chances of any of that happening?"

"Sixty percent."

"Bad odds."

"Not great." He unwraps another burger and takes a big bite.

I take a sip through my straw. "You know, in Tibet they have a good system. Before full moon, the wolves climb down rope ladders into the Tsangpo Canyon. Monks pull up the ladders, and the werewulves run totally free in this enormous gorge during the Change. After the full moon, the monks lower the ladders and help the wulves back up. They've been doing it for centuries."

"Well, good for them, but we don't live in Tibet," he says as he chews. He crumples the burger wrapper and stuffs it in the paper bag. "Then there's the other way."

"Which is?"

"Which is illegal. You don't register."

"Stay free," I say, even though I know it's not that simple.

"Sure. Unless you're caught or killed, which happens to most moonrunners eventually. Some of them get shelter by paying a keeper."

"Is that as bad as it looks in the movies?"

"It's probably worse in real life. You pay the keeper a lot of dough, then you get chained up—hands and feet—to bolts in the floor or walls of a basement. It's pretty disgusting. There's usually bad ventilation and little or no food. Lots of wulves die each month. Bodies get dumped in rivers or stuffed in landfills."

"Aren't *any* keepers decent people?"

"Not that I've heard of. And some of them just turn the wulves in to the cops or the LPCB. The keepers pose as neighbors, say they heard noises. Lo and behold, when the authorities check it out, they find a basement full of captive werewolves. The keepers get a nice fat reward, while all the wulves—the ones still alive in the basement—get hauled off to federal penitentiary."

I shake my head. Can this get any worse? "So the other choice is to be a moonrunner and try to hide somewhere."

"Right, and then we're back to getting hunted and killed, either by the LPCB or by poachers, who collect their bounties when they deliver your carcass to the cops."

"It sounds like we're out of options, if I don't register," I say.

"Well, there's one other way. A chamber."

"I thought that was just in movies."

"It's real, but rare. It's done in a private home with some-one who can be trusted. It costs money to build it right, so it's solid and escape-proof. And you need someone who's willing to keep an eye on you, make sure you have food and water. And since this is totally illegal, that person is technically an accomplice."

"Do you know anybody who would do that?"

He takes a deep breath. "Your mother might."

I laugh. "Are you kidding? I can just see it. You'll say, 'Thought we'd let you know, Danny's going to become a werewulf. And, oh, by the way. We were wondering if you'd be cool with us building a chamber in your basement, which means you and your family will be committing a felony every single month while you shelter a moonrunner.' Is that what you had in mind?"

"That's not bad at all. You can do the talking, slick."

He laughs, and I laugh, too. There's nothing funny about any of this, but being with him makes me feel a little less scared.

A little.

16
ALMOST TOVCHING

The last thing Dad told me before dropping me off was how important it was not to say anything about this to anyone. So what do I do, not twelve hours later?

"I'm not kidding," I say to Claire. "You can't tell anyone."

"I heard you the first twenty times." She's looking down at the path through the woods that we take to school. She can't be seeing much, because there isn't a lot of moonlight. But I've seen her do this—look down while she's walking—at times when she's trying to figure something out. She's in her own head now, working this over, but I need her to hear me about this.

"Claire, you can't tell . . . *anybody. On. The. Planet.* Get it? *No. Body.*"

"That's twenty-one."

"I'll keep saying it until I'm sure you get the point."

"Okay, I get it. Seriously. You think I'd tell?"

"I'm just saying."

She punches me lightly on the shoulder and we walk a few yards when she asks, "What about Juliet?"

"What about her?"

"Are you going to tell her?"

I stop walking. "What did I just finish telling you? Nobody."

"Okay. I'm just asking. I mean, you're so crazy about her, I figured you'd want to tell her."

"I want to, but the stakes here are just so big. I can't tell a soul."

"You told *me*."

"You're different."

She nods. "And this doctor is *sure* you're going to Change?"

"Yeah. Like I said, I already went through half of one. Or a Change Lite. It's going to happen. Soon. And I don't know what I'm going to do."

"You'll have to do *some*thing. Which choice seems the least horrendous?"

"All of them are terrible." Like Claire, I look down at the path as we walk, but unlike Claire, I can see rocks, bumps, and a tree root that she's about to trip on. I give her a push, and before she can curse at me I say, "Tree root. You didn't see it." She looks behind her, then doubles back, feeling the ground with her foot. "It's two steps ahead of you, but at your left foot," I say. She finds it, then squints at me, trying to figure how I could have seen the root in the darkness.

"I told you. My vision is sharper. All my senses," I say

with a shrug. "Come on, we're going to be late." We start walking again. "I don't want to go to the compounds, and I don't want to register. But my whole family could get in unbelievably serious trouble if they build me a chamber."

"And so could I, now," she says evenly.

"No. Nobody knows I'm telling you, so nobody could ever prove you knew anything."

"So you're thinking the chamber thing?"

"Maybe. We have to tell my mother what's going on first. She might notice major construction in her basement."

We come out of the woods and see the school on the other side of the playing fields. We walk under one of the goalposts.

Claire is still looking at the ground, but with the glow from the school windows, she can probably see the grass more clearly. "But if you do that, and you stay in that chamber for, like, three or four days during the full moon—"

"I know. I'll be out of school every month during the full moon, and they'll have to report it to the LPCB. We thought of that problem."

"And what's your solution?"

"Don't have one yet."

The halls are crowded and loud. Half these vamps look like they're still waking up; the other half make up for the quiet of the sleepy ones by shouting and laughing, hyped up like they just had a six-pack of SynHeme Triple Caf. Claire goes to A-wing, where her locker is, and I go to B-wing.

As soon as I turn the corner, I smell it. Something like cardboard and dust and, I don't know. Beef jerky, maybe.

152

I get to my locker. This part of the hall *really* stinks of it. I turn the dial on the lock, sniffing and trying to figure out what it is. I hit the third number, and as I pull the handle, I know.

Once the latch releases, the door swings open and an avalanche of small, dry brown nuggets, thousands and thousands of them, floods out. They scatter all the way across the hall. Some vamps laugh at me, some curse at me for stinking up the hallway.

Dog food.

Dry dog food.

It must have been loaded to the top of the locker. I don't know how it was done, but I'm pretty sure I know who did it.

"You okay?" I ask Juliet. "You looked like you were going to have a fit during Chem."

"I'm nervous about that test," she says.

"It's not going to be hard."

"Not for you, maybe." She's not looking me in the eyes, and from the way her shoulders are hunched forward, she's embarrassed, unhappy, or both. I feel bad for her.

"We can study together. If you want."

"When?"

"After school? We can get in a few hours before I have to leave to beat the sunrise."

"I'm leaving in a few minutes. And I can't stay up all night. Thanks, though."

She puts her books in her bag and pulls on her coat. I can't miss this opportunity.

"You know what?" I say. "I only have Health, lunch, and Gym left today. I can skip them to study with you."

She tilts her head and squints at me. "I don't want to be the reason for your academic downfall," she says.

"I'm fairly sure my downfall won't be your fault. Come on. I could use the studying, too. If your father's getting you, maybe he could drop us off at the diner."

"He only picks me up when he has to get fresh fish for the restaurant. But my parents like me to be home after school. We can go there."

"To your house, you mean?"

"Yes—where I live. That's usually why it's called home."

Oh, man. Phone calls and locker meetings. And now, going to her house? How have I not messed this up yet?

I must have scored some major points with her while we were studying. I found ways to explain stuff so she understood it better than she did in class. We worked for about an hour and a half, and now we're packing up our books.

I still can't believe I'm here. Juliet's living room has a lot of rugs, and the furniture is so soft, you just sink in. There are family pictures on the brick fireplace, which looks so much warmer than the slate one we have. In fact, this whole place is homier than my house.

She turns on the TV and puts her feet up on the couch so they're near my leg, almost touching.

"You won't get in trouble with your parents? I mean, they wouldn't be mad knowing we're down here alone?"

"No problem. They trust me."

I nod. I'm not sure what to make of that. Does she mean

that they're too trusting? Or does she mean that she *can* be trusted by them, in that she would never do anything with me to violate their trust, and I'm considered a total neuter?

Either way, if her parents knew that I was half-wulf, they might not be so easy about letting me hang out with their daughter. And if any of them knew I was going to Change . . . I don't even want to think about it.

"And anyway," Juliet says, "it's almost two in the morning. They're dead asleep." She puts her foot against my leg.

Then, finally, the long-awaited lip-lock. And it *is* all it's cracked up to be.

My right hand is behind her head, the left one on her hip. Should I make another move? Maybe not. She might not want that yet. Don't rush it.

She makes an *mmm* sound and pulls away. She smiles, looking happy and maybe almost sleepy.

"Are you tired?" I ask.

"Just relaxed. I didn't know if this would happen."

"Me either. To tell you the truth, though, I hoped it might."

"To tell *you* the truth? Me, too," she says. "You know, in a way, we owe it all to Mr. Morrison."

"What? Why?"

"Because he did the rebel yell, and you fell out of your chair and made me laugh. That was when we first talked at your locker."

"You remember that?"

"Well, yeah. It was when we met for real."

"You think we never would have gotten together if it wasn't for the rebel yell?" I ask.

"Who knows? But that's the way it happened, so we owe it to him."

"Well, fine. Here's to the rebel yell. You want me to try it right now?"

"Why? Are you planning to attack me?"

"Maybe. Maybe a nice attack."

"Then let's just skip the yelling part."

She pulls me in close and I can't believe this is happening. She likes me, definitely. *Definitely*.

But she also doesn't know me, not completely. She doesn't know the one big thing. And I hate that I'll never be able to tell her.

17
SVSPICIOVS

I get home and Mom is in her garden, kneeling on a rubber mat. She's tending her orchids, with the whole area on the side of the house lit up by floodlights. I still don't get what's so exciting about cultivating flowers, but she's been doing it for years, and never seems to get tired of it.

"How are they coming?" I ask.

"I have four that are thriving. This one, though . . ." she says, frowning. "No matter what I do, this one is just failing."

"Well, I would say that if four out of five look good, you're still ahead in the game."

She touches the petals on one of the orchids. I can't tell if it's the bad one or one of the successes. They all look more or less the same to me.

"Anyway, I'm going inside," I say.

"I was in your room today," she says ominously.

"Okay." I have nothing to hide in my room.

"Your Sol-Blok canopy was cracked. The one I just replaced."

Another one? "I don't know why. Restless sleep again, I guess."

"If I didn't know better, I would say you're breaking it deliberately, hitting it with a bat or something."

"Well, I'm glad you know better, then. Why would I do that?"

"Maybe it's some sort of passive-aggressive demonstration, to frustrate or anger me."

"I don't even know what that means, but I'm not trying to anger or frustrate you. I didn't do it on purpose. If you want, I'll get money from my bank account and pay for it to be fixed."

"They can't be 'fixed,' Dante. Once they're broken, they're useless. I had it replaced already. This time, I paid extra for the Sleep-Tite ultradurable model. So whatever the reason for its having been broken, I don't expect that it will happen again."

"I'm sure it won't." Not *so* sure, though.

She turns her head, her long neck elegant as a swan's. She looks at me and I can't tell what she's thinking. Her expression is blank. "You could use a haircut," she says.

"I think I'm going to grow it a little."

She shakes her head and gives me her annoyed smile. "I don't understand you. I've offered countless times to color your hair a nice ash blond, and you won't do it."

"I'm not dyeing my hair. That's ridiculous."

She gets a cold look, and when she speaks, her words sound clipped. "Coloring your hair is ridiculous, but keeping it brown and growing it isn't? You're going to look like a complete wulf."

I shrug. I'm not going to get into this with her right now.

"Speaking of which," she says, "your father called. He said he'd like to speak to you about doing some work on his apartment."

"He called the house?"

"Yes, he did."

"And you talked to him?"

"Only to take the message." She stands up and looks me in the eyes. "Why did he call you?"

"I meant to tell you. I've been in touch with him a little."

There's a flash of anger on her face, but she suppresses it quickly. "And why would that be?"

"I don't know. I wanted to connect again. Is that strange?" I put some concern on my face, as if I were worried that I did something wrong. It has the planned effect.

She turns back to her orchids. "I suppose not. I'm just surprised."

I look into the darkness of the nature preserve on the other side of the fence, then back toward the house shining in the night. "I guess I'll go in and call him back."

"That's up to you. But honestly. If he needs to do work on his apartment, he really should have his laborers do it. You're not some working-class lackey."

"I don't mind. The way I remember it it's kind of fun."

Mom looks at me and shakes her head. I can tell she's thinking, *How did I end up with a son who actually wants to look like a wulf and slum around doing manual labor?*

Maybe for the first time I know what it felt like for Dad when she looked at him the same way.

I get to my room and start changing my T-shirt when Jessica barges in. "Troy can be a real jerk," she says.

"Have you heard of knocking?" I ask.

She ignores me, tosses her hair, and stands in front of the window monitor, which shows a view of the sunshine in our backyard.

"Why are you in my room?" I ask her.

"Why wouldn't I come to visit?"

"How about because you never, ever come in here unless you want something."

Now she's walking around my room like she's browsing in a store full of tacky jewelry. She looks at the old Stake-n-Shake concert tickets on my bulletin board, picks up the baseball signed by three of the Cubs that's on my desk. Next, she's going to pick up my iPoddMaxx, look at my music, and sneer at that, too. "Well, I came in to say that Troy's an idiot." On cue, she picks up the iPodd and scrolls through my music, wrinkling her nose.

I get up and take it away from her. "I thought you said he's a jerk. Which is it?"

She shrugs, then opens my dresser and flips through my T-shirts.

"Do you mind? I don't go through *your* stuff."

She shuts the drawer and looks around. "How can you live like this? With all that stuff on your desk?"

"If you're looking for the door, it's right behind you. Don't feel like you have to stay."

"I guess Troy is both. A jerk *and* an idiot. Plus, he's a pain in the ass."

Jess is only talking to me because she's bored. She doesn't hate Troy, at least not more than any of the other guys Mom used to date, but she likes to interpret my indifference to him as dislike. "Jess, if you want to tell me why you hate him today, tell me. But I'm not going to beg you."

"He thinks he can tell me—tell us—what to do."

"Let me guess. Did he say he doesn't want you going out with Lane?"

"Not in so many words. It's just the tone of voice he uses when he talks about him." She's in profile against the monitor by the window, which is showing a view from the southeast, a shot of the sun shining through the trees of the nature preserve.

Jess really is beautiful, even if she is a total brat. She got a white car for her seventeenth birthday and insisted it be replaced with red, because red looks better with her hair.

"I wish Mother would just divorce him," Jess says.

"Tell her. I'm sure she'll do it if you ask. She got rid of William and Vaughn and Simon because of your nagging."

"She was just *dating* them. She's married to Troy. It wouldn't be that easy."

"Don't give up, Jess. You'll get your way if you really put your mind to it." I give her a hearty thumbs-up.

She narrows her eyes at me. "That's very funny, but I'm being serious. Mom is pretty into Troy. I don't know why. He's not exactly Mr. Exciting. I wouldn't mind him so much if he'd just stay out of my business. I'm sick of his attitude about Lane."

"Troy is harmless. Why can't you ignore him?"

"You wouldn't understand. If you had a girlfriend, you might know how it feels."

"Maybe I do have a girlfriend."

Jess laughs. "I'm sure there's a real live female who's interested in you," she says, her stupid perfect teeth flashing in a smile.

"Did you come in here just to be a complete bitch to me, or did you have some other purpose?"

"*Okay*, I'm *sorry*. Jeez, so sensitive. So what's this alleged girlfriend's name?"

"Never mind."

"That's what I thought."

"Okay, fine. Her name is Juliet."

"Juliet? Come on. That's not even original."

"That's her name."

"Right. What's her last name?" Jessica's getting excited, now. She thinks she's either going to get gossip or catch me in a lie.

"Walker."

"Uh-huh. So, is this a real person or a figment of your desperate boy imagination?"

"She's totally real."

Jessica narrows her eyes, trying to figure out what the trick is. "And she's your girlfriend."

I can finally say something to shut her down and end this. "Absolutely."

"I know pretty much everyone worth knowing in school," she says. "Even the ninth graders. I don't know any Juliet Walker."

I shrug.

"Dinner!" Loretta calls up the stairs.

"Dinner," I say. "Conversation over."

"What does she look like, this mythical girlfriend?"

"Well, she has brown hair," I start to move past her.

She grabs my arm and stops me. "Whoa, whoa, whoa. Wait. Brown hair? So she's not a vamp?"

"She's human."

"Oh," she says, and laughs. "Well, then. That explains everything." She's still laughing as she pushes past me.

As usual, Paige and Jessica have deeply important matters to discuss during dinner.

"I just saw on the entertainment news that it's true: Gwenbeth Paltroff is a vamp," Paige says.

"That's just a rumor. People have been saying that for years," Jessica says, like she's personal friends with the movie star.

"No, seriously," Paige says. "It's true. I saw it on *Celeb-Pretty*!"

"You're so gullible."

"Then why doesn't she deny it if it's not true?"

"Because she likes people to think it. It makes her seem more interesting than just some girl who happens to be pale and blond and pretty."

"Well, she's still a fine actress, even if she *is* human," Mom says to end the pointless debate.

"So what's the deal with you and Gunther Hoering?" Jessica asks me.

"What?" I try to keep my voice casual. "There's no deal."

"I heard that you guys are at war."

"How could I be at war with him?" I think I liked the celebrity conversation better. "He's, like, king of the school. Why would he even bother with me?"

"I don't know, but it's what I hear. He's in my grade, people talk."

"You're *at war* with someone in school?" Troy asks.

I raise my hands, palms up, like a bad mime showing innocence. "No. That is totally untrue."

Mom looks at me. "I hope so. I play tennis with Sabina Hoering."

Now it's Paige's turn to chime in. "Franz Hoering is in my class, and he says that his great-grandfather was a Nazi in that world war."

"That sounds like a tall tale to me," Troy says.

"It's true. He brought in this medal and it had 'WJ' on it, which he says proves that the guy was some kind of big shot."

If I remember right, WJ was an elite unit, like the SS. It stood for *Werwoelfejäger*, which was the Nazi group that rounded up wulves and sent them to extermination camps. Or just lined them up and shot them. It wouldn't surprise me a bit if Gunther came from such noble ancestry.

Jessica, of course, won't let it die. "I never heard anything about Gunther being a Nazi, but I still wouldn't mess with him if I were you. He could kill you in a second."

"He doesn't have any reason to kill me, and if I were *you*, I wouldn't believe every stupid rumor I heard."

"Well, at any rate," Mom says, "I do hope you aren't fighting or doing anything inappropriate. That may be fine for . . . other people, but not anyone in *this* family."

"Have I ever done anything to get in trouble at school?" I say, dodging.

"There's a first time for everything," she says.

I stab a piece of meat with my fork and put it in my mouth. This is unbelievable. Can I go one hour without being given a hard time, or having to deal with my werewulf issue?

I'm a little light-headed, which means my crit is dropping. I take a good drink of SynHeme and my stomach clenches. Hard. I'm going to puke.

I stand up suddenly.

"What's the matter?" Troy asks.

No. Not here, not in front of them. I get up and turn away from the table. Breathe. Breathe. "Nothing," I say. Don't run from the table. Don't. It'll raise questions and end up in a doctor's visit. Don't give in to the nausea. I put my hands on my neck. "Just something caught in my throat. I'm okay." I cough a few times to make it convincing.

I sit back down. I can feel Mom's eyes on me. "Have a drink, then," she says.

"I'm fine. Don't worry about it."

Loretta, back from the compound, comes in to clear the plates. There's a gouge above her eyebrow, and another on her ear.

The wounds are fresh enough that I can smell the blood. But it's strange: I don't salivate or get light-headed or anything.

I look over at Jess and see that her pupils are dilated. Paige is staring directly at the cuts on Loretta's face. Mom is breathing deeply, her eyes half closed. Troy gawks at Loretta's face, blinking repeatedly.

"Um, Loretta?" She turns to me. I tap my eyebrow and ear, then nod to her. She touches her eyebrow and realizes. She looks down at Mom and Troy, then Jess and Paige.

"Oh, excuse me. I'm so sorry. I'll put on some Hemo-Sealer and come back right away—"

"Don't worry about it," I say. "I'll clear."

"So sorry."

"No problem." Anything to get out of this room.

18
VIEWER WARNING

I sit in my spot on the gym floor while Mr. Carver checks attendance. Gunther is talking softly to the guy in line next to him. I think his name is Andre. They both look over at me and start laughing, then go back to their conversation. I can feel my face getting red.

"All right, ladies," Mr. Carver says. "We're going up the hill to the track, and I don't want to hear anyone complain that it's a cold night. It's not cold. I got them to turn on the lights, and we're doing it, so don't waste your breath whining. Get going."

We start moving toward the doors at the back of the gym. A side door opens nearby, and it's *Craig*. He hands Mr. Carver a note. Mr. Carver nods and puts the note in his attendance book. He pats Craig on the shoulder, then moves toward the doors with the rest of us. I leave the crowd to follow Craig, who's headed back to the side door.

"Hey, Craig, how you doing?"

He turns. There's a black patch over his left eye, with two deep, angry gashes above and below the patch. There are two more shorter, shallower ones on the side. All four gashes are parallel, with shiny black stitches holding them closed, the skin puckering around the sutures. It's horrible.

"Wow. What happened?" I ask.

"I got clawed at the compound."

"Is your eye going to be okay?"

"What eye? It's gone, man."

"What do you mean, it's gone?"

"Gone. As in, not there anymore? And the surrounding bones are so messed up, they don't even know if they can fit me with a glass one."

I think of one of Constance's words: *enucleate*, which means "to take out an eye." Nobody at the lunch table had ever heard it before. "Damn. I'm sorry."

He shrugs, looks down at the floor with his one eye. "Life sucks. What are you gonna do? At least I don't have to take Gym anymore."

He starts to walk away, but he only gets one step before a voice says, "Hey! Man, that looks bad!" It's Gunther. He and his pal Andre lean in toward Craig. "That happen at the compound?" Gunther asks.

Craig nods, turning his face to the side. I can tell he just wants to get out of here.

"So, what?" Gunther says. "Another crumpskull—oh, sorry—another werewulf just, like, came over and slashed your eye out?"

Craig nods. He doesn't look mad or offended. Just defeated.

"Wow. That's a shame." Gunther shakes his head. He takes a look at me before turning back to Craig. "A real shame, you know? If he'd gotten just a couple of inches to your right, he could've gotten the other one, too."

Andre laughs. Gunther holds his hand up for Andre to slap. "Oh, well," Gunther says, grinning. "There's always next month."

He and Andre head toward the door, still laughing.

I truly don't know what to say to Craig. He swallows hard.

"Hey, kid!" Gunther shouts from the doorway. "I'll keep an eye out for you." The idiot Andre laughs at this. Gunther howls, and it reverberates around the gym even after they're gone.

Craig starts walking away.

"Craig," I say.

He stops and turns to me.

"I don't know what to say. If there's anything . . ."

Craig looks at me, his one eye shiny, narrowed with anger. He snickers. "Anything you can do? Like what? What can you do for me?"

"I don't know. Whatever I can do." Which, I guess, is nothing. "Look. Guys like Gunther Hoering . . . He's just a specist scumbag. He has no idea what it's like—"

"But you do, right? You know exactly what it's like, after having gone to compounds for years and all that. I bet you know just what it's like to lose an eye, too." He shakes his head, then raises his slashed eyebrow. "You want to help me? To be my pal? Live the life of a wulf for a couple of years, then we'll talk."

"Did you see Craig Lewczyk?" Claire asks as we walk out the front doors into the night after school. She pulls her peacoat closed and buttons it.

I let out a long breath and shake my head. "He lost the eye."

"I know. That's so horrible." She shivers.

I shake my head. "Poor kid."

"I know, right? Awful. You feel like doing anything?"

"I have to go over to the Kray-Mart in North Haven."

"Eww. Why would you want to go to North Haven? And to the Krap-Mart, no less."

"I have to get this DVD, and it's not something I want anyone I know to see me buy."

"So download it."

"I don't want traces of it on my computer. I have to buy it, and I need to be totally anonymous. I figure a million people go through the Kray-Mart every day, so nobody would remember me."

"Yeah, but to go all the way there for it?" She pulls on her burgundy beret and studies me. "Okay. I *know* you're not talking about porn."

"It's not porn. I need to get *Faces of Change*."

"What? Haven't you seen it a hundred times, like everyone else on the planet? Why do you need to see it again?"

I grimace. "Because I'm not watching it for entertainment this time. I'm watching it to see my future."

Being in any other girl's bedroom would've been the thrill of my life, but being in Claire's is no big deal. I've been here at least half a million times, and I think of her like another sister, except not spoiled or snotty or shallow.

Claire puts the DVD in the player. "You want to watch the medical section?" She means all the computer-generated stuff, the MRIs, X-rays, and CAT scans. "Or go right to the action scenes?"

"Skip that. I just want the MTD film—it's the only part not shot in a lab or with the wulf sedated or something. That's what I need to see."

She advances to a freeze-frame at the beginning of the famous clip. It's an overhead shot of Michael Thomas Delaney, alone and naked in a small concrete cellar, his hands gripping his head. What a way to become famous.

"You sure you want to watch this?" Claire asks.

"No, I'm not sure I *want* to. But I need to. Go."

She hits PLAY. The narrator says: "The viewer is warned that the following segments contain graphic images that may be disturbing, especially for children. Viewer discretion is advised."

The clip is of worse quality than the rest of the show. It was filmed more than fifty years ago. Somehow, it never struck me before how bare the room seems, how lonely, as MTD paces in tight circles, as far as the heavy black chain cuffed to his wrist and attached to the cement wall allows.

The narrator continues. "Michael Thomas Delaney, twenty-six years of age, a native of Cleveland, Ohio, goes through the Change."

MTD drops to his knees and curls forward like he's praying. The camera zooms to the bumps of his spine getting bigger and wider.

171

A minute later the hair on his body grows thick. I feel itchy.

The shot switches to a close-up of his face. His eyes are squeezed shut. There's the sound of bone cracking. A ripple runs across his cheeks as the bones move. His nose and jaw start to push out.

I'm getting dizzy.

And that spray of blood from the corners of his mouth where his lips split and rip . . .

A different angle shows his hands curling, changing shape, joints bulging. Another angle shows the same thing happening to his feet.

Back to his face. More crunching of bone, and his brow flattens.

And then the scream, that scream that little boys playing vampyres vs. werewulves always try to imitate.

It starts as a human wail of pain, then gets scratchy and guttural, taking on an animal pitch, a sound that humans can't duplicate. It's the howl of misery. The agony of the Change.

In nineteen days, that'll be me.

19
BODY BAGS

As soon as I get in Jessica's car, I tear off the disposable Sol-Blok suit Claire gave me, ball it up, and throw it into the backseat. Jess sets her jaw and hits the gearshift hard, her coveralls making a crinkly sound. "My car is not your garbage can. Don't even *think* about leaving that there."

"Fine. Whatever."

She puts the car into gear and heads off down the street. "And you're welcome for the ride home," she says. "It's no problem."

"I'm guessing that Mom *made* you come get me. But thanks anyway." I look out the Sol-Blok-treated passenger window. The sun is starting to rise. That DVD really shook me up.

I hear the crinkle of her SB suit and I can figure that she's turned to look at me. "What's wrong with you?" she asks.

"Nothing. Just tired."

She drives for a while without saying anything. Then, "So

Alexis told me something interesting." I wait for it. "She said she saw you with this girl in school. A girl with brown hair, a human girl, she thought. She told me it seemed like you and this girl were . . . together." She takes her hands off the steering wheel to make air quotes around the word *together*.

"Yeah? And?"

Jess shrugs. "You were telling the truth the other night. You *do* have a little girlfriend. And even though she's a human, according to Alexis, this 'Juliet' was actually pretty normal. Decent looking, even."

"I'm so relieved that your friend gave Juliet a good report. I don't know what I would've done if she hadn't." I look back out my window.

"So," she says. "Dante Gray has a girlfriend. Amazing. I'm stunned. I'll have to talk to this girl and make sure she doesn't corrupt my baby brother."

"Don't even think of talking to her. Ever. About anything."

She looks at me. "Awww. That's so cute." She turns her attention back to the road but reaches over with her right hand to pinch my cheek.

I slap her hand away. "Don't think I won't punch you in the arm," I say.

She laughs at me. "Ooh, touchy touchy. Is someone in love? Is my baby brother becoming a man?"

If she only knew what I'm *really* becoming. In less than three weeks.

I figure I might as well hit the homework. I fire up the computer and open the paper I'm writing for History. On the news feed, they're doing the monthly tallies from the compounds.

"Compound W5-188-M in Bakersfield, Wisconsin, had the highest number of casualties this month, with a whopping twenty-eight confirmed. D8-402-M in Newark, T9-498-M in Oakland, and K4-296-F outside El Paso all come in second place with twenty-four confirmed. Rounding out the top five is M3-042-M in the Bronx, New York, with twenty-three confirmed. That's the forty-fifth consecutive week that M3-042-M has been in the top five. Federal inspectors are investigating the high mortality rate." This is all reported with the visuals of body bags being loaded into trucks, and a lineup of more trucks waiting for the compound gates to open. Then, of course, there's the "art shot" of the full moon glowing behind a guard tower.

That's a lot of dead wulves. They don't even bother counting the injured.

"Once again, this is outrageous and unacceptable," says Huey Seele. As usual, his head is shaved to show off all his bumps and cranial misalignments. No beard, either, because he wants his jagged cheekbones, flattened nose, and crooked jaw to be on display. He's always on the news, getting arrested at some rally or protest. Mom isn't the only person who thinks he's a loudmouth "agitator." Most vamps can't stand him. "The conditions at the compounds are deplorable," he shouts into a microphone, spit flying. "Not to mention the fact that this imprisonment of wulves—American citizens, mind you—is a complete violation of our civil rights. I don't care about the twenty-second amendment, executive orders, or any of that legislation. They're all unconstitutional and need to be repealed. This is fascism, pure and simple."

I can see why he'd be mad about the compounds and what he calls "illegal internment." But I'm not sure what else could be done. I mean, during the Change, wulves become feral. They're dangerous.

I guess I shouldn't be saying *they* anymore. More accurate to say *we*.

Then there's the whole thing that happened to Craig. What if he'd never made it out of the compound—if he was one of the casualties I just heard about on the news?

And there's other stuff everyone hears. Like about guards throwing the werewulves into pits and having "wulf fights," betting on who will win. I've heard about torture and medical experiments. Of course the LPCB claims the rumors are unfounded and that the compounds are strictly monitored for safety and humane conditions.

There's a knock on my door, and after I call yeah, Mom and Troy come in. He closes the door slowly.

Uh-oh. This can't be good.

"Dante," Mom begins. "We know there's something going on that you're not telling us."

"What?" No. I've been too careful. Nothing on my computer, no texts on my phone, no slips when talking around them.

"Come on, sport," Troy says. "We'd like to help. Whatever it is, you can tell us. We won't be upset."

That's what *you* think. "I don't know what you're talking about."

He looks at Mom, then puts his hands behind his back and leans against the wall. Mom looks at the image on my window monitor for a few seconds. It's a dark and cloudy day. There's fog in the nature preserve.

"You didn't swallow something the wrong way at dinner," she says. "You were nauseated."

"No. I wasn't—"

She holds her palm out to me, eyes closed. "Please. I know what I saw. You were ashen, and with your complexion, going pallid is *not* a sign of perfect health. Your Thirst seems odd. You've been irritable, argumentative with your sisters."

"We're *always* argumentative."

"I'm not a fool. Something is wrong and I want to know what it is. Are you doing illegal drugs? Coumidex?"

Troy stands up and puts his hands on his hips. "Dan. Straight and true: are you hooked in?"

I can't help but laugh, but I make myself get serious. This conversation could head into dangerous territory. "Look. I swear to you that I'm not doing any drugs."

"Well, be that as it may, I'm making an appointment with the doctor. There is *something* wrong and I won't leave it untreated."

The doctor. That'll mean a complete physical. And blood tests. "I'm not sick, Mom. If I were, I'd tell you."

"Well, considering that you don't have a medical license and aren't qualified to make that determination, I think we'll just leave it to an expert. I'll schedule an appointment for tomorrow night after school."

"Mom—"

"I'll tell you what time as soon as I know."

After they leave I lock my bedroom door and wait to hear them settle in to watch TV. I dial Dad on my cell phone.

177

"How you doing?" he asks. I can hear hammering and power tools. He's on a job.

"Getting by, I guess."

"Hang on, I can't hear you." The construction noises fade as he goes somewhere quieter. "Okay. What were you saying?"

"I said I'm getting by. But we have to do something about Mom."

"Something like what?" he says.

"We have to tell her. And *soon*."

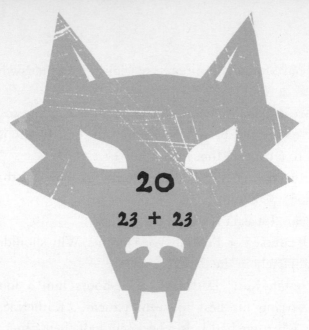

20

23 + 23

The girls are out shopping and Troy is in Romania on business, so it seemed like a good time to tell her. She is not taking the news well.

Mom screamed at Dad like it was his fault. He waited until she was done.

It's been a while since I've seen them in the same room together. One thing I notice now is that, even though they're about the same age, he looks ten or fifteen years older than she does. Vampyres don't age the same way wulves and humans do.

She pours herself a drink. Nothing for him.

"Look, Kat," he says.

"I've told you, I don't go by 'Kat' anymore."

"Okay, fine. *Katherine*. I don't know why you're acting like this is a total surprise."

She ignores his comment. "Who is this so-called doctor, anyway? Maybe he's wrong. If I had been *told* about this, I would have found a top-notch specialist. And that's what I'm going to do."

"Great idea. Your top-notch specialist is going to report Danny to the LPCB, as he's required to do. My guy is committed to a cause. Money can't buy everything."

She turns my way. "So clearly this is what all that odd behavior was about."

"Yeah. I wasn't ready to tell you. Yet."

"Of course not. I'm only your mother. Why shouldn't I be left completely in the dark?"

"Lookit. Kat," Dad says. She shoots him a look. He smiles, trying his best to seem patient. "Katherine, then. Listen. When we had kids, you knew half their genes would be mine. Twenty-three vampyre chromosomes and twenty-three wulven ones. It's biology."

"That's exactly why we did the genetic treatments. On both kids. Something you agreed to, I might add."

"Right," Dad said. "Because I didn't want them to suffer through the Change. Nobody would want that for their kids."

"We also didn't want them to grow up with the stigma. We didn't want the children to be wulven."

"No, Kat, *you* didn't want them to be wulven. That's *your* issue. I just didn't want them to suffer."

She glares at him. His jaw is set. He's not giving an inch.

She turns to me. Maybe I'm imagining it, maybe I'm being too sensitive, but I would say she's looking at me the same way she would look at a pig or a monkey that had run loose in the house and soiled her white carpet.

She turns away. "What am I supposed to tell Troy?"

"You don't tell him one damned thing. Nothing."

"You expect me to keep this secret from my husband?"

"Danny is your *son*. If word gets out, even by a slip, think of what could happen to him."

"I can't . . . I just cannot abide this."

That really pisses me off. "So, what do you want me to do?" I ask. "Disappear? Move out? Say the word, and I'll go live with Dad. Is that what you want?"

She stops for a couple of seconds, which is a couple of seconds too long, before she says, "No, of course not. I'm not saying that at all."

But I saw it. That hesitation. The right answer would have been immediate. Instantaneous. A clear *Absolutely not! We'll figure out some way to make this work. You're my son, and I love you, no matter what.* Not quite the answer she gave.

Now I *really* want to get out of here. Not just out of the room. Out of the house. I go over to Dad and whisper to him. "*Could* I stay at your place for a while?"

"I was thinking the same thing." He talks to my mother's back. "Maybe it's a good idea for Danny to stay with me for now."

"I'm not sure we need to do *that*," she says. "I'll certainly be able to come up with a solution once I have a chance to think. I just need a moment."

It takes me maybe five minutes to pack a bag and get out to his car.

I don't say good-bye. I don't say anything when I leave the house.

I sit on the bed and stare at the duffel I brought. Should I unpack? I mean, how long will I be here? When it comes down to it I have no idea what's going on anymore, where I'll be, or even *what* I'll be, a few weeks from now.

I'm in the room where I slept when I used to come on the weekends years ago. Same bed, same little dresser, same blackout curtains over the window. It's all the same, but everything feels different now. There's a soft knock, and Dad pushes the door open. He leans against the frame.

"I'm sorry it went that way with your mother." He squints at the door hinge and touches it like he's checking to make sure it's straight. I think he just doesn't want to look at me.

"Should I go ahead and put my stuff in the dresser?"

"I guess so. No reason not to."

I'm waiting for him to say, "Don't worry. She'll come around," or something, but he just sighs.

I get up and drag the duffel over to the dresser. It's a simple wood bureau, and the drawer squeaks when I open it. "I can't believe she's just going to give up on me."

He doesn't say anything for a while. I put my socks in the drawer. I probably should have brought more.

"Look," he says. "You know I try not to talk bad about your mother to you. But the truth is that she can be a difficult woman at times."

"She's not difficult with Troy. Or Jess. Or Paige."

"Well, I don't know about that."

"She's difficult with you and sometimes with me. It's pretty obvious why."

"Yeah? And why's that?"

"Um, duh? She's got a thing against wulves."

"I won't argue that. But I can't see her taking it out on you."

"Really? What just happened an hour ago?"

"We did take her by surprise with some pretty big news."

"It's not just that. She wants me to be blond, she wants me to be taller, more . . . She wants me to be a vamp."

"On the surface, maybe," he says, but if he's trying to change my mind about her, or make me feel better, it's not working.

"Come on, Dad. Seriously. She's disappointed that I didn't turn out all blond and vamplike. For her, everything turned to crap when my genetic treatments didn't work and she ended up with half a doglet."

"No," he says. "It wasn't like that at all."

I shrug. "Whatever. It doesn't make any difference now. We have too much other stuff to worry about."

"That's true. But we will get through this," he says. "That's one thing I can promise you."

That's a lie. He means well, but he doesn't know. He can't promise. Being a wulf means a lot of things, but it doesn't mean you can predict the future.

21
SERIOVSLY

Ms. O'Conner is in the front of the room, holding the Shakespeare book with her finger stuck inside to keep her place. "I know all of you read the first act of *King Wain* last night, as assigned." Um, no, actually. I completely forgot. "So we're going to look at Wain's monologue to Merinio in Act one, Scene four." She opens her book and waits for us to find the page. When almost everyone has found it, she starts to read:

> "Come, Merinio, bring my sword and dagger. Marry, I
> will gird myself and faithful, I will cut out their hearts.
> They are curs, the filthy wulves and devilish vampyres.
> Wherefore they doth breathe the air we breathe, walk
> in the light of our moon, under the heavens above man.
> They doth offend mine senses and spirit. Would that
> they had withered in their mothers' accursed wombs,
> never to sully the eyes or spirit of man."

All at once a hammering headache and a tidal wave of nausea hit me.

I make it to the boys' room and manage to ride out the nausea by splashing cold water on my face. By sheer determination, I manage not to puke. Over and over, I repeat in my mind, "Come, Merinio . . . they are curs, the filthy wulves . . ."

The nausea passes, but I'm still left with a pulsing head-ache. I don't know why I'm getting these symptoms in the middle of the lunar cycle, with two more weeks before the full moon. The end-of-period bell goes off.

I have to get my books and stuff from Ms. O'Conner's room before Math, so I work my way through the kids filling the hallway as I head back that way. I feel a firm hand on my elbow and I turn.

It's Juliet. "Are you okay?" she asks, her voice full of worry.

"I just got this really sharp headache and needed to get out of the room. But it passed."

"It must have killed. You ran out of class like you'd been set on fire." She puts the back of her hand softly against my cheek. She has a concerned look on her face, and I feel rotten for lying to her.

"It goes away as fast as it comes on. I'm totally fine."

"That's a relief." She smiles and her eyes crinkle at the corners.

"So you have a free period now, right?"

"Yup," she says.

"How about that. So do I. Feel like doing something?"

"Hmmm. Maybe." She pretends to mull it over, then turns

185

to me with her eyebrows raised. "What'd you have in mind?"

A few days ago, Juliet and I found a huge, dark storage room at the top of an unused stairwell that was at the end of a service tunnel at school. It's not like we were the first to discover it. Teachers don't typically explore dank tunnels and custodians don't care enough to check, so it's turned into a make-out room.

The only light is from a red exit sign by the door, which gives the place kind of a risqué atmosphere. Not inappropriate, given what people are doing in here. Juliet seems to really like kissing, and that makes two of us.

I've noticed that her tongue keeps going to my eyeteeth, feeling and exploring them. Today she pulls back after about five minutes and kisses my ear. It sends a chill through me. She makes a *hmm* sound and bites my earlobe. I jerk like I just got an electric shock.

She laughs quietly in my ear. "I guess you like that," she whispers, her breath hot and tickling. Okay, this is going to get me going. Since there's no cold shower nearby, I'd better put the fire out for now, or I'm going to end up with an awkward situation.

I break the kiss and pull a few inches away. "What's with those teeth?" I ask quietly.

"Which teeth?"

"Um, well you seem to go back to these teeth a lot." I point with two fingers.

"I'm curious, I guess. Those are *the* teeth, right?"

"Yeah, those are *the* teeth," I whisper.

"They feel the same as your other teeth."

"Why wouldn't they?"

"I don't know. I just thought they'd be different. I told you, I haven't really done this before. Not with a vamp."

"Not with a vamp, but with more humans than you can remember?"

"Yeah, with every guy in Millbrook." She punches me in the arm.

Down this road lies trouble. Change course. "Anyway. Those teeth are basically the same as all the other ones now."

"How often do you get them filed down?"

"Depends. Whenever they get longer and sharper than the other teeth. You think I need filing?"

"I can't remember. Guess I'll have to check again." She presses her lips back to mine.

We don't have much time before next period. I can see fine, even in this low light, so I take her hand and lead her to the steel fire door that opens onto the stairway.

We step out into the light and almost bump right into a couple heading in.

Gunther Hoering and Alana Gibson.

"Well, well, well," Gunther says. "What were you two lovebirds doing in there?"

"Excuse me," I mumble, trying to move past him. I grip Juliet's hand a little tighter.

"Whoa, easy there, Romeo. Slow down. Wait. *Romeo*. And your name is Juliet, right? How about that?"

"That's funny," Alana Gibson says.

"Yeah, hysterical," I say, trying to move past Gunther again.

This time he puts his fingertips against my chest. "Hold on," he says.

I don't push forward. I don't want to do this in front of Juliet.

"Let's look at this situation for a minute," Gunther says. He slowly wags his finger at Juliet, and talks like he's solving a calculus problem. "Now, you're human, I know that. And he's . . . well, we know what he is." He shakes his head, frowning with exaggerated disappointment. "Didn't you two pay attention in health class? Don't you know about the dangers of interspecies coupling?"

Juliet's cheeks are going red. I turn back to Gunther. "We have to go to class. Can you please get out of the way?"

He's standing one step below me and we're eye to eye. I can smell pizza and cherry Synheme on his breath when he talks. "Now, just relax. I'm doing a public service here. A little Sex Ed to make sure everyone stays safe." His eyes locked on mine, he says, "I mean, don't you think it's only fair that Juliet here knows what risks she's facing? *Do* you know, Juliet? Do you realize what genetic filth your little friend has in him? It's in every cell in his body. It's in every hair. And every body fluid."

I'm trying to keep my breathing steady, but my heart is pounding and I'm trying hard not to lose my temper.

But Gunther isn't done. "You don't want to be contaminated by him, do you? I mean even from just casual contact . . . you could get rabies. Or at the very least, fleas."

My hand clenches into a fist. I'd love to punch those stubby fangs right into the back of his throat.

"Don't do it," Juliet says. "He just wants an excuse to hurt you."

"Oh, I'm not going to hurt him," Gunther says. "I'm a lover, not a fighter. I'll let him hit me. And then he'll get expelled. And we'll be one step closer to a scum-free school."

Juliet puts both of her hands on my arm and moves in close, her mouth next to my ear. "Don't. He's right, you'll get expelled."

"I don't care." My voice is low. Quiet, but shaky.

"Well, I do. I don't want to be at Carpathia without you. And who knows where you'll end up?"

I swallow. She's right.

"I'm not going to hit you," I say. "I'll just stand here until you decide to get out of my way. You can spend the rest of the period talking to me instead of going up there with your girlfriend." I fold my arms in front of me.

Gunther tilts his head a little to the left, confused. I don't think he's used to things not going the way he plans.

Alana tugs at his arm. "Let's just go. This is boring."

Gunther looks frustrated, but he steps aside, pulling Alana by the hand. He makes sure to push his shoulder against mine as he passes. I ignore it.

The fire door shuts behind them with a clang.

Juliet smiles at me and squeezes my hand. I'm not sure if I won, but I know I didn't lose.

Juliet had to hurry to her locker, and I have to get to mine before Org Chem. At least the halls are mostly empty now, so

I'll be able to get there faster. Then, from the cross hall, I hear a female voice call, "Hey, stop. I need to talk to you."

Jessica. She *never* talks to me in school. She's going to want to know where I've been, but I can't get into the whole thing with her, not until we get everything worked out.

"You know, people can see you talking to me. We're in public," I say.

"What's going on?" she asks.

"Not much. I'm going to my locker." The kids in the hallway walk faster as it gets closer to second bell.

"Don't be funny."

"Can't help it. But I really am going to my locker, so if you want to talk to me—again, right out in public, where anyone could see—then you'll have to walk with me."

I start off down the hallway, and she follows. "Seriously," she says. "What's the deal? Why are you staying at . . . *his* house?"

We get to my locker. I shove my books under her arm and start turning the dial.

"Stop being a jerk. Did you move out permanently?" She frowns at my books.

"That would be a dream come true for you, huh?"

"Mom is all in a bitchy mood, yelling at me and Paige . . . She's snapping at Troy, too. And it all started the second you left, but she won't tell us what it's about. So what's the deal?"

I start digging through the mess to find my notebook for Math. "I guess that's between you guys and her," I say, wondering why Mom would be irritable. Guilt, maybe? Whatever.

Claire passes behind Jessica, does a double take, and widens her eyes like she saw a ghost. I shrug, like, *Don't ask me.* Claire smiles, shakes her head, and moves on.

"Something's going on and nobody's talking about it," Jess says.

She *is* my sister, and she probably has a right to know. I could tell her. That is, if I want the girl with possibly the biggest mouth in school to know stuff that could put my life in jeopardy.

There goes second bell. Well, I'm late now, and I have five more minutes before another point is taken off my grade, so I might as well slow down. I take a long look at my watch. "Now it's almost a minute we've been talking. I'm thinking they're going to banish you from civilization."

She turns red. "Danny, I'm serious."

"You're serious? I thought you were Jessica. When did you change your name?"

Now I can see the muscles in her jaw clench. "I'm asking you to please tell me what's going on."

"*Please?* Wow. Okay. Basically, my werewulf genes are coming out, so I'm going to Change any time now, maybe next month, which means I'll have to register or something, maybe go to a compound every month for the rest of my life, and our mother is disgusted and embarrassed, and that's why I'm living with Dad for now."

"You know, just once, it would be nice to get a straight answer from you." She looks at my books in her arms with an expression like, *Why am I still holding these?* and dumps them on the floor. Of course my binder pops open and papers spin out all over the hallway. She uses her six-hundred-dollar shoes to push a few of them even farther out of my reach. Now, *there's* the Jessica I know and don't especially love.

"So thanks for leaving me and Paige to deal with her all alone. Have a good time hiding at Dad's."

"Listen. I'll tell you all about it as soon as I can."

"Whatever. I hope you're happy."

She walks away. I start pulling the papers together, realizing I'm going to miss the next five minute interval and lose another point. Damn.

I'm packed in with all the other kids pushing to get out the front doors of the school. The cool night air feels good. Claire is waiting, leaning against the principal's car.

"Was I hallucinating, or did I see Her Highness Lady Jessica condescending to talk to you in public today?" she asks.

"I'm as shocked as you are."

"Did you tell her what's going on?"

I laugh. "I might as well put it on the evening news."

"Why are we still standing here? Let's go."

"I'm not walking to my house today," I tell her. "I'm still at my dad's."

"You're no fun."

"You can come over if you want," I say. "But it's a farther walk for you to get home. And we need to be quiet; he's on a day schedule for work, and he needs to sleep a few more hours."

"And then you have the place to yourself?" she asked.

"I guess."

Claire thinks for a minute. "I'll come for a little while. I can't stay out too early."

We walk a few blocks to the bus stop, then sit on a bench and wait.

After a while she says, "I know this wasn't exactly your choice, but maybe it's better for you to be with your dad for a while."

"Why do you say that?"

"No offense, but your mom isn't exactly what I'd call easygoing, and your dad must understand what you're going through."

"Maybe," I say, probably not sounding too convinced.

"I mean, there are worse things that could happen than having to live with your dad, right?"

"You mean like going through the Change and having to be locked up every month for the rest of my life?"

"Right. See, if that were . . . oh, wait. I forgot. That *is* going to happen." She snaps her fingers and shakes her head. "Oh, well. Too bad for you."

Only Claire could say a thing like that at a time like this and get me to laugh.

We watch TV with the sound turned down low so we don't wake Dad.

Keeping my eyes on the TV, I say, "Anything new with Virginia?"

"It's *Victoria*. And you know that's her name."

"Close enough," I say, trying to keep the smile off my

face. This is one area where I definitely have the advantage over Claire. Mention Victoria, and she goes all soft. "So, anything up with her?"

"She's awesome," Claire says. "I miss her so much when we're not together. Let's see. Right now, she's sleeping. She'll get up in a few hours."

I don't look at her while she goes on about the awesome things Victoria will do when she gets up—things like brushing her teeth and trying to decide what she's going to wear—because I still find it disturbing to see Claire in love, or whatever it is.

"Anyway," she says, leaning her head back against the couch pillow, "I'm sure you know what I'm talking about. You think about Juliet all the time?"

"A lot, yeah."

She laughs. "Who would've thought we'd both get girlfriends at the same time?"

"Not me. I wasn't even sure if *one* of us would ever manage it."

"It's pretty great, isn't't?"

"Couldn't be better," I say. We watch TV for a few minutes without talking. I'm thinking about it, and if I can talk to anyone, it's Claire. "Actually, it *could* be better."

She turns and glares at me. "If you say there's something wrong with her, I'm going to hit you so hard in the—"

"Take it easy. There's nothing wrong with her; she's great. The problem is with me: this whole Changing into a werewulf is going to be a real issue."

"And you can't tell her."

"I want to, but I can't. And I'm lying to her by not telling the truth."

"So what are you going to do?"

I lean forward and rub my eyes. "I don't know, Claire. We don't even have a plan for my Change."

Claire sighs. "If I had a solution, I'd tell you."

I nod. We just watch TV for about an hour. Dad gets up around five thirty so he can get to the lumberyard when they open, pick up some materials, then get to a work site. We hear him getting dressed and going into the kitchen. The crawl on the bottom of the TV screen turns red and flashes the words *Sunrise in 29:55*, the seconds counting down with each flash.

"I'd better get going," Claire says.

"I'll give you a ride home, Claire," Dad says, coming into the living room.

"Oh, thanks. I can take the bus, though."

He holds a doughnut in his mouth while he puts on his jacket. Powdered sugar snows onto his shirt. I point to it and he brushes it off, onto the floor. "It's no problem. Get your stuff."

Claire gets her backpack and they leave.

After doing my homework I get bored and start wandering around the apartment. Since it looked like I was going to be staying for a while, Dad put Sol-Blok shields over the windows that he hadn't already bricked over.

In Dad's room there are a couple of paperback mysteries on the table next to his bed. A metal urn sits on top of his dresser. It used to hold the ashes of his father, but he spread them in the woods years ago. Now the urn is filled with spare change.

There's something I want to look at. I open the top drawer, and there it is.

The collar is made of Fibrex that can stretch to triple its size and still return to its original shape without losing elasticity. Almost indestructible, it's tear-proof, with titanium clasps. It's a faded light green, like all of the collars in this region, with faint rust-colored stains that didn't wash out, clearly old blood. "Gray, Edward" and his Lycanthrope ID number are printed on it. It smells like sweat and animal musk.

I put the collar on. It's loose, though my neck will probably thicken a lot when I go through the Change. Feeling with my fingers, I find the embedded plastic square with the computer chip inside. My dad's entire medical history, blood type, ID info, next of kin—his whole life is encoded in there. It also holds the tracker.

"They keep track of where each werewulf is all the time?" I asked him a while back.

"Not every minute. It's more for making sure that nobody stays out on the compound grounds after their Change. And for recovery."

In other words, if someone gets hurt or killed in the woods or a cave, the tracker in the collar is used to find the body.

I take the collar off and put it back in his drawer.

After a shower I walk around the apartment in my boxers and T-shirt. I sure couldn't do this at home. Mom would have a fit. I feel like a bachelor or something.

The refrigerator doesn't have a whole lot to offer, so

I heat up some leftovers and take the plate into the living room. Eating in front of the TV.

I can watch whatever I want, walk around in my underwear, eat when I feel like it, and nobody's going to tell me what to do.

This isn't bad at all.

Maybe if I keep telling myself that, I'll start to believe it.

22
ALLIES

The loud buzz of the doorbell wakes me up. The clock says 7:43 p.m., which means I'm going to be late for school. It takes a second for me to remember that it's Saturday. There's another buzz. Who's here at this time of night? And where's Dad? Then I hear the sound of the shower.

One more buzz and I'm out of bed. I pull on a sweatshirt and go to the front door.

"Who is it?"

"It's your mother."

What? This is impossible. She has never, ever come to Dad's place.

"Really?" I call through the door.

"Yes, really. Could you please let me in? I'd rather not stand here and talk to you through a door."

Dad is standing in the living room, his hair wet. He has jeans on and is putting on a long-sleeved Henley shirt, which has wet marks on the shoulders. "Who's that?" he asks.

"Um, it's my mom," I say, still not able to believe it myself.

He raises his eyebrows and comes to the door. "Kat?"

"Would one of you *please* open this door? I'm standing in a disgusting hallway."

We look at each other for a second. "Fine. Let her in." Dad has what I guess is called a "wry" smile on his face.

She looks like she's been holding her breath in the hallway. She hurries in, then exhales loudly. "Thank you."

I lock up behind her.

"To what do we owe the honor of your presence in our humble home?" Dad asks.

She takes a look around. "Humble. I suppose that's one word for it."

Dad sits on the couch. "Have a seat, Kat. Unless you're afraid the furniture will soil your outfit."

"You know, you aren't making this easy."

"Making *what* easy? Why are you here? Want to tell us more about how ashamed we make you feel?" Dad asks, not exactly shouting, but not in a regular speaking voice, either.

She sighs. "I've been thinking. Thinking quite a bit," she says. She takes a few deep breaths. I'm not sure, but it looks like her lower lip is quivering.

Good. Go ahead and cry. You should.

She turns and walks to the window, facing away from us. The light from the streetlamp makes her blond hair glow like a halo. "One thing we always agreed on, Ted, was that we both wanted what's best for the children."

"That's true," Dad says.

"We may not have always agreed on *what* was best, but we did always want them to be all right."

"What's your point, Kat?"

"Well, argue all you want, but we both agreed for many reasons that we didn't want them to Change. We gave them the treatments to spare them pain. So forgive me for being just a little bit upset that it didn't work."

He holds his hands up. There isn't much to say. "Katherine?"

Her shoulders are moving in tiny little jerks. She's crying.

He goes to her and touches her back. "Kat."

I figure she's going to turn and smash him in the mouth with her fist. Instead, she goes into his arms and he holds her as she cries into his chest.

Hell just froze over.

It's too awkward to watch. I go into my room and lie down. What is going on here? Can things get any weirder?

A few minutes later there's a knock on the door. "Come in," I call.

She comes in and sits on the edge of the bed, while Dad stands in the doorway. She looks at me with red eyes. I don't think I've ever seen her cry.

She takes a breath. "I just wanted to say how deeply, deeply sorry I am about the way I behaved the other day. I want you to know that no matter what, I would never be ashamed of you. I love you."

We don't get along most of the time, but she's my mom, and I do love her. Oh man, I'm losing it. I've been so up and down over the past few weeks I keep feeling like I'm about to burst into tears or maniacal laughter. This time, it'll be tears. I guess she sees this, because her eyes well up again.

I sit up and we hug.

"Let's all go back to the living room," Dad says. "Then we can talk."

"Would you mind if we went back to my house, instead? I'm sure we would be more comfortable there."

He laughs. "I'm sure *you* would be. But that brings up another problem."

"What's that?"

"Troy. We can't have people knowing about this," Dad says.

"Look. He's my husband," Mom says. "He's in this as much as we are."

Dad lets out a heavy breath. "You're sure you can trust him?"

Her lips press tight. "I married him. Obviously I have confidence in him."

"Yeah, well, you married me, too."

"Good point," she says, and her mouth loosens in a smile.

"You're right. He's entitled to know. But maybe we should have the first conversation here, so we have a plan. We can eat and talk."

"Eat? Do you even have anything in your refrigerator?" She raises an eyebrow at him.

"Well, not *much*."

"Let me guess: half a jar of mustard, ketchup, three hot dogs frozen to the bottom of your freezer. Oh, and milk, with an expiration date from around when Danny was in elementary school."

"You think you still know me."

"Am I wrong?"

He shakes his head. "The expiration date on the milk is within this past year. Definitely."

"All right, then," she says. "If I recall, I have leftover duck, filet mignon, grilled vegetables—"

"Okay, okay," he says. "Your place is fine. I'll be ready in five minutes."

They say food heals all wounds. Okay, they say *time* does that, but I say food does it, too. As soon as we got home, we opened the refrigerator and took out everything that looked good, and as always there was a lot that looked good. We sat at the kitchen table, going at leftover pasta and shrimp and duck as though we hadn't eaten in weeks.

Troy came down and put his hand on my shoulder. "Are you coming back home now?"

"I think so."

"I'm glad to hear it. It's good to have you back, my brother."

Dad shook hands with Troy. "You're looking fit, Troy. Hitting the gym, are you?"

"Squash. How are you, Ted?"

"I've been better."

"What's wrong?"

Mom looked at Dad. He shrugged. "All aboard, I guess," he said.

She nodded. "Troy, have a seat. We have a lot to tell you."

And so we told him everything. He listened, he nodded a lot, and he asked a few questions. He called in to work to say he would be late and might have to take the whole night off.

Then it was down to business.

"I'm not sending my son to one of those compounds," Mom says. "Absolutely not, under no circumstances."

"No argument from me," I say.

"Okay, agreed," Dad says. "So what are we going to do?"

"I think we should find the best doctors and try a rest center," Mom says.

"Even the best doctors can't always avoid the . . . problems," Dad says. "And the other thing is, we can't just *try* it. He has to be registered to get admitted. Once he's registered, then he *has* to go to either a rest center or a compound every month. He's on the radar and there's no way off. Not while he's alive."

I nod and push my plate away.

Troy leans back in his chair and drums a paradiddle with his fingertips against the tabletop, deep in thought.

Everyone is thinking. The silence is going on too long, and it's getting loud. "Well, then. What do *you* want to do?" Mom asks me.

"Me?"

"You," she says.

I can't believe it. She's asking my opinion?

"This is your life," Dad says. "What do you think?"

The truth is, I'm not sure. "Well, the compound seems like the worst choice in every way. And I'm not too excited about the idea of blowing a circuit in my brain, so the rest center doesn't appeal, either. If I become a moonrunner I'll probably get shot to death by the LPCB. The only thing that sounds at all tolerable is finding a place to make a chamber."

"We'll do it in the basement," Troy declares without missing a beat. He pushes his chair back about a foot and crosses his right leg over his left. He doesn't look any more concerned than if he had just offered his house to host an anniversary party for friends.

"You mean here?" Dad asks.

"Of course here. Where else?"

Dad and Mom look at each other, then at Troy.

"I think we're all in agreement that we're not going to send him to a compound," Troy says. "The medical route is obviously too dangerous. The best idea—the *only* idea that's feasible—is completely clear. We'll take care of him at home."

Again, the three of us are pretty much dumbfounded.

"Harboring a fugitive wulf is a felony," Dad says. "It's a big deal."

"This whole situation is a big deal," Mom says.

"We're going to have to tell the girls," I say. "Right?"

"I don't see any way around it," Dad says.

Troy nods. "We'll make sure they understand how serious this is and that they absolutely cannot discuss it with anyone."

"One other thing," I say. "What about school? If I'm out during the full moon every month, they have to report it to the LPCB."

"How many times before they make the report?" Dad asks.

"I don't know the exact policy, but I heard about Millbrook reporting a kid after he was out two full moons in a row. That was the last anyone saw of him. So what are we going to do after two months?"

There's a silence, then Dad says, "We can't worry about that right now. Let's just get through this Change."

Mom shakes her head. "Why move forward with a plan if we know we'll run into a serious problem in two months?"

"Because we don't have any time to lose," Dad says. "We've got thirteen days to figure something out. At least he'll be safe, and we buy ourselves another month to think."

Troy starts nodding to himself. "Okay. I know a fellow. He's the brother of Stanford Chase." Troy turns to Dad. "A colleague of mine at the firm and a close friend. So Stanford's brother comes to play golf with us a few nights a year. He runs a private school in the city. And I've heard tell from Stanford that his brother has done favors for people—wulves, specifically—for whom he has some kind of affinity. I have a feeling what he was alluding to is that this school has been a haven for some who choose alternatives to registration."

"You're saying I would go to that school?

"It's a possibility. I'd have to look into it."

"What kind of school?" Dad asks.

"Top notch. Very wealthy and influential alumni—and consequently, the government doesn't audit their attendance or personnel files."

A private school? "So wait. I'd have to drop out of Carpathia and go there?"

"I know it's not ideal," Troy says, clapping me on the shoulder. "I'm hip to that. But it's better than going to a compound, wouldn't you say?"

"That's true," I agree. This would mean I'd have to leave my friends. Claire. And Juliet. We'd never see each other anymore. Would I have to break up with her?

"Are you still with us, bucko?" Troy asks.

"Huh? Yeah, I am. I was just thinking about how complicated this is going to be. Especially with my friends."

"Don't worry about it yet," Dad says. "Maybe down the road we'll think of another way."

"So what do we do now?" Mom asks.

Dad pushes his chair away from the table and stands up. "Let's take a look downstairs."

23
OFF THE FRAME

We watch while Dad walks slowly around the bare basement, checking out the walls and ceiling. "I'm surprised you didn't finish the basement. It's big, could make a great space."

Troy says, "We would have liked to, but it takes in water. Even with the sump pump, it's too humid down here."

"When we're done with all this, I might be able to fix that," Dad says. He starts to pace out the floor, getting rough measurements. He pulls a ballpoint pen from his pocket and writes them on his forearm. He paces it out in the other direction and writes that figure, too. Looks up at the ceiling, then the wall opposite him, and writes a third number on his arm. "I'll build the chamber. I'm going to start tomorrow."

"Are you going to bring your crew?" Mom asks.

"No. Can't tell them. I'll have Kevin help with some of it."

"Who's Kevin?" Troy asks.

"He's my partner in the contracting company. Not a blood relative—actually, he's human—but he might as well be family."

"I'll help too," Troy says. "I'm supposed to leave for Vienna tomorrow, but I'll cancel."

"Don't cancel," Dad says. "We don't want any changes in routine."

"But I'd like to help," Troy says. "I'm pretty handy with a screwdriver."

"Do you have a lot of construction experience?"

"Well, none, really," he says with a smile. The fact that he's not pretending to be "one of the guys" kind of impresses me.

Dad says, "That's okay. Believe me, you'll help in other ways. Just keep up appearances, go about your work as usual. You know what could be helpful? I don't know if I have the cash on hand to get all the materials. . . ."

Troy waves his hand and shakes his head. "Money is absolutely not a problem. Don't give it another thought."

"Great. Thank you."

Troy shrugs and smiles.

Dad tucks the bottom of his Henley into his jeans. The shirt is tight across his broad shoulders, chest, and arms. It's funny: when Mom first married Troy, I imagined play-by-play scenes of cage matches in which Dad slowly beat the crap out of him. Now, we're all working together. Weird how things turn out.

Dad looks around one more time. "I'll need to be here pretty much day and night. Sorry, but you're going to have to get used to having me around."

"I can help build," I say.

"You have school," Mom says.

Dad says, "Maybe we can skip a day here and there when I need a pair of strong hands?"

"No problem," I say. I look at Mom. She shrugs and nods.

"I'll have the first materials delivered tomorrow."

"The neighbors will notice," Troy points out.

"True. Let word get out that you're finishing the basement. The basement will be smaller because of the chamber, but nobody would ever be able to tell, not without checking against blueprints."

"Wait a minute," I say. "I just thought of something. What about Loretta? What do we tell her?"

Dad's looking at me, confused, and Troy says, "Our housekeeper. She's here every night. That could be a problem."

Mom shakes her head. "I don't think so. Loretta never, ever comes down here, not since that raccoon got in. We can tell her the same story: that we're finishing the basement."

"And she'll be gone during the full moon when I'm down here."

"I'm not worried about her," Mom says. "Anything else we should be doing?"

"Tomorrow you need to go buy two large dogs."

"What?" she says. The last thing she'd ever want in her house is a couple of dogs shedding all over the furniture. Okay, well maybe the *last* thing she would want in her house is an adolescent werewulf, but dogs would be next on her list. "Is that a joke?"

"Have to do it," Dad says. "I'm going to put heavy

soundproofing in the chamber, but there's still a chance people could hear Danny howling."

She shakes her head. "Of all the animals, dogs. They're so high-maintenance."

I could make a comment about the fact that she never complains about Jessica, the absolute *queen* of high-maintenance, but this is no time for jokes.

For some reason, Troy has a little smile on his face.

"What's funny?" I ask him.

"Nothing. It's just that I always wanted dogs, and this is a horrible reason to get them."

"Well, I never wanted pets," Mom says. "But we'll do what we have to do."

Dad shows us where the new walls will go, where the door will be, ventilation, everything. It feels like we're planning a war. Which, I guess, we are.

Building the chamber has been a good distraction for me. Lola and Poe, the two Siberian huskies we got, stayed downstairs with us while we worked. They seemed to like me a lot; probably because I was the one who walked them most. It was a good time to think, just walking with the dogs in the quiet of the night.

What with the Change, Juliet, building the chamber, school, and now this completely weird thing of Mom and Dad being back under the same roof every day, there was a lot to think about. "It's crazy, right, Poe? Lola, what do you think?" They looked up at me whenever I talked, and I almost wondered if we would understand each other in a different way after I've been through the Change. Maybe we'll have in-depth conversations about literature and politics.

It was a bad scene when we told Jess and Paige. We were all together. Troy stayed in the background and let Dad do most of the talking.

"I don't get it," Paige said. She sat back into the corner of the couch and put her bare feet up, knees to her chest.

"He had the genetic treatments," Jess said. "How can this happen?"

"You know he wasn't able to finish them," Mom said. "We thought he made it past the critical point, but apparently he didn't."

Paige swallowed. "What's going to happen to him?"

"We're going to make sure he's okay," Dad said.

"Hold on," Jessica said. "We're not sending him to a compound, are we?"

I tried to laugh. "Come on, Jess. Getting rid of me for a few days every single month? This is what you've been waiting for. What could be better?"

"Don't be an idiot," she said. "This isn't funny." There was a quaver in her voice.

"Jess?" I said. "It's going to be okay."

"Shut up," she said, punching me in the arm. "You don't even know what you're talking about. I want to hear that from *him*," she said, hooking her thumb at Dad without looking at him. I could see that she was scared. She twisted a lock of hair around her finger. "We can't send him to a compound."

Dad looked at Mom, then at Troy, eyebrows raised. Troy held out his hand toward Dad, palm up, like, *go ahead*. Dad turned to the girls. "Okay, here's our plan. It's really, really important—I can't tell you how important it is—that you don't tell anyone about this. Not friends, nobody. Danny's life depends on you keeping this completely secret. Do you understand?"

They both nodded.

He explained the plan to them. We went over the fact that there would be deliveries, and there might be times when work would be done day and night. At a few points in the discussion, the girls looked at Troy to gauge his reaction, but he was totally with us, nodding, occasionally asking questions about how to work things out. Dad explained the cover story of finishing the basement.

And so we started the next day and stayed at it practically around the clock. Dad ate dinner with us a lot, since we didn't have any time to waste while building.

We drilled deep into the cement floor and built a lattice of rebar, floor to ceiling. We put up a set of steel forms on both sides of the lattice, leaving an opening for a door. We drilled twelve two-inch holes around the doorway, putting eighteen-inch solid steel bars in each one—these would anchor the steel door frame. That's what we've been doing for the past forty-eight hours.

I hold the last of the bars in place while Dad secures it. "You don't think this is kind of overkill?" I ask.

"The door could be a way out if it isn't completely solid."

"You said it's going to be a steel fire door, like the one in the boiler room."

"This'll be much sturdier than that. But if you can pull the door off the frame, then all this is for nothing."

I laugh. "Like I'd be able to pull a steel door off its hinges."

He doesn't laugh. "You'd be surprised."

Dad moves a portable cement mixer into the garage during the day when the neighbors are asleep.

Kevin Baker comes over for the cement part. "How you doing, kid?" he asks.

"Getting by," I say. I always liked Kevin. Looking at him, most people would probably assume he was scary, maybe the leader of a homicidal biker gang. Hardly.

He used to be a cop in town, but about ten years ago there was some bogus brutality charge against him. Dad said it was a setup, which I believe. Still, he quit the force before the trial, and the charges were dropped. He went into business with Dad, grew a beard, a ponytail, and a bit of a gut, and he's always seemed a lot happier than he ever was as a cop.

He squeezes the back of my neck. "Don't you worry, champ. We're gonna take good care of you."

It takes almost seven hours for us to pour the high-performance concrete inside the forms. This is going to be a fortress.

The vicious glares Gunther throws my way in Gym are getting to me. The bell rings, and I just want to go upstairs to the locker room, change, and go to English.

I'm the first one up, and I should be able to get out of here before Gunther and his crew come in. I strip off my sweaty T-shirt as I walk toward the freshman lockers. I glance into the huge mirror as I walk.

I stop and look back at the mirror. There's hair on my chest. Not a huge amount, but enough to see from a few yards away. I turn and look over my shoulder: hair on my back, too. And of course, now I see that there's more hair on my forearms than vamps typically have. But it's totally natural for wulves.

When Constance gave us the meaning of the word *hirsute*, I knew I'd remember it by thinking "hair suit."

I don't know how I didn't notice this before. Is it possible that it just grew today?

Dozens of footsteps thunder on the metal stairs, and students flood into the locker room. Nobody pays any attention to me as they swarm past, shouting and laughing. I realize I'm just standing here like a statue. Not a good idea with my new hirsute condition. I pull on my damp T-shirt before anyone notices.

But I'm too late. One person is staring at me.

It's Gunther. And he looks suspicious.

After working on the basement while I was in school, Dad's ready for my help when I get home. I was planning to take a shower right away and shave my chest and arms, but I'll have to do that later.

We take the metal forms down, leaving a twelve-inch-thick concrete wall crossing the basement. All these structures took three days and nights of hard work to put in place.

"Not bad for a rush job," Dad says.

"Can we really get it all finished in ten days?"

"We'll have to." Dad hands me a short sledgehammer. "Let's see how strong it is. Give it a solid hit."

I give the wall a nice shot with the hammer. It doesn't even make a mark.

"No," he says. "I mean really smash it. I want to see if it chips or cracks."

I wind up and take a good hard swing. The sledgehammer bounces off the wall and out of my grip. My hands buzz like beestings all the way to my elbows. And there's not the tiniest dent in the wall.

"I guess that'll hold," he says.

"Yeah, I'd say it's pretty solid." I shake my hands out and smile at him, proud of our work. He's not smiling.

I realize why. For a while there, I forgot the reason for all this.

It's going to be my prison every month, maybe for the rest of my life.

24
COVPLES

At the end of the school day, Juliet gave me a naughty smile when she met me at my locker. That smile meant just over fifteen minutes of fun in the room over the stairwell. Except, as great as kissing her is, the closer we get, the guiltier I feel.

"You okay?" she asks after pulling away a little.

"Better than okay," I say. "Why?"

"You seem distracted." She lifts my wrist and pushes the button on my watch that makes the time glow. "I have to go. My father's probably already waiting for me out front."

I walk with her to the entrance in B-wing, holding her hand. She stops before we turn the corner into the lobby. "Say good-bye here. My dad may be watching."

"You could always tell him I'm just a friend."

She smiles. "He'd know I was lying."

I shrug. "Fair enough." We lean in for a last kiss, then she hurries to the door. I go right up to the corner of the wall, trying to peek around it to watch her leave.

"You're seriously going to make me vomit."

Heart attack! I spin around fast enough to get whiplash. Claire is sitting on the floor of the hallway about ten yards away, her back against the wall and her legs out in front of her.

My hands are on my chest. My heart is pounding from the quart or two of adrenaline running through my body. "What the—"

"I'm not kidding," she says. "That was completely nauseating. No offense."

"Why are you sitting in the hallway spying on people?"

"I'm not spying on *people*. I'm spying on *you*. And I'm not even spying. You're late. I've been waiting for you almost half an hour, and if that wasn't bad enough, I have to sit through a creepy peep show, too."

"Hey, I never told you to watch. And it's not like we were going wild here in the hallway."

"Yeah, well. It was more than I needed to see." Her eyes are half closed and a little red around the edges.

"What's going on?" I ask.

"Let's just get out of here and I'll tell you on the way home." She drags herself to her feet and swings her backpack up, making sure it hits me in the stomach before settling it over her shoulder.

We're on the narrow black asphalt path that goes by the tennis courts, and I feel really bad for Claire. "What exactly did she say?" I ask.

"Just what I told you. 'We don't have anything in common' and 'I don't mean this in a bad way, but you're really too young for me.' What difference does that make?"

"Wait, she called and told you this, or she texted you?"

"I just *said*. She texted. She didn't even have the decency to do it in person."

"Would that have been any better?"

"Yes. I don't know, maybe not. But it would have been a little classier, more personal. I mean, seriously. *Texting* a breakup?"

"That's pretty cold." When we come to the end of the path, we go left on Judson. Instead of splitting off on Summit, tonight I'll walk her all the way to her house and go home from there, unless she wants me to stay and keep her company.

She lets out a long breath. "Remember we were just talking about how amazing it is that we're both in relationships?" She shakes her head. "I should've known better. Oh, well. One down, one to go."

"Thanks for the optimism, but I haven't given up yet."

Claire lets out a short breath, like *huh*. "Oh, really? And so, what'd you decide to tell her about your little secret?"

"I'm still thinking about it."

"You're going to end up breaking up with her. You'll have to."

"Not if I can help it."

She nods over and over, like she agrees. "Okay. But just a little advice from someone going through it this minute: if you're going to do it, do it soon."

I'm not sure if she's saying that from a misery-loves-company feeling or if she's so unhappy that she has a bleak attitude toward everything.

"Considering how *you* feel now, I'm surprised to hear you advising me to break up with her at all," I say.

"If we had been together longer before she dumped me, it would have hurt even worse. I'm just saying: Don't drag it out. If it has to die, kill it fast."

She pulls up her hood and covers her head. I take it as a signal that she doesn't want to talk about it anymore. That's fine, because I don't, either.

25
JAGGED

The lobby of the apartment building is dark and grim. "This isn't where we saw him before," I say to Dad.

"This is where he said to come," he says. If I think this place looks run-down, I can only imagine what Mom thinks. We trail behind Dad while he walks down the hallway, checking the numbers above the doors.

He finds the right one, then knocks. After about half a minute, I hear footsteps, then the sound of a peephole cover being raised. The locks turn and the door opens. "Come in," Dr. Mellin says. He holds the door open, and after we walk through, he takes a look down the hallway, shuts the door, and turns the locks.

"I'm sorry for the location change," he says. He leads us into an office that looks a lot like the one in his first place, but with even more books. There's a musty smell, though, and light-brown water stains on the ceiling.

We take seats, and Dad introduces Mom to the doctor.

"So, do you have any questions before we do the procedure?" he asks.

"How long will it take?" Mom asks.

"If all goes well, I'd say about ninety minutes," Dr. Mellin says.

Dad massages his temples. He's getting worn out. "It won't hurt much." He turns to the doctor. "Right?"

"He'll be asleep for the procedure. There will be some soreness for a few days. But his vampyric regeneration will speed healing and shorten the period of discomfort."

"Maybe this isn't a good idea," Mom says.

"It's up to you," the doctor says. "We don't have to do it. But when he goes through the Change, the bones in his face could break in irregular ways. If I score marks into the bones, they should break cleanly. Right along the dotted line, as it were. They slide back into place after the Change. No deformities."

"I think we should just do it," I say. "We don't want to risk ruining my good looks, do we?"

Mom smiles, but it's tight. She's been totally nervous since we got here. I can hear her heart beating fast, close to human rate, like seventy beats per minute.

"There's only eight days left until the full moon, though," Dr. Mellin says. "We can't put it off, even for another day."

"Let's do it," I tell him. I wouldn't say I'm scared, exactly. Petrified might be a little more accurate. But I give Mom and Dad the best smile I can manage before following Dr. Mellin out of the office.

He takes me into what looks like a small operating room, except it isn't white and sterile-looking like the ones on TV.

Some of the tiles are missing from the wall, and the rest of them are cracked. There are deep dripping sounds as water falls from the leaky faucet to the bottom of the metal sink.

"Um . . . why did we come here for this operation instead of the other office?" I ask, while I take off my shirt.

"I think my office is being watched. This is a colleague's place."

"Watched? You mean by the LPCB?"

"Maybe. I didn't want to take any chances. This office will serve our purposes." Dr. Mellin pats the table and I lie down.

"Nervous, eh?" he says.

"A little."

He puts a sheet over my body, up to my neck. "We're going to do everything we can to take care of you, Danny."

"I know. Thanks."

He pulls on one of those blue surgical gowns and moves behind me. I hear the snap of rubber gloves.

He opens up a wrapped tray of equipment, but I can't see what's on it. I hear metal clinking.

"What's that?" I ask.

"Just the instruments," he says. "I'll start your IV in a few minutes. Any new symptoms?"

"I still have major aches. Bones, joints, face, head."

"Anything else? Are you eating and drinking normally?"

"I get a little sick after drinking SynHeme."

"That isn't surprising," the doctor says. "I'll check your blood today, but what I believe is happening is a sort of war between your vampyric Thirst and the wulven part of you, which reacts to SynHeme almost as if it's a poison."

"So what do I do?"

"I'll prescribe some medications that will prevent most of the nausea. Anything else?"

"Just that my senses are really, really sharp."

"And all of these things are happening all the time, independent of the moon phase?"

"Pretty much."

He comes back within my view. Now he's wearing a blue surgeon's hat and mask. "That's unusual. Typically, you'd be symptomatic only around the period of the full moon, right before and after. I assume your symptoms have something to do with the interruption of your genetic treatments. Little pinch now," he says. He puts the IV needle in the back of my hand. "Okay?"

"No problem. So why would my treatments cause this stuff between full moons?"

"I couldn't say. The truth is, genetic treatments alter your DNA in a fundamental way. When the treatment is stopped midway? Who knows?"

"Okay. So, um, not to change the subject, but do you use a chisel for this?"

"Not exactly a chisel, but the principle is the same. Here comes the anesthesia. See you soon."

I start to float. I feel . . .

I open my eyes. I'm tired and my limbs feel like stone. "He's not going to do the operation?" I ask.

"He already did it," Dad says. "How do you feel?"

"Sleepy."

I touch the skin behind my ears. There's a tiny wet scab

forming next to each one. There are more, concealed in my eyebrows and along my hairline. A few more in my mouth, between my cheeks and upper gums.

After a few minutes, Mom and Dad help me to my feet. I feel a little weak standing up, so I lean on them while we walk. We all go back into the doctor's office. I sit in the chair.

The doctor comes in. "It went perfectly," he says. "Here's the post-op X-ray." A front view of my skull comes up on the screen. Along my cheekbones, jaw, and forehead are a series of dotted lines that look like armies of ants marching across my skeletal face. "From my point of view, total success," he says.

Total success, huh? I now have score marks to make the breaking of my skull easier.

Painkillers and sleeping pills get me through the day and the whole next night. Now, waking up at 4 a.m., at least I'm rested.

So I'm just lazing in bed, the sheets damp with sweat. The joints in all my fingers are killing me. This must be what humans feel when they have arthritis. My teeth ache as if I'd been grinding. I check them with two fingers and feel a bumpy ridge, as hard as bone or teeth, under the gum line. It's got to be close to the roots of my teeth.

In the bathroom I take a look in the mirror. My face is a tiny bit swollen, but not bad at all.

"Can someone take the dogs out for their last walk before it gets light outside?" Mom calls up the stairway.

I might as well do it. Getting some fresh night air will probably do me good.

It hurts to put on my sneakers. To add to all these body aches and joint pain, my fingernails and toenails are really sensitive.

Downstairs I get the metal leashes. In the short time we've had the dogs, they've quickly learned that the sound of the leashes coming off the hook means they're going for a walk. I hear them come running from the living room.

They turn the corner into the kitchen, and once they see me, they try to stop running, skidding sideways on the tile floor. They come to a halt about five yards away, both looking at me. Poe tilts his head a little to the side, breaking eye contact. Lola does the same. Both of them lower their tails.

"Come on, guys. Walk time!" I clap my hands loudly, which usually gets them all excited.

They lower their bodies halfway to the floor, eyes averted, but still keeping me in their peripheral vision. Their ears go back flat against their heads, and I can hear their hearts beating fast. Their black noses are twitching as if they smell something.

"Let's go. Time to walk."

No barking, wagging excitement at all.

"Poe! Lola! Come!"

They turn and run.

I have no patience for this. I follow them into the living room, where they've backed themselves into a corner. When I get closer, I see they're both trembling.

"What's wrong with you guys?" I lean down to put their leashes on, and both of them start whining, making high-pitched squeaking sounds. Their chins and chests are on the floor, back ends in the air, tails down.

I go to the family room, where Paige is watching *What Never to Wear*. "Paige, you need to take the dogs for their walk."

"Why don't *you*?"

"They don't want to go with me."

"Well, I'm watching this. Get Jess to do it."

I think my fever is back, and a headache is coming on fast. I'm not in the mood to argue with dogs or little girls.

"Paige, just do it!"

She looks up at me, startled. "Why are you yelling at me?"

"Because the dogs need to go out and they're afraid of me, and I don't want to stand here and debate it with you. Stop arguing, and please just take the damned dogs out for a walk."

She looks at me as she slowly gets up. I hold the leashes out and close my eyes.

"I'm not picking up poop, though."

"Paige!"

"I'm just saying. I'm not."

She takes the leashes and leaves me with my headache.

"Come on, dogs," she calls, walking out of the room. "Let's go for a walk."

They run to her, claws clicking on the wood floor in the next room.

"Good doggies. Don't worry about him. He's just being a meanie. You come on and walk with Paige. That's good."

She shuts the door, the sound making me cringe for a second as it echoes in my head along with the whimpering sounds of the dogs' fear.

I know I don't look any different or sound any different. But the dogs sensed something. To them, I'm a predator.

It's become a daily thing, Juliet and me going to this new make-out room at the end of the day. We found this place, a book storage room in the basement. It's a little humid, and it smells kind of like mildew, but we're less likely to run into Gunther Hoering here. And this place is less crowded, too.

A few minutes before we got here today I asked Juliet why she didn't give me a heads-up about Victoria for Claire.

"I would have, but I didn't know Victoria was going to do that," she said. "We're not *that* close."

"She texted her the news," I said. "That's pretty low."

"Very. Don't ever break up with me by text. In fact, don't ever break up with me."

"I don't plan to," I said as we slipped into the room and the door closed behind us.

Lying to her hurts. At least it's dark in here and she doesn't see my eyes when I say it. She drapes her arms around my neck and our mouths meet.

I have no right to do this with her, not when I know that I'm going to hurt her. I make myself sick.

Juliet puts her hands under my shirt and presses her palms against my (shaved) chest.

But we're so good together. How can I let this go? She's breathing fast and moves her hands, her fingers in my hair, holding the sides of my head. Now I'm breathing faster.

But maybe we don't *have* to break up. I get that I can't tell her the truth. But if I'm going to a different school, I can probably find ways to dodge the issue. Technically, it would be lying, but maybe a little dishonesty is better than breaking both of our hearts.

She breaks the kiss and whispers, "Hey. You're really hot."

"So are you."

"No, seriously. You're burning up," she says.

"You light a fire in my heart," I whisper loudly in a movie-romantic voice.

"Oh, man," some guy shouts. "The talkers are here again. Would you get lost?"

Juliet grabs my sleeve and pulls me out of the storage room.

I blink in the light. She wipes my forehead and shows me her hand. It's slick with sweat.

"So what?" I say. "It's hot in there and you got me hotter." I smile to reassure her.

"You have a fever or something. Do you feel okay?"

"I feel great," I say, which is a total lie. I feel like a selfish scumbag, but since she brought it up, I do feel warm.

"Let's go to the nurse," she says. She takes my hand, which hurts. My knuckles are swollen and sore. All reflex, I yank my hand away.

"What's wrong?" she asks.

I flex my fingers. "Nothing. My finger got jammed yesterday in Gym. It's fine." I take her hand and give a little squeeze, which sends a jolt of pain into my fingers.

She touches my face, my cheeks, runs her hands back over my ears and through my hair. I'm kind of getting a little turned on, even though I don't feel so great.

She looks deeply into my eyes.

"What?" I ask.

She shakes her head and smiles. "Nothing," she says. "I'm happy."

No, I'm not going to break up with Juliet. I'll make it work. Somehow.

She wipes my forehead again. "I hope you're not getting sick."

"Hey. Don't worry about it. Vampyres *can't* get sick." I try to laugh, but to my ears, it sounds forced and false.

I need to get to my locker and get my stuff, fast. Right before second period, I promised I'd go to the city with Claire after school, and there's a good chance she'll murder me if I keep her waiting again.

I quickly spin the dial, make a mistake, and have to start again. I throw my books in and reach for my jacket, and then I see the black spray paint on the back, stretching from one shoulder to the other. A werewulf's head on a big red circle. The wulftag logo.

26
RALLY

Claire heard about a guy who supposedly has tickets to the Rubber Crutches concert. She heard this from Hugh, who *didn't* manage to get the tickets through his father's great connection. The fact that Hugh gave her this tip means it's almost certain to be wrong. But she's determined to go to the concert.

All five shows sold out within minutes of going on sale, no doubt due to the group's number one song, "Thicker than Water," which seemed to be on every radio station every minute of every day last summer. Terrible lyrics, typical of the worst vamp headbanger crap. But just like everyone else, I was a victim of the melody, which got in your head and dug its claws into your brain.

And so we're wandering around the business district. All the humans and wulves around here are wearing coats, because it's chilly in the early morning dark. I'm cold in just my shirt, and still pissed about my jacket, which is now stuffed inside my backpack.

"How much are you going to pay for those tickets, assuming they even exist?" I ask her.

"I don't know. Maybe one-fifty? Two hundred?"

"You're out of your mind."

"Like you know anything about music."

"I know enough to know that two hundred bucks is one hundred and ninety-nine dollars more than those tickets are worth. You realize that the amazing Rubber Crutches aren't even really vamps? It's all bleached hair and a lot of posing."

"That's just a rumor. And even if it were true, I don't care. Stop being a killjoy."

"I'm just making sure you're an informed consumer," I say. We walk another half block, and I'm starting to think that Claire has no idea where we're going. "Where is this guy, anyway? At this rate, we're going to be wandering around until sunup."

"He said to meet him at the Chill Grill. I know it's around here somewhere."

"Why didn't you tell me you're looking for the Chill Grill? We're on the wrong side of the square. Come on."

We walk to Brookline Street. There's a candlelight vigil in front of the courthouse. I see a lot of blue clothing, and as we get closer I realize they're all cops. The square is packed with them. And they're each wearing the gray armband that means they're in wulf divisions.

"Hang on," I say, stopping. "I want to see this."

Claire seems surprised but stops next to me.

There's a guy in uniform at the top of the steps, calling down through a megaphone to the assembly in front of him.

"How is it possible that, in this day and age, we still have a segregated police force? What does that mean, other than that the brass and the mayor don't think we're good enough to serve next to every other cop who wears blue?"

There's a roar of cheers from the crowd.

"Why are we on a different pay scale? We do the same work, we take the same risks, we get shot just like anyone else. And why should we have to use our sick days for time spent on the compound? Is that fair?"

Big shouts of "No!" from the crowd.

"Are we going to stand for this?"

"No!"

"Are we going to demand a new contract in January?"

"Yes!"

"I can't hear you! A new contract for wulf police officers? Integrated squads? Equal pay? Fair treatment?"

"Yes!"

I tug on the sleeve of Claire's navy peacoat. "Hey—look." I point toward the podium. "The bald guy. That's Huey Seele."

"Really? How can you see that far?" Squinting, she evidently sees that I'm right. It's the famous wulf-rights guy, in person.

The cop who got the wulf-police crowd cheering hands the megaphone to Seele. "Hello, gentlemen . . . and ladies. Some of you may have heard of me. I'm—" But the crowd of cops goes nuts before he can say his name. "It's good to see a turnout like this. Wulves give so much to society but get so little in return." He waits for the cheering to settle. "You men and women in blue are another example of how wulves are treated as second-class citizens in our country. From birth, our government marks us as different, actually tattoos us, so everyone who sees us knows: 'That's a wulf. I'll keep my distance.' Or 'I can offer this one a lower salary.' Or 'I don't want to get involved with him.' We're branded. Like criminals. Like animals."

His bald head is shiny with sweat. Even from here I can see he's gripping the microphone so tightly his knuckles are white. "Land of the Free, huh? Sure, except for us during the full moon, when it's the Land of *Imprisonment*! Is that what America is about?" More crowd reaction. "Is that the American way? Lock up innocent citizens? Why should we let the human and vampyre fat cats in Washington make 'full' and 'moon' into four-letter words for us? Along with other four-letter words, like 'hate' and 'poor' and 'bias.' Well, let me tell you something. 'Wulf' may have four letters, but it is not a dirty word!"

Loud cheers echo between the marble buildings around the park.

"You may be wondering why we're holding this rally now, at this early hour, under this waxing gibbous moon. It's because we are gathering before the light of a new day. A new day when wulves have rights like everyone else. And we will meet that new day together, as one people, victorious."

Lots of shouting. Seele bellows into the megaphone. "Who are you? Come on, I want to know. Are you animals?"

"No!"

"Are you people?"

"Yes!"

"I can't hear you. Let's go, now. You know what I want to hear!" He shouts the chant we've all heard him lead on TV news reports. "*We* are *wulves* and *we've* got *pride*. We *won't* let *our* rights *be denied!*" By the third repetition, the gathered cops join in. He alternates it with his other catchphrase: "You. Can't. Kill our hopes. Power to the lycanthropes!"

The chanting echoes in the square, the sound reverberating off the buildings. This is when he usually gets arrested.

But these cops are wulves. Who's going to arrest him?

Claire and I leave the square and take a left onto Brookline Street.

"Since when are you into politics?" she asks.

"I just wanted to hear what he had to say. It's important."

"I didn't say it wasn't. It's just the first time I've seen you pay any attention to wulf-rights stuff."

"Are you saying that I only care because it affects me now?" Wow, that came out a lot sharper than I meant it to. Claire stops walking and gives me a dirty look. Which is totally justified. I say, "Well, you know what? Even if you didn't mean that, it's true. I should have cared more about this a long time ago."

She starts walking again. "Hey. Better late than never."

"I guess."

We walk a block without talking. The rally is still going on with Huey Seele shouting through the megaphone, followed by rousing shouts from the cops. The sound barrels down the streets, echoing off the expensive Sol-Blok-glass-covered buildings. Not one vamp, male or female, who's walking by takes a look down the street to see what the noise is all about. Being so used to wulf public protests—on TV, on the news, in the paper, in public—most vamps don't even hear them anymore.

Claire looks back toward the rally for a second, then shakes her head. "It's so sad," she says.

"That wulves don't have the same rights as anyone else?"

"Well, yeah, that. But also that they really believe they'll ever get those rights."

"You don't think they should?"

"Easy, pal. Of course I think they should. But it's never going to happen. And I think it's sad."

I don't say anything. She's right.

27
TORN AND TWISTED

Of course, the rumored ticket scalper is nowhere to be found at the Chill Grill. Since we're already here, we decide to get something to eat. We go inside and sit in a booth.

"I'm so pissed," Claire says. "I really wanted to see that concert."

"Believe me, not getting those tickets is the best way for this to go. Now I can still be your friend."

"What a relief. I'd rather go to the concert."

"Hey, there. What can I get you?" asks the waitress. She's human, with red hair, maybe in her early twenties. She's very good-looking.

"Hi," I say. I nod to Claire to order for herself.

"Um, you go first," she says.

"I'll just have a grilled cheese."

"Sounds good. To drink? SynHeme?"

"Sure. Thanks," I say automatically. It still makes me sick

to my stomach, but the waitress might take notice of a vamp who didn't want SynHeme.

"And you, hon?" she says. When Claire glances up to give her order, she sits up straighter. Taking in the waitress, Claire says, "Uh . . ." at least three times. She starts blinking, like she's communicating in Morse code and can't stop. I'm afraid she's going to have a fit.

The waitress smiles and dips her head a little, keeping her eyes locked on Claire's.

"What can I get for you?" the waitress asks again.

"Oh, just whatever he's having."

"Grilled cheese and SynHeme?"

"Fine. Oh, diet SynHeme. Please."

"Sure thing. Not that you need diet."

Claire watches the waitress take the menus and walk away. Her cheeks are red.

"Looks like *some*one got swept off her feet," I say.

Claire shakes her head and shrugs. "I don't know what you're talking about."

Now she's all embarrassed, and I wasn't even trying to tease her. "Well, anyway, for the record, I think she's hot, too."

"Whatever," Claire says. "I miss Victoria. I mean, she was my first real . . . you know, serious thing. And I thought it was going so great." She looks out the window into the late-night darkness.

"I know it sounds like a cliché, but it really is her loss." I peel the paper sleeve off the straw and tear it into tiny strips, seeing how long I can get them before they rip. I know how she feels. Boy, do I. And I'm thinking a little about that rally and Huey Seele. *We are wulves and we've got pride*, he said.

"Claire, are you, like, cool with the way you are?"

"The way I am what?"

"You know what I'm asking." I lay each little paper strip on the table, trying to make them perfectly parallel. "I mean, not this minute—I know you feel rotten right now—but usually. Do you . . . do you like being the way you are?"

"I don't know. Kind of. I'm still getting used to the idea, I guess."

"When did you know?"

"I'm not sure."

"Was it the locker room thing?"

She doesn't react. I know it's a sensitive subject, and we've never actually talked about it.

"The locker room thing wasn't what everybody thought," she says. "It was before Gym, and I was thinking about that song 'Drone'? I forgot the lyrics, and I was just sitting on the bench, you know, in my underwear, kind of spacing out and trying to remember. And, yes, Patti Chapman was standing there in front of me. And, yes, she was wearing just a thong, and, yes, she's totally hot. But I wasn't staring at *her*."

I don't say anything.

"Then the rumor started, and nobody would talk to me, and they called me lesbo and all that. The thing is, even though the story wasn't true, I guess that's when I started thinking about it in a serious way. And the more I thought about it, the more I started to realize. I mean, I can see when a guy is good-looking, but I was never *attracted* to them. All the people I had real crushes on were girls. So I guess that means what it means."

"So, when you first figured that out, were you like, Okay, I guess that's what I am? Were you totally fine about it?"

"No. I'm still not sure how I felt, or how I feel now. It's just who I am. I mean, what's the use of fighting it?"

The waitress comes with our food. "Hey, guys," she says. "I put a rush on it. Sunrise is in forty minutes, in case you need to travel to get home."

We thank her, and Claire starts eating. I open my SynHeme but don't drink.

"Why did you suddenly want to know about that?" Claire asks. "You never asked before."

I run my fingers through my hair. It's getting longer, starting to cover the tops of my ears, the way Dad said it would. "I don't know. I'm thinking about a lot of things these days."

She peels open her grilled cheese, then lets the top drop back. She looks at it for half a minute, takes a bite, and swallows. "How much time left?"

"Five days."

"Are you scared?" she asks.

"Pretty."

She nods. "Well, if you die, can I have your brown leather jacket?"

"Sure. Enjoy Gunther Hoering's artwork on the back."

"Oh, right. Forget it. There's nothing else of yours that I want. So you might as well live."

"Thank you. But please try to rein in your sentimentality. It's embarrassing." I look out the window. "I can't believe I'm going to have to go to another school."

"That sucks in a really big way."

I nod. I wipe the condensation off my glass of SynHeme and put my hand flat on my paper napkin. I touch my wulf-tag. I can see the abstract werewulf-head emblem under the surface, but that's only because I know it's there. I was always happy about the fact that it wasn't immediately obvious to people that I was part-wulf. But now, after that rally, after talking to Claire, I'm ashamed. I almost feel like I should get the tattoo repunched so it would be visible. But I couldn't do that, even if I wanted to. The vamp part of me would reject it.

I look up. Claire has been watching me. I put my left hand over my right.

She smiles and shakes her head. "Hey. It is what it is."

It is what it is.

You are what you are.

Simple.

We are wulves and we've got pride. . . .

I wonder how many times you have to say it before you start feeling it. Because as much as I want to, I sure don't feel a whole lot of pride right now.

28
CONCEALED

We're making progress downstairs. Kevin's been running the job sites while Dad works here day and night. I take two days off school to help him. The basement's nearly done. Drywall covers almost the entire cement wall we built, and Dad was right: it's impossible to tell that the basement is smaller now.

The only obvious sign is the steel door that we mounted yesterday, but that'll be covered up by a removable panel of drywall and a bookshelf. There's a big slot in it so they can pass food and water through to me.

There's a small hole in the chamber's ceiling where we're going to mount a video camera and microphone so Mom and Dr. Mellin (who she hired to be around in case of a medical emergency) can monitor me when I'm down there.

We're attaching paneling to the walls and ceiling. It's soft enough that I can't bash my brains out, but coated with something I won't be able to claw to pieces. Dad said it's also good for soundproofing.

About an hour ago, Troy was trying to help us, but the guy could barely figure out which was the business end of a hammer. I had to keep redoing his stuff so it lined up the right way. Dad noticed and caught my eye. I shrugged.

Finally, Troy said, "Hey, Danneroo, don't think I haven't noticed that you're following me, fixing all my work."

"I'm just making little adjustments."

"It's okay," he said. "I know I'm not great at this. Is my helping making more work for you guys, Ted?"

"Well, we appreciate the effort. . . ."

"But it might be better if I just let you boys do it?"

"Maybe."

"Fair enough. I'll be upstairs. Give a shout if there's anything I can do."

"Thanks, Troy."

He went to the stairway, then stopped. "I almost forgot." He came back to where we were working. "I've been talking with that fellow who runs the private school. You're in. It's called Talbot Prep, by the way."

"When do I have to start?"

"Maybe after this full moon," Troy said.

I nodded. "Thanks."

Troy puts his hand on my shoulder. "Hey. I know you're not happy about having to switch schools, but we agreed that there isn't much of a choice. Right?"

I shrug. "Unfortunately not, I guess."

"Thanks, Troy," Dad says. "That's a lifesaver. Literally."

Once Troy leaves, we move much faster and start making headway. I'm almost done with a panel when I lose my grip on the nail gun, drop it, then catch it in midair. The bad part is that I catch it by the handle just as the front part hits my leg and accidentally shoot a nail into my thigh. I yelp.

"What's wrong?" Dad asks.

"I nailed myself." He comes to look. The nail is sticking about half an inch out of my jeans. He takes hold of the nail head and yanks it out.

"How'd you manage to do that?" he asks.

"My hands. I dropped the nail gun."

He checks my knuckles. They're all swollen. "Okay, you're done," he says.

"What should I do with the nail gun?"

"Just leave it with that stuff by the boiler room door. Get the camera and the cables. We'll take care of that as soon as I finish up with the panels."

I get a tube of Factor Fourteen from my pocket, but the bleeding stops before I can even get the cap off. Weird. Then I remember that Dr. Mellin mentioned that I might not bleed like a vampyre. The little blood that did come out has left a small round circle on the knee of my jeans. It's exactly the size the red-moon tattoo around my wulftag would be.

"Dad. What's the deal with the red moon?"

"The deal?"

"Why does the moon look red when we Change?"

He shrugs. "It's just something that happens. It has to

do with the rods—or cones, I always get them confused—in your eye. The full moon affects your night vision, and the moon looks red."

"But not everything that's white looks red?"

"Just the moon. Nobody knows why."

"And even though you forget most of what happens when you're Changed, you remember the red moon?"

"Oh, yeah." He nods his head slowly a few times. "*That*, you remember. It's like the image of it gets burned into your mind."

I must have a worried look on my face, because he smiles and pats me solidly on the shoulder. "But you'll be in here," he says. "You won't even see it."

For days, probably weeks, it's felt like I had no control of my thoughts. No captain in the wheelhouse. And one of the more frequent ones is in my mind now. "Dad? Remember I told you a while back that there was a girl I liked?"

"You told me that night we got together again, right?"

"Yeah. Well, I forgot to tell you how things went. We've been going out for a while now."

The nail gun makes a loud bang each time he fires it. "You never told her what's going on, right?"

"No, no."

"And how'd it go when you broke up with her?"

I don't say anything. He stops nailing in the panel and turns to me. "You didn't break up with her."

"Not yet."

"Not yet? There are three days until the full moon. What exactly are you waiting for?"

"Well, see, she's really great. And I know she would never, ever do anything to—"

He shakes his head. "You have to end it. You know that."

"Here's the thing. I was thinking about it. And I don't like the idea of lying to her, but I think it's possible for her not to find out."

"You don't think she'll figure it out when you disappear every month during the full moon, then come back with cuts and wounds?"

"Right. But I'm going to that new school, so I won't see her nearly as much. I could time things so I only see her when I look okay. And during the full moon I can make up excuses."

"That doesn't sound realistic."

"But it *could* work. It's possible."

He closes his eyes for a couple of seconds, then asks, "You love her?"

"I don't know. Maybe. I'm telling you, she's a good person. She would never do anything to hurt me."

Dad shakes his head. "I can hear it in your voice already: you want to tell her. And the thing is, if and when you really do fall for her, you're not going to be able to keep it a secret. And at some point you and this girl will break up, and she'll have really dangerous information."

He sighs and sits next to me on the chamber floor. "There's another thing to think about. If she knows and doesn't report you to the LPCB, she could get in a lot of trouble. Do you want to put her in that position?"

"I know, I know." What else would he say? "I was just hoping there was some way around it."

He puts a hand on my knee. "I don't think you need me to tell you what to do here."

"I have to break up with her."

"Sorry, pal. And you don't have a lot of time."

29
POLITICS

Dad has been worried that I've been spending too much time working on the chamber and not keeping up with school, so I'm doing homework in my room now, banished from the basement for the rest of the day.

But I can't concentrate. I keep thinking about Juliet.

I glance at the computer and see the little news window showing crowds throwing rocks and bottles at rows of green-uniformed cops. It says "Shanghai Wulf Riots" on the bottom of the screen. I maximize the window and turn up the sound.

At one thirty local time, protests in Shanghai's Hongkou district turned violent when wulf demonstrators confronted squads of Peoples' Army police.

Jessica comes into my room and shuts the door. "One of those stupid dogs got into my closet and tossed my shoes around. It's a total mess now."

"Shh. I'm watching this." The image cuts to a female reporter standing safely around the corner from the riots.

"The demonstrators were protesting conditions at several Chinese wulf compounds, demanding that they be shut down. Police and two national guard units opened fire on the protesters. We have no report on the number of wulves injured or killed at this time. United States wulf-rights leader Huey Seele had this to say . . ." Cut to Huey Seele, in a badly fitting suit: *"The members of the American Association for Wulf Rights and Advancement fully support and stand behind our brethren in Asia as they fight to have these deplorable compounds shut down."*

"Dream on," Jessica says.

I mute the volume. "Did I ever tell you what a compassionate person you are?"

Jessica switches one of my window monitors to mirror mode and looks at herself. "Spare me." She holds her hair up at the top of her head, then turns sideways, trying to decide if she likes it. "So you agree with Huey Seele? It would be good to just let werewulves run free every month? I get that it's personal for you now, but look at the reality. Werewulves hunt. They would *kill* people, genius."

"He's not saying that wulves should be running free. He's saying they shouldn't be treated like criminals and kept in dangerous compounds."

She lets her hair down and wanders away from the mirror. She doesn't bother switching the view back. "So what's the solution, Mr. Political Activist?"

"I don't know. He says government should pay for more research into medical solutions, finding ways to give wulves more choices."

"Sounds likely."

"Someone has to come up with *some*thing better than the way it is now. At least he's trying."

"So, what's next? Are you going to be shaving your head and wearing an I Heart Huey T-shirt? You'll be with his crew, making bombs in basements."

I shake my head and turn back to my math work.

"So?" She says it like I'm supposed to answer. I'm not sure what she's asking.

"So what?"

She doesn't say anything for a while, then lets out a long, long sigh. One of those pay-attention-to-me sighs. "This thing with you. Really sucks."

"Tell me about it."

"Well, you did say I always grab the spotlight for myself. Looks like you have it now."

"I didn't want it. Definitely not for this."

"I'm sure." I swivel around in my chair and watch her think. She goes to my bureau and pretends that the loose change on top is fascinating. This way, her face is away from me when she says, "I know you supposedly can't help this."

"*Supposedly?*"

"Okay, fine. You can't help what's happening. I just hope you know what this is going to mean for me."

"Maybe get in the way of your shopping trips?"

"Do you have any idea how this is going to affect me? I mean, what are all my friends going to think, knowing I have a lunadog for a brother?"

Ah. Got it. I see a hint of a smile there. "An unregistered outlaw one, at that. A moonrunner," I say.

She puts on a face of exasperation. "That's what I'm saying. You think my friends would tolerate such a disgrace?"

"Hey. How do you think all *my* friends feel about me having the school's biggest prima vampyreena for a sister?"

"Yeah. You don't *have* friends. None that matter, anyway."

"Oh. Hmmm. I guess that's mostly true." There's a look on her face that's different from the tone of all this play. I'm pretty sure it's real worry.

I turn back to my math book. I might cry.

She doesn't say anything. I hear her breathing. It sounds like she's working to keep it steady. She grabs my ear and gives it a twist.

"Yeah. Well. You'll live." She goes to the door. "You'll live."

She closes the door behind her, and my tears come.

30
A WHOLE LOT WORSE

Walking near the pond I can hear every nocturnal animal: frogs, crickets, owls, the field mice. I can smell the damp earth, a dead animal decomposing somewhere nearby, algae, methane from the mud at the bottom of the pond. It all makes me feel like puking.

"You don't look good," Claire says.

"I feel a lot worse than I look."

She pulls her beret lower on her forehead. "You want to stop and sit?"

"If I sit, my knees will lock and I won't be able to get up. Let's just keep going. We're almost at school."

"You have a headache?"

"Bad. Stomach, too."

"Like you're going to puke? Because if you are, I need to get away from you. Nothing makes me sick to my stomach like the smell of a big, steaming puddle of fresh vomit."

My stomach churns. She had to say that. "You know what? Can we talk about something besides . . . barfing?"

"Really? I was enjoying the subject so much."

"There's something I do need to talk to you about. I've been thinking. I'm going to have to break up with Juliet."

Claire nods. "I thought you were going to say that. No way around it, I guess."

"In two days I'm going to turn into a werewulf. I don't think I'm going to be able to hide it from her month after month. She's kind of observant. I need to end it before the full moon. I just don't know how."

"You're talking to the wrong girl. I'm the one who *got* dumped, remember? I don't know the right way to do the deed."

"I thought you might have some deep wisdom, some idea for me."

"Well, all I can tell you is not to do it via text message." Claire shakes her head. "You're definitely going to that other school?"

"Yeah. It's done. No way out of that, either."

She crouches down and picks up a rock. She switches it for another, stands, and throws it into the woods. "We'll hardly see each other."

I pick up a rock, too, and throw in the same direction. She throws another. I start to speak, but the words catch with a little gulping sound. I clear my throat. "We'll see each other all the time. Just not in school."

"It won't be the same."

"No. But it'll be okay."

She picks up another rock, winds up to throw it, but stops.

She starts walking again, holding the rock. "We're going to drift apart. You'll see."

I'm half a step behind her. "Never."

"It'll happen. We'll have less day-to-day stuff in common, and we'll start talking less, and it'll get awkward, and . . ." She throws the rock into the woods. "I mean, don't get me wrong. It'll be a big relief to get you out of my life. It's you I feel sorry for."

"Being deprived of your charm and wisdom."

"Exactly." The moon hasn't gotten high yet, but I can see clearly in the darkness. Just before Claire turns her head to look toward the woods, I catch sight of a tear on her cheek, shining in the moonlight.

The moon: my enemy in the sky.

Actually, it's not the moon that's my enemy. The moon is the instrument. The enemy is in every cell, in every twisted strand of DNA I have, in the blood running through my veins. My own body is my enemy.

I wasn't lying this evening before school when I told Juliet that I had a crushing headache and couldn't talk. She could probably see it in my face, and she let me suffer without any more talking after I assured her that I had a doctor appointment.

The first three periods at school are pure torture. I can't even begin to concentrate on the work. Every noise—a cleared throat, a pen clicking, gum being chewed—sounds like it's being broadcast right into my ear. My eyes burn. My stomach is churning. I'm hot inside. And this headache is killing me.

I raise my hand, and Mr. Wells calls on me. "Yes, Danny?"

"I need to get a drink. Is that okay?"

He sighs. "It's fine, but you'll miss this next problem. And there could be one just like it on the test, hint, hint, hint."

Everyone in the class starts writing quickly in their notebooks.

"I'll get it from someone," I say.

I walk down the hall and find a water fountain. I can't drink. Not SynHeme, not water. Nothing. I run the water from the fountain on my face, then sit on the floor with my back against the lockers. At least it's quiet here in the hallway. I can close my eyes and try to cool down.

Relax.

Relax.

"Who left a pile of garbage in the hallway?"

My head hurts so much I can't concentrate enough to place the voice.

"Oh, wait. That's not garbage. That's wulfboy. So, I guess it *is* garbage. Get up, vermin."

I open one eye, then the other. Gunther is looming over me like a giant. I'm blinking against the light, which causes swirls of dizziness. I want to keep my eyes closed, I want total darkness, I want sleep.

"What are you, stalking me?" I mumble.

"I have people keeping an eye on you. I heard you were staggering through the halls like a drunk. Or maybe a rabid dog. Now, get up on your hind legs so I can talk to you."

I close my eyes and wave at him with the back of my hand, like, *Just go away, leave me alone.*

"You don't dismiss me," he says. "Get up. Or I'll kick your head clean off your neck."

The thought of anything touching my head is unbearable.

I grit my teeth as I push back against the lockers and work my way up to my feet. My head swims, and I have to lean back against the lockers.

"I'm on to you," he says. "Genetic treatments? I doubt it. I think you're a scumbag moonrunner. And I'm going to prove it and make sure that you—"

"Man, what is your *problem* with me? Why don't you just live your own life and leave me alone to live mine?" Even talking hurts my head.

"I'll tell you why. Because I believe that your kind are what's wrong with this world. Something I learned from a very honorable man. I have a little history lesson for you," he says. "Are you listening? Open your eyes and look at me when I talk to you." Gunther just about shouts into my ear. His words seem to bounce off the inside of my skull.

I open one eye.

"Good. That's better. Now. This is about my great-grandfather."

Is he kidding? Can he possibly believe that I care at all about his great-grandfather? I guess so, because he keeps talking. "He came from Europe. He was there during the war, during the purges, you know? And he told me all about the moonrunners—or in German, *die Mond-laüfers*—and how a lot of them tried to pass as human and escape with fake passports. My great-grandfather taught me that wulves can be very sneaky. That they'll lie, cheat, and steal to get ahead. And if they feel threatened, they'll sell their own mothers down the river to escape."

I'm light-headed. His voice gets stronger and his blue eyes bore into me.

"Wulves hide, and pretend to be something they're not. Luckily there are people like my great-grandfather who look out for the public good. He was on a squad that flushed out wulves who were lying and hiding, flushed them out like rats, then exterminated them. I learned a lot from him, a lot about the ways of wulves, and I believe in what he did. He was a hero."

"Yay," I say, my voice weak. "A hero."

"Sarcasm is going to get you hit. And you'd better not use that tone when referring to my great-grandfather."

I feel like death. "Look. Don't take this the wrong way, but I couldn't care less if your Nazi great-grandfather got caught in the sun at high noon and ended up a smoking piece of charcoal. All I want is for you—"

Of course I don't see it coming. The flat of his hand catches me on the temple.

I once saw a documentary on TV about these monks who forge huge bells that ring so loud the sound can be heard for miles and miles throughout the valley.

That's the inside of my head.

My eyes are shut from the pain, and then everything goes white and I feel a pressure in the center of my head, building . . . building . . . building . . .

Then a huge spurt of blood bursts from my nose and hits the floor.

This time my eyes are open when he moves to hit me a second time. The looping arc of his punch looks like it's in slow motion, so I just step to the side.

His fist hits the metal vents of the locker, splitting the skin on his knuckles. He steps back and shakes his hand out, splattering droplets of blood on the floor.

He avoids looking at my blood and glances at his own instead. He shouts and charges at me. He's taller than me, heavier than me, and meaner than me. But it doesn't matter.

Because I deliver what must be the most perfect—in aim, timing, and power—kick in the balls in the history of the world.

He drops to his knees, grabs his junk, and hunches over.

For some reason there's an air raid siren. Or maybe it's an ambulance wailing. Good, maybe they'll take me away and put me out of my misery.

No, it's the end-of-period bell.

And now, all is chaos. The hall fills with vamps who immediately see and smell all the blood. Some try to get a look at it, others are shoving through the crowd to get themselves away from it before the aroma drives them mad.

The hallway is filled with screaming and shouting.

Then there's another voice, deep and bellowing.

"Hold it right there. Don't you move. I saw that!" It's a teacher. He grabs my left arm and pulls Gunther to his feet by his right arm. "Both of you, come with me."

Away from all this noise? I'll go anywhere you want.

PART III

PART III

"It's cool, bro. So what if the dulls call me a moondog-howler-surfing freak? Dude, I am a moondog-howler-surfing freak! Ar-oooooo! Ha, ha, ha . . ."

—Shawn Fenn as wulf-surfer Jimbo Pirelli in
Crazy Days at Elwood High, © 2005, Universal Pictures

If the wulves are going to be rioting and making a big fuss over this, I say they should be relocated. A few centuries ago, England shipped off its criminals and undesirables to Australia. Maybe it's high time we deported all our wulves. This is America, the greatest nation on Earth, and if they don't think they're being treated fairly, we can happily assist them in getting the hell out of our country.

—Senator Latham Winthrop III,
NeoRepublicrat, Kansas

You can't kill our hopes—Power to the lycanthropes!

—Wulf rally slogan,
popularized by activist Huey Seele

31
SVSPENDED

No doubt about it, my nose is broken. So I won't have to worry about that happening during the Change. It didn't bleed after that first spurt. My headache was still pounding, though. I didn't get a good look at Gunther, so I don't know how badly he got hurt, but I'm willing to bet he won't be spending quality time with Alana Gibson anytime soon.

We both got one-week suspensions.

When the principal called home, Dad was there, testing some things in the chamber, so he came along with Mom to get me.

"Thank you for not yelling at me," I say from the backseat. "My head would explode." I try to keep my eyes closed and hope we're on a road with no bumps.

"Well, it doesn't sound like it was your fault," Mom says.

"And the timing is perfect," Dad adds. "If you're going to get suspended, the day before the full moon is the time to do it."

I open my eyes and see Mom glare at him.

"What?" he says. "This gives us a perfect excuse for his being out of school." He puts on a straight face. "I am not saying you should fight. But if you do, always do it right before the full moon." He's trying to irritate her and lighten things up at the same time.

Mom ignores him. "He won't need to. This is the ideal opportunity to make the transfer to Talbot Prep."

I can't get into it right now, so I just nod, which makes my head swim. The streetlamps light up the inside of the car like a strobe every time we pass one. It makes me dizzy, so I close my eyes, but that's worse. I need a distraction.

"Could you put the radio on, please? But really, really soft?"

Dad turns it on, switches from an oldies station, tries to find something. He stops for a second on the news when he hears the words ". . . *witnesses report hearing four gunshots. Police cornered the suspect three blocks south of the incident, but he shot himself before he could be apprehended. Again, wulf activist Huey Seele has been assassinated by a lone human gunman at a construction-workers'-union rally. Seele suffered two shots in the head and one in the chest. Efforts to revive him were unsuccessful, and he was pronounced dead at the scene.*"

Dad turns off the radio.

I can't believe it. Huey Seele has been out raising hell about the plight of wulves since before I was born. Even when we ignored the stories, his presence on the scene was a part of life. Whether he was being thrown in jail or beaten up, Huey Seele wouldn't back down. And now he's gone? "I just saw him at an uptown demonstration," I say.

"When were you uptown?" Mom asks, reminding me I wasn't supposed to have been there.

"I mean, on TV."

"This is terrible," Dad says.

"It was bound to happen," Mom says.

"The guy may have been a little over the top at times," Dad says, "but he did a lot of good. Now that he's a martyr, there are going to be nuts coming out of the woodwork to avenge him. There'll be demonstrations. Riots, maybe."

We hit a bump and my head throbs. I can't help moaning.

"Head is bad, huh?" Dad asks.

There isn't a word to describe how bad it is. "Uhh . . ." is all I can manage.

"Did you try the Lupinox?" he asks.

"Doesn't . . . work," I say through gritted teeth.

"We can fix that," he says. The best thing anybody ever said to me.

Dr. Mellin unnecessarily uses an alcohol pad on my arm where he gives me the shot. Must be habit, since most of his patients don't have vampyre immunity to infection. "That's a painkiller and a sedative. You should start feeling better very soon."

He's right about feeling better. It doesn't take more than five minutes. I feel lighter, almost like I'm suspended in midair. I don't know what's in that shot he gave me, but whatever it is, sign me up for more.

32
GOOD-BYES

Dad brings us home. He says there are some things he needs to discuss with the whole family before he leaves for the compound tomorrow. It's so weird to be in the chamber with them. Dad, Mom, Troy, Paige, Jessica, and me. Dad has just finished explaining about the cages over the light, how the camera and intercom work, the feeding slot, and all the safety features. I'm trying to pay attention, but I'm feeling a little loopy from Dr. Mellin's medicine. Anyway, the information isn't important for me to know; I'll be the tenant here, not the landlord.

"Well, that's it for the chamber. Let's look at the door." We follow Dad out of the room into the main part of the basement.

"So this is the door. Obviously." He's trying to keep this all business, I think, so he doesn't get upset. Mom is the same way. They're trying to hold it together. If anyone cries, we're all going to lose it and we'll drown in tears down here.

He closes the door. "It's heavy. Solid. It'll hold. There's no knob on the inside." He pulls a six-foot-long metal bolt along the slides. "You really need to yank it the last foot or so, to engage the catch. . . ." He pulls hard and it slams home with a deep, metal clang.

It makes me jump.

"If you have any trouble, Kevin will take care of it. He'll be staying here. He's a strong guy and an ex-cop." He says in a mock-announcer's voice, "And Kevin Baker will be providing security for our event." It doesn't lighten the mood like he'd wanted. But not much *could* lighten it. He looks at his watch. "Okay, sunrise is in a couple of hours. Six o'clock, I think. Sun*down* is at six thirty-seven. Kevin will get here by six to help get everything set."

"Will that be enough time?" I ask.

"You're not going to Change as soon as the sun sets. It usually happens around nine o'clock, when the moon gets higher. You should have plenty of time if you go in by seven thirty or so."

I nod. That's in less than sixteen hours. This is really going to happen.

"You arranged for the doctor to stay, too?" he asks Mom.

She nods. "He's coming at five to set up some equipment, in case something . . . just as a precaution."

Dad claps his hands, then rubs them together. "Okay, then. That's it. I need to get going. I have a bus to catch in the morning."

He shakes hands with Troy. He hugs the girls. He even hugs Mom.

"Walk out with me," he says, tapping my shoulder.

I follow him out through the garage and we stand next to his truck.

"So," he says. "I think you're all set."

I nod. I can't speak. I just can't.

"Did that shot the doc gave you help at all?"

"Oh, *yeah*."

He laughs, just a little. "All right, then. You take care. It'll be over before you know it."

"Dad . . ."

"It's okay. I know." His lips go tight over his teeth. He holds his arms out. I go to his chest and we hug. I forgot the smell of him up close, his aftershave, his flannel shirts, his skin, his hair.

He lets go and turns his face away as he gets in the truck. He starts the engine and rolls down the window. "If there was any way I could stay here to be with you," he says, "you know I would."

"I know." Damn, I'm scared. I want to be a little kid again so I can sit on his lap, lean back into his strong arms, and feel totally safe. But those days are long, long gone. He can't make this go away.

He lets out a long breath. "You'd better get inside. It's going to be light soon."

"I'll see you in a few days, Dad."

He nods twice, forces a tight smile, puts the car in gear, and backs out of the driveway. He gives me a wave and heads off down the street.

I'm alone now.

• • •

After Dad leaves I go right to my bed. It's 4:30 a.m., and I'm so tired. I want to sleep, but there's one thing I really have to do before I can go to bed. I pick up my cell phone and dial.

"Where have you been?" Juliet says. "I left about ten messages for you."

"Long story."

"Did you really get suspended? For fighting with Gunther Hoering?"

"I guess it's *not* that long a story. That's pretty much it."

"Are you okay?"

"More or less, yeah."

"How could you let him bait you? He told you he wanted you to hit him so you'd get expelled."

"I'm not expelled. I'm suspended."

"Well, you *could've* been expelled. And then we wouldn't be together at school anymore."

I can hear her breathing into the phone. And then it comes to me.

It's perfect. "Juliet, there's something else. Something I need to tell you."

"What?"

"My parents are sending me to another school. In the city."

"Why?"

"They've been talking about it for a while, and they're convinced that it's a good move. And they decided that, with this suspension from Carpathia, the time to do it is now."

"If they've been talking about this with you for a while, how come you never mentioned it?"

Good question. "I didn't know if it was really going to happen, and I didn't want to upset you."

"Well, I'm upset now," she says.

So am I. Looking at the monitor over my Sol-Blok shade, I see a car pull into our driveway. People always use our driveway to turn around and go back up the street. Why our driveway? I'm getting distracted. The drug Dr. Mellin gave me for the pain is making me zone out a little. And I need to do this. "The thing is, with me going to school in the city, it's going to be pretty much impossible for us to see each other. I'm thinking it's going to be too hard to . . ."

"To what?" she asks. There's a quaver in her voice.

The doorbell rings. I hear my mother's heels on the hardwood floor, then the door opening and a deep male voice. I could probably hear what they're saying if Juliet wasn't talking.

"Hello? What are you saying? Too hard to what?" Juliet asks.

"I think it's going to be hard to keep, you know, seeing each other."

"Are you kidding me? You want to break up?"

"It's not that I want to." I put my hand over my eyes. "It's probably just going to be too hard."

"And you don't think we can work through it?"

My door opens and Paige comes in, looking very worried.

"Hang on," I say into the phone. "What's wrong?" I ask Paige.

"There are two scary-looking men downstairs," she whispers, "and I think they have guns!"

270

"What?"

"I'm really scared," she says.

"I'll find out what's going on. Just go back to your room and close the door. Everything's going to be fine."

She leaves. Juliet is talking. "Are you there? *Hello?*"

"Listen, I have to go. There's something happening here."

"We're in the middle of a pretty important conversation, don't you think?"

"I know, but there's kind of an emergency here that I have to look into. I'll call you back."

She lets me go. I head down the stairs and hear a higher male voice say, "I hope we're not interrupting your dinner."

"No. It's not even seven," Mom says. "We don't usually eat supper before it's light out. What's this all about?"

As I walk down the stairs, I see there are two serious-looking humans in suits. One is tall, the other short. Guns are holstered to their belts. Mom and the men turn toward me as I walk down the last few steps.

"What's going on?" I ask.

The short man has a deep voice, no emotion, no friendliness at all. "I'm Agent Boothe, and this is Agent Swerski. We're from the Lycanthrope Protection and Control Bureau. We need to ask you a few questions."

33
VISITORS

Did my heart just stop? Doesn't matter, because now it's about to burst out of my chest.

Mom, to her credit, keeps amazingly cool. "Again, what's this all about?" she asks, without a trace of fear in her voice.

"The local Bureau office received an anonymous phone call a short while ago, with an allegation that there's an unregistered adolescent lycanthrope living at this address," the tall, higher-voiced agent says. "Is that true?"

"Well, my former husband was a wulf, so my daughter and son are half-wulf by birth, but they had Lychromosomal Repression Therapy as infants, so they're not subject to registration requirements."

"We can tell you, ma'am, that we're not here to investigate your daughter. The call came in about your son."

"Are you Daniel Gray?" Agent Tall asks.

I take a breath. I feel really calm. That's got to be from the sedative.

"Actually, it's Dante. Maybe you have the wrong guy."

Agent Little answers in his deep voice. "Well, the call came in about Danny Gray. So, that's our mistake, assuming 'Daniel.' But it was at this address."

All I have to do is make sure I keep my voice steady. "Did the caller know that I had genetic treatments?"

"The caller said there's reason to believe that you did *not* have the treatments, and we've checked to confirm that you are not, in fact, registered."

"Wait, *who* said this about me?" I ask, as if I were more curious and amused than mad.

Agent Tall says, "As I said, it was an anonymous call. Now, it's a second-degree felony if you did *not* have successful treatments, and you're not registered."

"I had the treatments," I say at the exact same time that Mom says, "He had the treatments."

The other agent, with a lower voice, says, "If you can show us the medical records verifying that each child had successful LRT as infants."

"Well, I don't keep my documents in the house. They're in a safe deposit box."

There's a short silence, then the smaller guy speaks. "If you'll excuse us for a moment?"

I can hear the agents talking to each other but can't make out what they're saying. Where's Troy? Oh, right. He said something about picking up a suit he had made at the tailor's. Not that Mom hasn't been doing a good job of handling these guys. I'm going to take a stab at this.

"Excuse me?" I say. "If I didn't have treatments, my wulftag would be dark and clear, right? Well, look."

The agents come back toward me.

I'm not sure why, but Mom takes my wrist and pushes my hand back down to my side. "Now, listen," she says to the agents. "I let you in here and you've asked questions, and I allowed this without even asking to see a warrant."

"Ma'am," Agent Little says with a patient smile. "If you'd like, we can have warrants faxed immediately. Warrants to search the entire house. That tends to be disruptive, and unfortunately once in a while an accident happens and things get broken. But we can just look at your son's hand, examine the lycanthrope identification emblem—or lack thereof—and put this whole matter to rest."

I look to Mom. She shrugs. Even doped up as I am, I can tell she's faking indifference to show the agents she's not intimidated.

I put out my hand for them to see. Agent Tall reaches into his jacket pocket and takes out a pair of rubber gloves, which he starts to put on.

Mom lets out a disgusted *Harrumph!* "I would expect that you, being experts on all matters wulven, would know that being a wulf is not contagious."

"Thank you," says Little. "We're well aware. But when you touch as many as we do on any given day, it doesn't hurt to be hygienic."

Agent Tall holds my hand up, turning it slowly back and forth. "I don't see anything."

Little reaches into his pocket for a small flashlight, which he uses to shine a blue light on my hand. My wulftag shows up more clearly, now. "There's still a trace here, which isn't the standard vampyric ink rejection."

Without missing a beat, Mom says, "When the tag didn't fade away completely the pediatrician checked Dante's blood and found him to be severely anemic. Because of that his V-beta541 cells were deficient, and we were stuck with the trace elements of the tattoo. We're just glad it faded enough to be unnoticeable."

Agent Little nods. "I've heard of that happening." He flicks off his little flashlight and puts it away. "So what happened to you?" He nods toward my face.

"I got in a fight at school." It hits me and I can't believe I didn't think of it sooner. "And I would be willing to bet anything that the so-called anonymous tip came from a guy named Gunther Hoering. Maybe you should go after *him*, nail him for obstruction of justice or something."

Agent Tall smirks. "That's a good tip," he says. "We'll take it under advisement."

Little says, "We're sorry for the disturbance. You understand, we're just doing our job. We appreciate your cooperation."

"You have yourselves a nice day," Agent Tall says.

Funny that she would mention anemia. As soon as the outer door closes behind the LPCB agents, I feel light-headed and dopey. I plop down in a chair.

"What's wrong?" Mom asks.

"Globin crash. Either that or the drugs Dr. Mellin gave me."

She grabs her purse and takes out a porta-hemometer

that she slips over my index finger. She waits for the readout. "Hmmm. Not too low. It's probably the medication."

"I think I'm going to lie down for a while." She reaches to support me when I stand up, but I shake my head. "I'm okay now. Maybe I can sleep it off."

I make it upstairs fine. When I get to my room, I see a note taped to my Sol-Blok canopy. It's Paige's handwriting:

Danny,
    I really, really, REALLY don't want this awful, terrible, sucky thing to happen to you. It's totally and completely not fair. I hate that you have to be locked up in that disgusting room for so long. This whole thing just really bites and I feel bad for you. I hope you're going to be okay.
    Sincerely, Paige (your half-sister)
P.S.
I'll miss you.

I go into her room and tap on the door before opening it. I lean in.

"Thanks for the note. And everything's fine downstairs. See? Just like I told you, nothing to worry about."

She looks unconvinced.

I have to call Juliet to end things right. Wait. Did I tell her that we have to break up? I don't remember. Hang on. Think. I told her about changing schools. Oh, *then* I got into the breaking-up part. How far did we get?

I can't do it now. That stuff Dr. Mellin gave me is really kicking in, and I can't think clearly. I'll sleep a little and call her later. I get into bed. Lots of time before sundown. I'll get back to her. I'm not even worried. If I close my eyes, I'm sure that before I know it, I'll . . .

Beep beep beep . . . Beep beep beep . . . Beep beep beep . . .
I wake up and my cell is on the floor, beeping and turning in a slow circle from the vibrating. My Sol-Blok shields are covering the windows, which means it's still light outside. The clock says 4:47 p.m.

It's Juliet. I was all zoned out and didn't call her back. But my mind is clear now. "Hi. I'm *so* sorry. I know we were in the middle of a pretty intense conv—"

"An intense conversation? Yeah. We'll get back to that." Her voice is tense, her words clipped. "But right now, you need to go to your computer and look at what I just sent you."

"What is it?"

"Just go look. I'll hold."

I turn on the computer and bring up my e-mail window. Right up top is the forwarded e-mail from Juliet:

> **Fwd:** Dantesinferno@mrnt.com
> **From:** GHoermaster@crt.net
> **To:** Jewelyet3@loa.com
>
> Dear Animal Lover
>   u backed the wrong horse—or dog. your little howler is due for a trip 2 the aspca 2 get neutered.

but Im writing 2 u bcuz u r in need of punishment
2. it is tru, u r not a vamp, just a human, but itz
still disgusting 2 see a mixing of species. would
you also go out with a monkey? a mule? its called
bestiality and u r a tramp and u r disgusting. u
r an offense to humanity and u will pay, u little
skanky . . .

It went on, but I didn't need to read anymore. It was all curses and threats.

"Where are you now?" I ask Juliet.

"I'm home. I'm not going to school tonight. I don't think I could concentrate in class, thanks to your little bombshell and your friend's love letter."

"Listen, I don't know what's going to happen with us . . . I'm really sorry I didn't call you back. I'm sorry. Sorry about everything. But I'm absolutely going to take care of this. And I promise that it won't happen again."

"I don't want to get e-mails like this. Or any other—"

"I'm on it."

"Jess, I never ask you for anything. Please just do it."

Jessica squints at me from her bed. "What are you talking about? It's still daytime. I'm sleeping."

"You'd be getting up in a couple of hours anyway. Come on. It's important."

She doesn't even open her eyes. "Just call her on the phone."

"I don't need to talk to Juliet. I need you to help me."

"Forget it. I'm not going to get in a Sol-Blok suit right now. I'll take you later."

"It can't wait until later. Tonight is it. I won't be . . . able to go later."

She looks at the clock on her Sol-Blok canopy. "You're crazy. It's five in the afternoon. You're going to . . . you know, Change, really soon. Mom would never let us go out now."

"You heard Dad. It won't happen until, like, nine. That's four hours. Lots of time. We'll sneak out the back. Please, Jess. I'm asking you. Please."

She sighs, thinks for a minute, and then throws the covers off. "Grab my stupid Sol-Blok suit from the closet. Get yours on, too. I'll meet you in the car."

34
LITTLE MOONS

"I never should've agreed to this," Jess says. "Mom's going to skin us alive if she finds out."

"It's not going to take long. The faster you get there, the sooner we'll get back."

"I can't fly over other cars," Jess says.

"Then go another way."

She shakes her head. "Are you wearing Troy's Helio Guard running suit?"

"Yeah, and don't remind me how much it cost. I know."

"Why didn't you just put on a regular Sol-Blok suit?"

"Because I may need to move fast and I can't do it in a Sol-Blok suit."

She turns the wheel and heads up a side street.

"What do you mean about needing to move? You *can't* get in another fight."

"I can if I have to. I think that's your left turn up there."

She turns to look at me. Through her faceplate, I can see worry in her eyes. "Put on your gloves and headgear."

I'm hot, even though she has the AC on. That's the problem with all the sun-blocking clothing: it's heavy and a little stiff. "I don't need that until I get out of the car."

"And if my windshield or windows break? Then what? You fry. Put the headgear on or I'm stopping."

"Fine." I pull the black head sleeve on and adjust it so the speaking grill is over my mouth and the hearing grates are over my ears. I put the goggles on, check all the seals. I must look like a ninja going out for a run. It's ridiculous, but that's not my concern right now.

"You know for a fact that he's at home?"

"Oh, yeah." Before I woke Jess, I got his number and called him. *"This is Danny Gray."*

"Hi, pal. Good to hear from you."

"Are you at home?"

"Yes I am."

"Good, Stay there. We have some business to address."

"I can hardly wait."

That's what *he* thinks. I'm just this side of pure rage. And my muscles are all pumped and primed. "Can you drive a little faster?"

She shakes her head. "This is a bad idea." She takes a left turn, a shortcut.

Out of nowhere, it feels like a hot nail has been driven into the end of my index finger. "Ow!" I shout.

"What?"

There's a small spattering of blood on the dashboard. I

look at my hand and can't believe what I see. A short, sharp, curved black thing has pushed out through the bottom edge of my fingernail.

Jessica turns to look and gasps. "Holy . . . What the hell is that?"

"I think it's a claw. Don't worry about it. Just hurry."

"Don't *worry* about it? You said you're not supposed to change for another three or four hours! What's going on?"

"I don't know." A tiny bit of blood wells up at the base of the claw, then stops. The bottom of each nail is purple with blood, like each one was hit with a hammer. What's that curved white part of the nail called? Oh, right. I remember, courtesy of Constance, of course: the *lunula*. Little moon. How perfect. I'm bleeding into the little moon.

I pull on the Sol-Blok gloves as Jess makes a left turn. "We should just turn back and get home."

"No! We're only two blocks away from his house. There it is. Make the second left. Go."

"I'm going," she says.

She doesn't even slow down for the turn and I'm thrown against the door. "Good job," I say. "That's it up ahead. Green house on the right."

She slows the car and I jump out before it's totally stopped.

"You have two minutes," she says, trying to sound firm in spite of the quaver in her voice.

"That's all I'll need. Hit the horn," I tell her, and she does. The middle of the five garage doors starts to open. It's so slow, I wonder if it can somehow sense I'm in a rush and is taking its time to spite me. I look at the sunlight sensor strips on my sleeves. They're still red.

The door lurches to a stop when it's fully open. And there, standing in the shadows at the back of the garage, is Gunther Hoering. No Sol-Blok suit.

I stride toward the garage, and as I get closer, he bursts into laughter. Still in shadow, he says, "Is this Halloween? What are you wearing?"

"Come on out and see."

"Oh, I can see fine from here. It's a Helio Guard running suit. From the fit, I'd say it looks like you borrowed Daddy's. It's an awful shade of green, and the blue stripes are doing nothing to help. Oh, wait. Now I get it. You're wearing a running suit because . . . you're . . . a *mooon-runnnner*. Clever."

"You crossed the line and I'm here to tell you that it's going to stop." It's kind of hard to sound tough while talking through a voice grate. I look at the sensor strips: purple. Still traces of sunlight.

"I crossed the line? What about you telling LPCB agents that I phoned in a tip about you? I don't know where you came up with that flat-out lie, but I can tell you—"

"You did phone in the tip. Anonymously. Like a coward."

"Prove it."

"I don't have to. I'm guessing they went back and traced the call."

"Even if I did make the call, the tip wasn't false, mongrel. You *are* a moonrunner."

"Yeah? Prove it." I check the strips. Darker purple, but not blue yet. "I'm not even here about the LPCB." I walk into the garage. "I'm here about the message you sent to Juliet Walker. You have a problem with me, you deal with me. Leave her out of it."

Gunther Hoering laughs at me again. "I don't take orders from anyone, much less from dogs. Usually you discipline a dog by smacking it on the nose with a newspaper. But since I don't happen to have one available . . ." He reaches into a tall bag next to him and pulls out a golf club. "Now get the hell out of here."

"I'm not leaving until I get it through to you that—"

He swings the golf club at my head. My mind says run away, but my body has other plans. Before I know it, I catch his wrist in my left hand and twist, so the other end of the golf club is in my right hand. I drive him back against the wall, pushing the shaft of the club hard against his throat, pinning him.

Gunther is pushing against the golf club as hard as he can, but it's not moving me back even one inch. In fact, I press it harder against his throat, making him cough.

"Listen to me," I say. "Juliet Walker does not exist to you anymore. Neither does Claire Yates, if that was your next move. And add my sister to the list. You don't talk to them. You don't e-mail them. You don't call them. You don't even look at them. Clear?"

His lips move, but no sound comes out. He might be surrendering or he might be cursing. No way to tell, and it doesn't matter much to me. I made my point. I give the golf club one more shove against his throat before I let it clatter to the cement floor. I walk backward, watching him as he coughs and sputters.

Jess beeps the horn, telling me to move.

I'm still backing away from him. I step out of the garage.

"I'm done messing with you," I say. "Push me and see what happens."

On my next step back, I hear a sound like a thick branch breaking. But it's not a branch—the sound is inside my head, and it feels like ice picks being jammed in my ears. I double over for a second, but force myself to straighten up. He might charge me.

The sensor strips on my Sol-Blok suit are solid blue. It's night. The full moon is coming fast.

I run to the car.

Gunther Hoering shouts at me from his garage. "I know what you are! I know! And you're not going to get away with . . ."

But I don't hear the rest of what he says. All I hear is the car door slam and the engine roar as Jessica hits the gas.

35
CRVSH ME

It hits me hard, all at once. The pain, the shakes, the fear.
I'm in the front seat, next to Jess, and she's doing her best to
drive home fast without freaking out.

Every joint feels like it's exploding. My shoes are getting
tight.

My throat feels like it's closing up.

And that killer headache is back.

"What should I do for you?" she asks.

My body starts shaking, like with chills, only much stronger. "Just get me home."

"I'm trying."

"I know." The shaking gets worse.

"Why is this happening?"

"I don't know. I can't talk right now. Just go."

It's killing me. I can't take this.

Then we stop.

"What's going on? Why are you stopping?" I can't even see straight.

"I don't know. I see flashing lights ahead. It looks like an accident."

I stomp on the floor. I want to pull my hair out.

"What do I do?" she shrieks. She's losing it, too.

"Get us out of here!"

"I can't. There are cars behind us now. We're boxed in."

It feels like the whole car is closing in, crushing me. All I can do is groan.

Jess is crying.

It's dark out now.

"Are those flashing lights from police cars or tow trucks?" I ask.

Jess leans her head out the window to look up ahead. "Cops, it looks like. They're all over the place."

I try to breathe. "Jess, if I don't get into the chamber really, really soon, we're going to have a big problem."

I try to swallow. Can't. "Call Mom." My throat is filled with iron filings and slivers of glass.

"What?"

"On your cell. Call Mom. Tell her to be ready."

"For what?"

"For me. I'm going home."

And I'm out of the car.

36
RVN

Through the woods. I'm trying to beat the moonrise.

I can barely stay on my feet—it feels like they're being stretched, pulled apart.

I fall and yank off my sneakers, then pull off the gloves, hood, and goggles, too. The zipper on the running jacket is snagged so I tear the jacket open and throw it aside. Just the running pants and T-shirt now. Much better.

Now I can run.

Man, I can run *so* fast.

The woods are glowing orange, which means I'm in trouble; the sun is almost down.

My T-shirt catches on a branch. I can't unhook it. I tear it off and keep running.

A darting rabbit catches my eye. And a raccoon staring at me.

Whoa!

I dive to the right and barely miss a tree, but fall and hit the ground hard. Need to keep my eyes to the front. Don't look at the animals. Just ignore those tiny heartbeats.

My hands make cracking sounds. They're lengthening.

There's fur growing on my forearms. I touch my face. Different, but I can't tell how. And my hair is longer.

I need to get up and *run*.

The woods are dark, but I can see okay.

I'm getting close to home. There's a faster way, but I can't remember it.

Don't think. Just go. *run run air in lungs good. run just run.*

What the hell was *that*? Now I'm hearing voices in my head?

The bones in my face hurt.

There's a tall chain-link fence ahead. No problem: I can climb that in a second.

I jump high and catch on with my fingers, then go stiff.

I hit the dirt—hard. I'm on my back, body buzzing, totally rigid.

That fence is electrified. I think I'm paralyzed.

I'm Changing. And now, not even one mile from home, I can't move at all.

37
SHORTCVT

I'm lying next to the fence, shaking like crazy. All my
muscles contract, then all at once, they loosen. Now I can
move again.

Stand up and shake it out.

The fence is very high. At least twenty feet.

Damn. This is the fence that runs the perimeter of the
nature preserve. It has an electric current running through it.
Not lethal, but enough to wake you up. Craig Lewczyk and I
used to see *Lewczyk wounded wulf weak broken* who could
touch it the longest. The record was maybe two seconds. I'll
have to run around *fence metal pain no climb stuck trapped
danger* What *is* this? Why are my thoughts . . . stuttering? Is
that some part of the Change? Is that how I'll think when I'm
a werewulf?

Ah! Stabs in my vertebrae. I drop to my knees. There are

tiny cracking sounds from my ankles, which burn.

I'm not going to make it all the way around the fence, but if I could cut through the preserve, I could *run hunt small prey all around no big animal no human to hunt*

Uh. Happened again. Where was I? Oh, yeah—I could get to our house in a couple of minutes. If I can still talk—or yell—they'll hear me, maybe short out the fence or cut a *deer's throat pulsing feed blood hot human blood better find human tear stomach get inner*

Yah! Okay, so touching the fence and getting shocked breaks off the werewulf thinking. That's good to know.

If I can get to that long branch on that tree, I'll climb out and drop down on the other side of the fence. Can I climb all the way up? Twenty feet?

I look at the black claws on my hands and feet. They give me the grip I need, and with my extra strength, I'm up the tree in seconds. I crawl out onto the branch . . . and . . . drop.

Pain shoots from my feet to my hips on impact. Ignore it, there's no time to waste. *Get up*

just run.

run run.

eyes better wide view smell skunk muskrat too small need big prey big deer run fast need big slow human

That light, through the trees. It's far, but I can see it. That light is from our house. I have to get there before I can't think clearly anymore. *move to light human prey at house*

I have to outrun the Change. *Faster.*

run strong legs strong heart

Let me keep my mind clear, just long enough to get

to get

to get

to kill

38
THE CHANGE

Walnuts cracking. *That's what it sounds like strong pain*
And it's my face. My cheeks are breaking *shake run fall
leaves sticks rocks look up round red glow calls me*
    moon my moon full
    That's it. The moon is actually red. It's a bloodred moon
and it's rising *love me moon red moon*
    more pain blood from nose
    Wait. *teeth long now fur warm muscles hot strong fast
sharp ears long* I understand what's happening s*trong heart
power strong wulf* It's clear . . . *this is*
    This is the Change *my Change.*

Get up and run home. *Now run faster jump run light there*
    Light from my house *go to it metal strings fence fence*
    I have two sets of thoughts *a wall of metal fence* like two
radios playing different stations at once *go over grab metal
pain pain jangle buzz pain*

Of course that hurts; it's an electric fence, genius *touch again*

No, *don't* touch it again! back away *no fence get to house human prey in house*

If there's some way to get to the house Kevin will be *fence in way* able to get me inside *no can dig under fence* the chamber *find fence end find end go around* the end is all the way on the other side, too far *find end* you can't find the end, that's what I'm saying *run*

A car door slams *machine near house* That's a blue Porsche *male white hair walk to house* Is that—it is. That's Gunther *hit door knock knock* What's he doing, coming to my house? *knock knock squeak female voice*

"Yes?" That's Mom talking. "Can I help you?"

"I'm here to see Danny."

"He's not home right now."

"Really." *hostile male voice hostile* What does Gunther want? "And where, exactly, might he be?"

"He's out." *Female voice fear try dominance but fear*

"Just 'out' somewhere."

"Who are you?"

"Let's just say I'm a concerned friend."

"You're Sabina Hoering's son. Gunther. You made that prank call to the LPCB."

"We both know it was no prank."

"Do you know where he is?" *fear big fear* she must think he found me after I ran out of Jessica's car, that he's holding me prisoner or something.

"Do *I* know where he is? I thought *you* did. He's *your* son. Poor kid must be lost. I sure hope he's okay. Maybe the

294

LCPB would be able to help find him. Or, if you *do* know where he is, you could just tell me the truth." *male aggressive* You scumbag. If I could get to you right now *whitehair male threat threat to make adult female submit*

"You do whatever you want. This conversation is over."

Loud noise She's slammed the door in his face. Nice!

whitehair enemy kill kill now kill

PAIN

fence in way male looks up here

I must have made noise when I ran into the fence. Can't do that. Wait. He's walking across our side lawn. *Grrrrr* don't growl. He's looking at me, standing *challenge* a few yards from the fence, keeping his distance. Maybe he doesn't know if I can tear through the fence to get him. *Grrrr Don't make noise. Stop it. Male whitehair heart beats faster*

"Well, look at that. I'd recognize those green-and-blue running pants anywhere. Moonrunner."

GRRRRRRR Stop. Back up away from the fence, or you'll charge it and get shocked again.

"It makes sense that your family would set you up in the woods, practically right in the backyard."

Standing tall dominant smile white teeth
kill kill kill
SHOCK metal shock. Howl. Howl.
whitehair jump back away smiles close again

"Whoops. Careful of that fence, pal."

whitehair enemy must die What does he want? *tear out teeth rip off jaw*

"Well, I have a really cool present for you. You'll love it. Stay right there."

whitehair pulse in throat runs back over grass to car What's he doing? *want throat tear him crunch bones hot blood* Now he's opening the trunk and taking something out of a long leather case *tear head slash throat* He's walking back this way *long metal stick* What's he carrying? *come to fence kill you* The red moonlight glints off the long thing in his hand *closer come here* He's smiling *hear heart pound*

That thing he has, that's a rifle! *Run! run into woods* Get better cover *quiet run in shadow*

This is far enough, stop here *crouch*

"Aw. You ran away. I guess you're kind of stuck all alone in there. Maybe you need some company. Hey! Let's play a game. I've got more toys in my car. You just stay where you are and I'll find you."

go low ground He shoves the rifle in the backseat, gets in the car, and starts the engine *follow watch low quiet* He drives down the street, then stops well out of view of my house. He's out *goes to back end of car* He's opening the trunk again *steel string hangs from metal smile* That's not a steel string, that's a chain *puts metal smile down on street* clang clang *takes metal stick* I can't tell what those metal things are. He's crossing into the woods and coming closer *wait wait for him then kill* He's crouching down on the other side of the fence. And he's got a wire cutter or something.

"A hunting we will go, a hunting we will go . . ."

kill him kill him now No, don't kill him, just get away. *away run run muscles hot run for moon then come back and kill*

run run heart fast hard good for hunting
red light up stop look

red moon high
look look look No, don't stop here to stare at the
moon red moon red moon
love
red moon

39
RED MOON

Mother red help

The moon won't help; it can't stop bullets. And I might not be able to hide from him *hunt enemy* Offense is defense *better hunter than enemy more quiet more fast more strong* He's human and he must be nervous *human weak slow* Get close *stalk stalking hunt* get up close and disarm him, disable him *faster than enemy quiet stalking* That should work. Go. Find him.

    run

    run

    run

    smell

    whitehair There he is *quiet low* He's facing the other way. Follow him. *hear him breathing hard heart beating fast* Flank him from behind *slow slow closer* Don't rush. Get closer *time to attack* no, *not close enough*

    attack run run He's raising the rifle. Go all out. Attack!

CRACK *bright flash from metal stick PAIN top of arm PAIN burns* I'm shot in the shoulder and he's backing away *enemy scared*

howl again howl loud

He's taking aim again, hurry up and *run run to kill him loud sound . . . burn in leg*

enemy turns runs slow easy catch prey He's running away! Just forget him *run to catch* Let him go and check that leg wound *kill him*

run

fall I can't run on this leg *pain hurt stand fall* It's bleeding like crazy *pain white pain* Will my regen work if the bullet's still in there? *claw in hole dig pain hard inside* That's it, that's the bullet *pull out metal hold hole keep lifeblood in*

tired rest rest

sleep fast . . . sl—

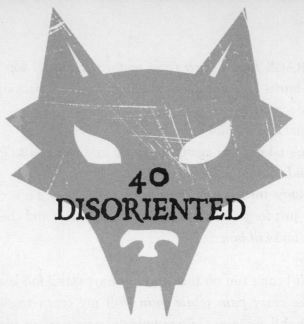

40
DISORIENTED

Where am I? Somewhere outside. It's mostly dark, but I can see. It's probably just after sundown. Trees all around. Yeah, I'm in the woods—on my back in the leaves and dirt. I sit up and feel a dull ache in my thigh. No shirt. Whoa! That's a lot of hair on my chest. My forearms, too.

There are little black nubs sticking out from under the bases of my fingernails. And the tips of my fingers are caked with dried blood.

Wait, I remember now. The Change. I touch my face and it feels different. Some fur, sharper teeth, and—

There's a piercing shout from somewhere. It echoes in the woods, but I can tell it's not far and coming from the left. It's a person in pain.

"Please, please, help me." It's Gunther.

And now I notice that it hasn't gotten darker out. It's gotten a tiny bit lighter. Which means this isn't dusk: it's dawn.

I have to get to shelter before the sun rises.

"Can anybody hear me?" It's him, and wherever he *is* is not where I want to be.

Wait: I know where I am. I'm in the nature preserve. Not sure exactly where, since I'm deep enough that I can't even see the fence. The sky is lightening a little bit on my right side, darker when I look left. West is to my right, and that's where home is.

And that sun is going to come up really fast.

I start running toward my house. The ache in my thigh throbs, but it's not bad enough to stop me. Small mammals dash away from me. I can hear them; I can hear their tiny racing heartbeats.

"Please! I'm going to die out here!" Gunther wails.

I stop. I don't know why he needs help, but he sounds desperate.

Damn it. He's even farther east, closer to the sunrise. If I go to him—toward the rising sun—we could *both* incinerate.

I start running again.

41
TRAPPED

He's not really shouting for help so much as screaming hysterically. So it's easy to follow his voice. And there he is.

He's sprawled out on the ground, his left calf caught in the steel jaws of a bear trap. It probably crushed his shinbone. The lower half of his pants leg is soaked with blood. I can't help but notice the dark stain around the fly of his pants, but that one's not from blood.

His eyes go wide when he sees me. "What . . . are you?"

I grunt at him.

"I mean, what the hell? I can see it's you. The running pants. And your face is . . . but you don't look totally like a werewulf. You're not . . ."

I grunt again and start to turn away.

"You can't leave me here," he shrieks. "Please! The sun is coming up."

Look back his way. "Why would there be a bear trap in a nature preserve?" I say. But my mouth is all different on the inside, and I can't form words.

"I don't know what you said, but help me! Please."

I point at the trap and then hold my hands palm up, like *what's going on?*

"I'll explain later. I'm begging you. I can't get this thing open."

And now I remember. A hunting rifle next to him. *Metal stick . . . loud noise.* And the metal smiles with chains, those were bear traps. He got in here somehow, set traps, and then went hunting for me. Literally.

He tried to run away but got caught in one of his own traps. How's that for poetic justice?

So this guy tried to kill me, and now he wants me to *save* him?

Gunther whimpers, then says, "You have to stop staring at me. Please. Do something, like now, or I'm a roaster."

I look down at the trap clamped tight on his leg. It looks very strong. I probably wouldn't be able to open it even if I wanted to.

"Okay," he says. "I'll admit it. I tried to kill you. Or at least shoot you. I thought you were a moonrunner, and I was going to . . . Well, you *are* a moonrunner. But I don't care anymore. Really. It's not my business. Do whatever you want. I swear on my life, I won't tell a soul if you'll just please, *please* help me."

Uh-huh. This specist informed on me to the LPCB, and he shot me with a rifle. Twice.

"Please. Please." His eyes are pleading, desperate.

Damn it.

I still don't think I can open that trap, but I kneel down to look at it.

He whips his head from side to side. "It's getting hot. I'm starting to feel the sun. Do you feel it?"

I say *no*, but I'm not sure even the single word is clear, so I shake my head, too. And it's true: I don't feel anything. It's getting lighter, but the sun isn't high enough for direct rays to hit us, not yet. But it won't be long, and he's panicking.

I get my fingers between the jaws of the trap, right next to his leg, and pull to open them. They open just a little, maybe two inches. Not enough. And if they close again, this guy is going to die of agony. I can't get the jaws wider, but I don't want to let them go. I start trembling.

Gunther is moaning and writhing. "Look. Please. If you can't get me out, I'm begging you: shoot me. Take my hunting rifle and just shoot me. Don't let me burn to death."

I can't hold it anymore. The trap starts to inch closed again.

Gunther screams, shrilly enough to set birds flying from the trees. And I pull those jaws with everything I've got. They're opening. I ease the open trap down over his foot, stand up, and yank my fingers clear as I shove the thing away from me. It makes a solid clang before hitting the ground.

Gunther is barely conscious. I check his leg, and lucky for him, his regen has stopped the bleeding. But the wound is bad, and I can see jagged shards of bone—too severe for the regen to close and heal.

We don't have time to deal with his injury now. The sun will come up in minutes, and we're way out in the woods. I get him upright and he groans. I pull his arm over my shoulder and start moving toward the house.

The sky is definitely getting lighter. I pick up the pace. At least moving through the woods going west—away from the rising sun—the trees will block the sunlight, buying us a few more minutes.

Gunther groans with every step, and he's not moving fast enough. Tiny patches of sunlight are coming through the trees. I can dodge the light, sticking to the shadows. But we're running out of time, and his bad leg is slowing us down.

He starts shouting, shrieking. I look and there are three small spots on his face that are smoking and turning black.

Sunlight.

We're going to die if we can't move faster.

I drop low and heave Gunther over my shoulders in a fireman's carry.

I can move almost at a full run. Definitely a fast jog. He's moaning and gasping, but I can't stop for that. I hear the sizzling sound as pinpoint beams of sunlight burn the side of his face. I duck my head, even though the sun somehow hasn't hit me yet.

I see the fence. We still have at least a hundred yards until we get to the spot where the fence is closest to my house. But then what will we do? Even if I could scramble up the fence fast enough to endure the shock, there's no way I'd be able to do it while carrying Gunther.

Wait. This can't be too far from where I saw him walking

into the woods with his traps, gun, and tools.

I jog to the fence and start to run alongside it. If I haven't overshot, I should be able to find the place where he got in.

Shafts of light start to cut through the trees, and I look left and right to avoid running through them. Gunther cries out.

"Pull your coat over your head," I say, or try to say. I pin his arm and leg across my chest and reach back to pull his coat up, giving him a little more cover.

The sun is getting higher. My face and arms start to feel warm, then hot.

Gunther is silent now. He must have passed out.

I stop running. There it is: a four-foot cut in the fence. There are wire cutters with insulated rubber handles on the ground on the other side of the fence. But however he pushed it open, the flap of fence has settled back now.

I can't squeeze through without getting shocked, especially with him as dead weight. I'm standing here, trying to figure it out, and then I hear sounds like bacon dropped on a hot skillet, as another shaft of sunlight catches his neck.

I put him down and curl him so there's no exposed skin.

I can see the corner of my house through the trees.

The sun is rising fast. And we're so close, but I don't know how to get us through. This space is going to be bathed in sunshine any minute. We can fry by electrocution or we can fry by sunlight.

I have an idea.

I pull the sneaker off his right foot and put my clawed

hand inside, palm down, thumb toward the heel. I squeeze and bend the sneaker in half. It's like an oven mitt, but the thick rubber sole will insulate me from a thousand volts of fun coursing through the steel wire. I hope.

I bend the sneaker and hold it over the jaggedly-cut edge of the fence and squeeze to get a grip, tensed to be electrocuted. I clamp it closed.

Not even a tingle. I grip hard and pull it back, folding it up. I get it to hook onto itself. And now we have an exit.

Grabbing Gunther by the back of his jacket, I drag him to the opening and push him under. Once I'm through, I grab his wrists and pull them over my shoulders. I crouch, put my right shoulder against his stomach and bend him as I push up. He's hanging over my shoulder. He smells like burned steak.

It's maybe forty yards through the sun-dappled woods until I get to the edge where our lawn starts. There's my house, Sol-Blok shields already closed tight over the windows.

I've got twenty yards of blazing sunshine to cross before I can reach the shade at the back of the house. No other way.

I run.

I feel the sun on my neck, arms, and face. It's hot. The sunlight is directly on my skin.

In no time, I'm in the shade.

But the shade won't last.

I let Gunther down, and he lands with a thud. Oh, well. I pound on the back door, checking the sun creeping along the deck, getting closer and closer to me.

I bang on the door.

The videocam buzzes and rotates to face me. I hear Mom shouting inside. The door unlocks. I drag Gunther inside the outer Sol-Blok photoshield doors. They close them just as sunlight reaches the spot where we were standing.

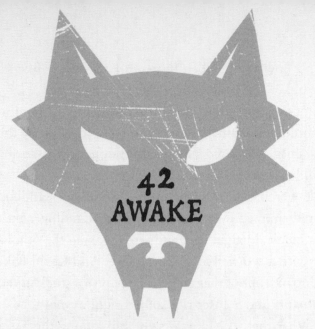

42
AWAKE

I'm on my back. Hard floor is under me, cold against my shoulder blades. It's dark. No, my eyes are closed. I open them and I'm staring straight up into a light.

Weird paneling on the ceiling and the walls. The floor feels like concrete.

Right. I'm in the chamber.

It's completely silent in here. I'm tired and I don't even want to sit up. How did I get here? What happened?

I was in the woods. Maybe during the Change?

It *was* during the Change. I remember the full moon. The moon was red.

Gunther was there.

Right. He shot me. Then he got caught in a trap or something.

I carried him. There was an electric fence or something.

Somehow, I picked him up and ran to the house.

And now I remember. It comes back to me like seeing a movie again after a long time. It's coming back. . . .

I got the inner doors open and burst into the family room. I was holding Gunther Hoering, unconscious, up by the front of his shirt. I lowered him to the floor, slowly, so his head wouldn't crack on the tile.

We weren't alone in the room. Mom was standing there, with red-rimmed eyes. Dr. Mellin was standing next to her with a medical bag in his hand. Troy was on the other side of Mom with a worried look on his face. And Kevin Baker was standing in front of them with a huge pistol stuck in the waist of his pants and a Taser rifle aimed right at me.

"What the . . . ?" Kevin said, still aiming the Taser right at my chest.

Mom's hands went to her mouth, and tears ran down her cheeks. Troy put his arms around her shoulders and whispered something to her.

I started to raise my hands, and Kevin instantly put the stock of the Taser rifle against his shoulder.

My hands were up high and I waved them to say, *don't shoot.*

"What's going on?" Mom said. "He doesn't look like . . ." She trailed off. "What's happening?"

"I . . . I don't know," Dr. Mellin says.

"He just came in from the sun," Troy said, "but he didn't burn."

Kevin kept the Taser rifle aimed at my chest. He said, "I don't know what's going on here, but the first thing we need to do is get him secured."

"I need to examine him," Dr. Mellin said.

"Nobody's going near him until he's restrained. If I could get him to lie down, after we get cuffs on him and move him downstairs, you can sedate him and do your exam. I don't know how to get him to comply, so I might have to stun him with the Taser."

I got to my knees, then lay prone on the floor. I put my hands behind my back.

"He understood you," Mom said. "What is this?"

I heard Kevin take a few steps, then pick something up, then the *ka-shuck* sound of a shotgun being racked. I felt the heel of a workboot over my spine, right below shoulder-blade level. Just enough pressure so it took some effort to breathe. Then I felt the twin metal circles press firmly behind my ear. "Just relax, buddy," he said, almost under his breath.

"Please be careful," Mom said.

"Troy, give me a hand here," Kevin said. "Right there in my bag's a pair of handcuffs. Grab them for me?"

"These? Are they strong enough?" Troy asked.

"Those are extra-heavy LycanoLock handcuffs. Believe me, they're strong enough. Now you're gonna have to put them on him. Don't worry. If he so much as moves one muscle fiber, this'll take his head off."

The shotgun barrels pressed a little harder against me, and I started to breathe heavier.

"I think he really does understand us," Dr. Mellin said.

"That's fine with me," Kevin said. "If he understands, then he knows what'll happen if he moves. Go ahead, Troy. Just like bracelets. Ratchet them nice and tight."

The cold steel tightens around my wrists. Kevin says, "Nice job, Troy. He's not getting out of those."

"While you have him immobilized, let me give him the sedative," Dr. Mellin says.

"What are you giving him?" Mom asked.

"Ketamine. It's a tranquilizer," Dr. Mellin said.

"Make sure you give him enough," Kevin said. "Cuffs or not, I don't want him going wild on us."

"The dose I'm giving him? It would put two grizzly bears to sleep for days. Okay, Danny. If you can understand, you're going to feel a pinch in your leg. Nothing to worry about. You just have a good sleep."

And that's the last thing I remember.

Wait, hang on. I'm thinking clearly. Perfectly rational. Werewulves can't think like that.

Which means I've been asleep here for a couple more days and passed completely through the Change.

Relief floods through me. I'm alive. I'm back to normal.

I hear the metal door bar sliding, and the door opens. Kevin is standing there. "Good morning, sunshine. Looks like Sleeping Beauty has awakened, or whatever. Feel like coming upstairs?"

Music to my ears. Now if I can just get the energy to sit up.

I scratch an itch on my chest. And a small tuft of fur floats through the air.

Fur?

I look at my hand.

Tips of black claws poke through the nails. But they should have fallen out when I reverted back.

"Come on, you lazy bastard," Kevin says. "You've been sleeping down here for a solid ten hours."

Ten hours. *Ten hours?* But that would mean that I *didn't* sleep through the whole Change, that I'm still—

Wait. I'm thinking clearly. So then why do I still . . . ?

I touch my face and—

What the hell is going on?

43
HALFWAY

My legs are achy and my balance is off from the sedative, so it takes both Kevin and Troy to help me walk upstairs.

First thing I want to do is get a look at myself and see what's going on, and the hallway mirror happens to be right outside the basement door.

Whoa. *Not* what I was expecting.

I have two dark purple streaks under my eyes, probably from my nose breaking. My eyes are golden with big black pupils. That's pretty freaky. My nose is not its usual shape, but it's not completely deformed or anything. I move the hair away from the top halves of my ears, so I can get a look. Weird. They're definitely elongated and come to dull points. But with my hair down, it's not easy to see.

My mouth looks fine closed, but I can feel the pointy tips of werewulf teeth poking out from my gums, all the way around.

At least there are no facial ridges or bumps. My

314

cheekbones do look sharper and more prominent. I move my fingers to touch them.

Dr. Mellin waves his hand back and forth. "No, no. Don't touch. Your facial bones aren't fused yet. They broke perfectly along the seams I created, but right now they're still mobile. If you touch them, they could shift, and we'll have some severe ridging to fix."

There's still a lot of the dark hair—or fur, I guess—on my chest, shoulders, arms, and legs. But I shed it really easily. All I have to do is rub or scratch. And now there are tufts of fur on the floor. Mom's going to love that.

My legs look weird. The bones between my toes and my ankles are longer than usual and angled up, so my heels are a couple of inches off the floor. There are scars forming on my thigh and on the shoulder where Dr. Mellin took out the second bullet. My regen is already at work healing the wounds.

Jess and Paige look scared, but relieved that I'm more or less okay.

We figure out pretty quickly that nothing I say is understandable. It takes a little work for me to grip a pen, but I write a note asking where we are in the full-moon cycle, where I am in the Change.

"You got through the first night and most of a day," Dr. Mellin says. "You have two more nights to go."

Two more nights? I'm in the middle of the Change right now? I write on the pad, *Confused. Thinking is clear—writing!!!—but I look like this. Why?*

"We'll get to that," he says. "But you should sit. You don't look too steady."

They help me to a chair. I write a note asking what

happened to Gunther. Troy explains that he drove Gunther to the hospital while I was unconscious. Troy told the ER staff that he'd been driving and saw this kid in the street, smoking from the first rays of morning sun. On the way, Troy reminded Gunther that I saved his life when I could have let him fry, and that between my rescuing him and the fact that Gunther had tried to kill me—on federally preserved property—it would be a good idea to keep his knowledge of my condition to himself. Gunther agreed.

We're all anxious to understand what's happening to me. Dr. Mellin clears his throat. "Let me first say that almost all the conclusions I've drawn about Danny are only educated guesses. Based on initial results from blood, cerebrospinal fluid, skin and muscle biopsies, and physical examination, this is what I believe is happening." Dr. Mellin explains his theory.

He goes into a lot of scientific detail, but I think it boils down to this: because of my failed genetic treatments, I had a severe gene mutation that made everything—to use the technical term—go haywire.

I didn't have a complete Change. My vampyre traits and my wulf traits are fighting it out—a raging cage match, the cage being me.

We start firing questions at him—me writing, and everyone else calling out.

Which is stronger: the wulf side or the vamp side? Dr. Mellin says, "It could change month to month. But I don't know."

Why did I have so much regular human thinking, and why did I think it at the same time as the primitive werewolf thoughts? Dr. Mellin's answer: "I've never heard of that phenomenon before, but I suspect that because you didn't have a complete Change, some of the reasoning and language centers of your brain didn't degenerate."

Since I didn't have a complete Change, will my future Changes be more extreme? "They could be, but I don't know," he says.

When this full moon is over, will I revert completely to normal? "I don't know."

Why am I not violent and feral right now? "The hormone lychancholomine, which causes werewulf aggression, is below typical levels." Why? "I don't know."

Since I didn't burn in the sun this time, does that mean I never will? "Maybe. I don't know."

Will I have to be in the chamber the whole time during every Change? "I would think so. But I don't really know."

In the end, will either the wulf side or vamp side take over completely? "It's possible. But I don't know."

This goes on for a while. There's a silence and then Kevin says, "So, when it comes to how this whole thing works, you just don't know."

"Exactly," Dr. Mellin says. "Look. This is incredibly rare. I can't even find cases of it in the medical literature. Everything about this is abn—" He stops and glances at me. "Unusual. Danny is a complete specian anomaly."

Which, I figure, is a polite way of saying I'm a total freak of nature—something Claire has been telling me for a long time.

I have one more question, which I write on the pad, but this one I pass to Mom.

She reads it, then smiles, her lips tight and her eyes crinkling.

"What'd he write?" Paige asks.

Mom reads, "*Not to be demanding, but I'm starving!!! What're the odds of a werewulf getting something to eat around here?*"

She smiles. Her eyes shine with tears. "I'd say the odds are pretty good."

44
SVNSHINE

After I finish an enormous meal, Jess says, "By the way, Claire called about five times during the night and earlier today."

I still have some time before sundown. I go up to the computer in my room and IM Claire.

i'm fine, I type when she finally signs on.

it's the middle of the day, she types. u couldn't wait? u had to wake me up?

Nice try. I'd bet a million bucks that she wasn't sleeping.

I type, u do need your beauty sleep—desperately—but i thought i'd check in

so. anything new?

not much, I type. just the usual

There's a lag of almost a minute before she types again: u ok?

That's a really good question, and I don't know how to answer it fully. The best I can do for now is type, more or less, yeah . . . a lot happened, a lot going on

wait—it's still the full moon . . . how can you be chatting?

I type, long story. can't put it all down right now

u'll have to tell me all about it

promise i'll give you every detail

u better. hey. so where are things between u and miss juliet?

not sure. up in the air, i guess

There's a rap on the door, and Kevin pokes his head in. "Sorry, chief. It's getting to be that time. You need to go downstairs."

I give him an okay sign. He nods and leaves.

gtg, I type.

take care. i'll see you soon, right?

definitely

and you better not im and wake me up again!

or what???

or you'll see. Claire signs off. I get up from my chair to go down to the chamber.

They're all waiting for me downstairs. Kevin stands by the door that leads down to the basement.

"If all goes right," he says, "we'll be able to bring you back out tomorrow when the sun is up. But for now . . ."

I hold up one finger, like *I need a minute.*

"We're already cutting it pretty close," Kevin says.

"Go ahead," Mom says to me. "But hurry."

I go to the back door so I can do something I've never done before.

Coming out of the Sol-Blok doors, I step out onto the back deck.

I come outside into the light of the sun, and for the first time in my life, I have nothing to fear. I don't have to cover up, run, or hide. I'm perfectly safe out here.

I look directly into the sunset, then close my eyes and let the last rays of sunlight bathe my face.

It feels warm.

It feels good.

GLOSSARY

MEDICAL TERMINOLOGY

Anadiploidy shock: negative reaction from LRT
   anti-codominance treatments (see Lychromosomal
   Repression Therapy)

Bi-specian: a species hybrid, e.g. vampyre-wulf, wulf-human

Burr's Ridge: superior aspect of ear with pointed cartilage,
   site from which lupine cartilage grows during the
   Change. Named after Dr. Edward Burr (1889–1943).
   This is the structure that gives wulves slightly pointed
   ears when in human form.

DNA-mRNA Mutation Syndrome: negative reaction from
   anti-codominance treatments

Globin Crash (colloquial): a severe drop of hemoglobin;
   acute anemia that afflicts vampyres, which requires
   immediate infusion of iron and oxygen in their blood.
   Symptoms include weakness, disorientation, and
   fainting. Intake of synthetic blood products will typically
   resolve the condition within minutes.

Haemophilesis: vampyre's excessive bleeding due to decreased clotting factors

Hemodipsia: a vampyre's need for increased hemoglobin intake (Gk: *heme*=blood + *dipso*=thirst)

LMPI (Lycan-Metamorphosis Prodromal Illness): a varied set of flulike symptoms (headache, nausea, fever, vomiting, body aches) that some wulves suffer for a few days before a Change

Lycan-metamorphosis: the Change (Primitis Lycan-metamorphosis: first Change. Pseudo-Lycan-metamorphosis: partial Change before Primitis)

Lycardiomegaly: the naturally large size of the wulf heart; typically 30–40 percent larger than a human or vampyre heart

Lychondrocytosis: growing of cartilage in ears as they take on elongated lupine shape

Lychromosomal Repression Therapy: genetic therapy performed to repress lycanthropic phenotype traits (including Lycan-Metamorphosis)

Metahematosynthesis: blood cells during the Change

Soladurisis: (vampyre) burning in sunlight (Latin: *sol*=sun + *aduro*=to set on fire, burn, singe)

Vamporphyria: when heme levels decrease, porphyria is induced, causing a toxic buildup of porphyrins in the blood. Vamporphyria is a chronic, severe, and potentially lethal form of porphyria. It is an inheritable trait of all vampyres.

Vampyrolytic anemia: breakdown of red blood cells—and lowered heme—naturally occurring in vampyres. This is the reason they need to have an increased intake of *VampHematin*.

MEDICAL AND CONSUMER PRODUCTS

Coagudine: coagulation medication, used to slow or stop bleeding (effective only in vampyres)

Coumidex: blood thinner. Typically given after Coagudine to regain hemostasis. Used illicitly as a way to "get high."

DermaWhite: a product that temporarily whitens skin by use of a bleaching chemical

Dial-a-Canopy: commercial company specializing in express delivery of Sol-Blok bed canopies

Factor XIV: coagulation agent, used only for small injuries

Fibrex (collar): Fibrex collars are worn by wulves at compounds. They are extremely flexible to expand when wearer's neck thickens during the Change, and the material is exceptionally durable, untearable without industrial-strength cutters.

Hemometer: instrument that quickly measures basic blood composition status such as hematocrit, red blood cell count, hemoglobin levels, etc. Units range from sophisticated hospital models to personal, portable units for consumer use.

Hemo-Sealer: an ointment that quickly dries into a rubbery, waxy substance when applied to cuts or scabs. It prevents the scent of blood from arousing vampyres.

Lupine Fresh: deodorant formulated specifically for wulves

Lupinox: an over-the-counter treatment for the aches and pains of LMPI

Lycano Lock handcuffs: (police use) extra-strength carbon steel restraints; legally available only to police forces and units of the LPCB

Photoshield: chamber by doorway to prevent sunlight from entering house (similar to revolving door of a darkroom)

Sangre-Vin: wine infused with real blood; highly addictive, outlawed in the U.S.

Sol-Blok: Leading U.S. manufacturer of light-blocking products (window treatments, canopies that close over beds, body-cover suits, etc.)

Somnambulex: prescription sleeping pill for vampyres

SynHeme: commercial beverage, synthetic blood (developed by Sandor Bartlett)

SynHemesicle: dessert; frozen fruit-flavored SynHeme on a stick

Tylenol-V: Acetaminophen 4000 mg, formulated for vampyre use

Vamp-EYEr: producer of blue-hued nonprescription contact lenses, sold at malls and online

VampHematin: the agent in all forms of artificial heme; active ingredient of products such as SynHeme and VeniHeme

VeniHeme: synthetic blood for medical use; intravenous (IV) used when a vampyre is hypovolemic and needs an infusion

SLANG

Blood-flood: copious bleeding after an injury, due to vampyre decreased clotting factors of haemophilesis (also known as *speed bleed* and *heme stream*)

Blue-tooth: one who drinks too much SynHeme Caffeine
 Plus (Blue tooth stains can be removed by a dentist)
Crumpskull (strongly derogatory): a wulf, specifically one
 who has post-Change cranial deformities (named after
 comic-strip character "Crump" who is an unlucky wulf
 boy with a lumpy head) (see *Face-case*)
Doglet (derogatory): young wulf
Face-case (derogatory): a wulf, specifically one who has
 post-Change facial deformities (see *Crumpskull*)
Fang-banger: one who prefers to (or will only) have sex
 with vampyres
Furburger: a werewulf corpse (esp. as food for scavengers)
Hamp: human who is a vampyre wannabe; gets blue contact
 lenses, dyes hair blond, etc. (see also *Wamp*)
Hooked in: the state of a vampyre who is addicted to
 blood
Howler (derogatory): wulf
Howler-prowler: one who sexually pursues wulves
Keeper: person who illegally rents cage space (usually
 unhygienic and cramped) to unregistered wulves during
 full moon (high mortality rate for these wulves)
Lunadog (derogatory): wulf also *lunabitch* (f)
Moondog (derogatory): wulf also *moonbitch* (f)
Moonrunner: an unregistered wulf who evades the
 authorities
Mutt (mildly derogatory): wulf
Poacher: a civilian hunter of unregistered wolves, often in
 league with local police
Prima vampyreena: a conceited and spoiled wealthy female
 vampyre (also, *PV*)

Rabies baby (derogatory): infant wulf (most common in
    plural, as *rabies babies*)
Regen: vampyres' heightened healing abilities
Roaster (derogatory): a vampyre
Sun-scorch: soladurisis (vampyres' severe burning in
    sunlight)
Throw a clot: to get anxious, upset, or excited (vampyre
    use)
Wamp: wulf who is a vampyre wannabe (see also *Hamp*)
Wulftag: tattoo of a wulf symbol, legally required to be
    applied to the right hand of every wulf at birth. A red
    ring is added when the wulf registers for a compound.
Wulf-whacker (derogatory): someone who is sexually
    promiscuous with wulves

ORGANIZATIONS AND AGENCIES

AAWRA: The American Association for Wulf Rights
    and Advancement. Social action group dedicated to
    protecting rights of wulves
LPCB: Lycanthrope Protection & Control Bureau
LRC: Lycanthropic Rest Center. Medical facility as an
    alternative to going to compounds. Very expensive;
    technique (drug-induced coma) highly dangerous.

ACKNOWLEDGMENTS

So many family members and friends have been supportive of my writing, that it's going to be hard to list them all here. But I'll give it a try: many thanks to members of the families Tiven, Kohn, Bihaly, Moore, and Shenfeld; thanks to pals Abi Morrison, and amazing writer Kevin Baker.

Thanks to Alessandra Balzer, who welcomed the book to its home at Hyperion. And thanks to all the other people at Hyperion who made the book look good and read smoothly.

Huge thanks to my phenomenal editor, Ari Lewin. Her excellent judgment, sharp eye, keen wit, and unbreakable tenacity kept me honest. She accepted nothing less than my absolute best, and the book is much better for it. And big thanks to Catherine Onder, the final member of my Dream Team of editors, who joined us late in the game, but still ran the book all the way into the end zone.

I'm fortunate and grateful to have the best agent on the planet, Jodi Reamer. As smart as they come, Jodi has given me sage guidance, candid and valuable criticism, and unwavering encouragement. Always protecting my interests, she is my literary bodyguard.

Thanks to my at-home consultants and moral supporters: Jake, whose instincts for good writing are as sharp as a vampyre's fang; and Hedy, who supplied much-needed fashion advice (for the characters, not for me).

And finally, deepest thanks to my wife, Ellen. When she first heard my idea for the story, she said, "Vampires and werewolves? Um, you're kidding, right?" In spite of initial . . . *concerns*, she became an unending source of enthusiasm, support, and inspiration for me not only in the writing of this book, but every day of my life. She is my SynHeme: I couldn't live without her.

DON'T MISS PETER MOORE'S
NEXT ACTION-PACKED NOVEL

CONFESSIONS

OF A

TEENAGE
VILLAIN

FLASHBANG

Gym class at the Academy—Physical Training or PT for short—is kind of like a microcosm of the real world. If you have enhanced strength, you get an A. If you don't have it, you get broken bones and bruises. Since I was in the second category, I didn't exactly look forward to the forty-four-minute periods dedicated to Survival of the Physically Fittest.

The Flyers were using the gym, practicing for the Flight Maneuvers provisional certification tests that a lot of the seniors would be taking within the next few months. So the rest of us who had PT were out on the Flashbang field. Not that the kids outside were second-rate, in terms of powers. Every one of them was a solid Hitter—Hero-in-Training— teen. Some were playing hard because that's just how they were. Born hero types. Others were playing hard so they could score points for their PT cumulative grade. As far as I could tell, I was the only unenhanced kid on the field, and that meant I would have to play hard, too, just to get off the field intact. Or I could try to stay out of the way of the action and survive the period.

"Hey, Baron!" Mr. M. bellowed at me. The former Mr. Mastodon (of the Liberty Sentinels) had voice-amp powers that could rattle glass when he shouted, which made him perfectly suited for a PT teacher. "What's the deal? You stuck?"

"Huh?" I called, without a whole lot of effort or volume. I knew what he meant. I was sticking around in the left backfield, not wanting to get too close to the middle of the field, where the four offensive players from the opposing team were trying to break through our forward line.

Mr. M. shouted to me, "You think Blake Baron would've been caught dead standing still for one second during a game of Flashbang?"

"I'm not Blake," I said.

Mr. M. laughed, way louder than necessary. "No, *Brad*, you're not Blake. Blake would be charging down the field, mixing it up, getting physical," he boomed. "You should be ashamed of yourself. If your brother saw you just standing there like that, he'd puke."

"I don't think he'd really care," I said. Which was a lie. He'd either be embarrassed, disgusted, or both. Blake played hard when he went to the Academy. He was a star. Even then, he was twice the size I am now, and busting out with new powers practically every day: enhanced strength, invulnerability, speed, and dexterity. Me? I had brains, but that wasn't going to do me much good in a game of Flashbang. Cunning wasn't valuable in a situation that called for brute force.

"Wrong, chief. He took pride in being here, he worked hard. *That's* what it takes to be a hero. Now get your butt in the game or I'll put you in as goalkeeper. How's that sound?"

It sounded to me like a guarantee that I would get killed. "I read you, sir, loud and clear. I'm getting in the game right now," I called. "I am *pumped*! Ready and rowdy, sir." I even saluted. Not really as suicidal as it might sound: Mr. M. probably couldn't spell *irony*, much less recognize it. Still, I trotted away from where I was, but kept my distance from the action, figuring at least a little movement would get me off Mr. M.'s radar.

Unfortunately for me, a completed pass to Donna Dersh sent her running toward my new position, followed by a stampede of kids right behind her. Midfielders from her team ran in a flanking formation, blocking for her, keeping my teammates from reaching her and stealing the rugby-ball-shaped flashbang. She threw a lateral to her left midfielder. He caught it with one hand and did a quick pivot and straight-arm block away from a player on my side. He juked left, then right, and came running in my direction, and I saw his face.

It was Rick Randall: a likely contender to get recruited to the Dawn Patrol or another coveted hero-league position straight out of high school. I could see the flashbang gripped tight to his ribs with one hand. It was glowing green, which meant it wasn't set to go off anytime soon. Randall would have to pass or make a straight run for the goal right away. He had more than enough time to cut across to my side of the field. Clearly, he figured he had a much better chance of getting past me than any of our other defenders. He was right.

Rick Randall was big. Whether from working out, surgical enhancement, or doses of Myomegamorperone, the guy was 6'2" and probably 220 pounds of solid muscle.

Coming straight at me.

Not having a single physical enhancement power, there wasn't a whole lot I could do to stop Randall. I ran through my options: A) try to slow him down enough for the other defense guys to get to my side of the field and take him on. B) square off with him and hope not to die. Or C) just get the hell out of his way.

Maybe the stuff Mr. M. said had gotten under my skin—instead of moving as far away as possible from this hurtling locomotive, I ran toward Randall from a flanking position, hoping that he would change direction. Not because I believed he was afraid of me, but at the least I might be an irritant that he'd rather avoid.

It was when I saw him glance down at the flashbang, notice me, and start to slow down that I knew I had made a big, big mistake.

The flashbang had just switched from glowing green to glowing red. And that meant it could go off at any second. Randall was still a good thirty yards away from our side's goal. He must have decided that he didn't want to risk going for the goal with a live flashbang in his hand.

I didn't realize what he was doing until it was way too late.

His tackle was perfect, his shoulder square in my solar plexus. If that hadn't knocked the wind out of me, then hitting the ground would have. Before I knew what was happening, he drilled his knee on my chest and pinned my right arm to the ground. He executed a perfect force reception, and I could only watch as he pressed the flashbang's contact plate against the lock plate on my wristband. The high-pitched squeal signaled that the flashbang was locked on.

"Nice one, Rick!" Mr. M. called. "That's the way to do it."

Rick Randall rolled to the side, got to his feet, and ran like hell to get clear of me. The ball was flashing red. Forty-five seconds left before it would go off. Anybody dumb enough to look at the ball when the flash went off would see floating white spots for the rest of the afternoon. Anyone who was within ten yards when it detonated would have ringing ears for at least twenty-four hours. But the real fun part was the bang: anyone within ten yards would be hit with a concussive force blast that would cause full-body aches for a couple of days.

The others on the field would just shake it off after a day or so. But for someone without powers, someone un-enhanced, the effects of the flashbang would be much more than an annoying penalty for slowness, hesitation, or bad tactics. For me, it would be temporary blindness, loss of hearing, and profound pain right down to the bone marrow—not my idea of a good time. So I wasn't just going to stand there and wait for the damn thing to go off. But with the flashbang locked and activated, the only way to disable it was to run it through the opposing team's goal. Not kick it, not throw it, which I couldn't do anyway, since it was locked onto my wrist. Run it through. And that meant I had to get past everyone on the other team.

Not too likely. But still, there *was* a chance, however

small. And this was a chance for me to impress the other Hitters, to show them that even if I didn't have great physical powers, I could make a run and maybe even the score. That would show them.

But Hitters don't like to lose. They especially don't like to lose face. And they most especially don't like to lose face to kids with no real powers. They ran at me—eight of them? ten?—and started bodychecking me, one by one. They dashed away, no one staying long enough to risk being caught in flashbang range. Bumper cars. I was getting knocked all over the place, but not making much progress toward the goal. My teammates kept their distance, keeping out of the whole thing to avoid the blast of the flashbang, which would be going off any moment.

Suddenly, the blue lights on the posts lining the field started to flash. At the same time, my feet felt the humming and vibration from the electromagnetic lattice under the field as it powered up. The power field engaged and pulled down on our vests, wristbands, and ankle bands, making us feel heavy, like we were fighting against increased gravity. I took a look at over at Mr. M., who, being a typical sadistic gym instructor, was grinning. The purpose of Gravitygain was strength training, but I always believed the PT teachers used it to amuse themselves.

Kids with enhanced strength obviously had an advantage and were able to power through it. All I knew was that I was stuck to a beeping, blinking flashbang that was set to go off if I didn't get rid of it fast, and the last thing I needed was to be slowed down.

And the Gravitygain was sure not going to work to my

benefit if one of the guys knocked me to the ground: I'd never be able to get back up.

"Let's go, Hitters!" Mr. M. shouted. "You gonna let a little extra gravity slow you down? Get moving. Look alive."

If I could make a straight run, lurch past the three guys who were between me and the goal only twenty yards away, maybe I would have a chance. Just dodge a little bit and not get slowed down.

If I really dug in, I had a chance of diving through the goal and deactivating the flashbang before it detonated. It wasn't completely impossible. There was a chance I could make it.

That chance evaporated when I heard a shout from my left, turned, and Rick Randall slammed into me with a perfect form tackle.

I hit the ground. And I mean *hard*.

A loud crunch reverberated in my head. It was the sound of three vertebrae in my neck exploding when they smashed against the hard-packed ground. A chill like ice water shot down my back—temporary spinal shock.

I heard the sound of Mr. M.'s baseball-mitt-sized hands clapping. "Nice tackle, Randall. Nice! But I'd get away from there if I were you. Look alive, kid. Run."

I could hear a bunch of Hitters laughing and clapping, and the sound of Randall's double-heavy footsteps retreating as he ran for safety. That's when it hit me: the worst was still to come.

The flashbang suddenly vibrated and let off a high-pitched squeal. Then there was an astonishingly loud percussive sound like a prolonged gunshot in my ears. My eyes were clenched shut, but it didn't matter. The bright light easily penetrated my closed eyelids; it was like looking directly into the sun. The concussive force of the detonation rattled every atom in my body, and just before I blacked out, I had one last thought:

I really, really, really hate this game.